House of the
Hanging Jade

Books by Amy M. Reade

Secrets of Hallstead House

The Ghosts of Peppernell Manor

House of the Hanging Jade

House of the Hanging Jade

Amy M. Reade

LYRICAL UNDERGROUND
Kensington Publishing Corp.
www.kensingtonbooks.com

LYRICAL UNDERGROUND BOOKS are published by

Kensington Publishing Corp.
119 West 40th Street
New York, NY 10018

All Kensington titles, imprints, and distributed lines are available at special quantity discounts for bulk purchases for sales promotion, premiums, fund-raising, educational, or institutional use.

Special book excerpts or customized printings can also be created to fit specific needs. For details, write or phone the office of the Kensington Sales Manager: Kensington Publishing Corp., 119 West 40th Street, New York, NY 10018. Attn. Sales Department. Phone: 1-800-221-2647.

Lyrical Underground and Lyrical Underground Reg. US Pat. & TM Off.

First Electronic Edition: April 2016
eISBN-13: 978-1-60183-558-1
eISBN-10: 1-60183-558-2

First Print Edition: April 2016
ISBN-13: 978-1-60183-559-8
ISBN-10: 1-60183-559-0

Printed in the United States of America

For Kalolina, Lepeka, and Iokua

ACKNOWLEDGMENTS

I wish to thank my family for their constant support, and especially my husband John, without whom I wouldn't be able to do what I love.

I wish also to thank all the wonderful people I've met in Hawaii, from *kanaka* to *kama'aina* to *haoles* and tourists, young and old. The island of Hawaii is indeed a place of beauty, peace, and restoration, and I am very lucky to have experienced its aloha.

Chapter 1

I knew I should have stayed home.

I bent my head as the wind whipped down Massachusetts Avenue, hurling snowflakes at my face, stinging my cheeks with hard, frosty pellets. The icy sidewalks were treacherous, making my walk to work precarious and slow. There were very few others brave or foolish enough to be out in this weather. I passed one man out walking his dog and silently praised him for being so devoted.

I finally arrived at the restaurant. I stamped on the snow that had piled up against the front door and slipped my key into the lock with fingers stiff and clumsy from the cold. Once inside, it only took me a second to realize that no one else was there. On a normal day, one without a blizzard, my assistant Nunzio would already have come in through the back and flipped on the kitchen lights before I arrived.

I groaned. Even Nunzio, whom I could always count on, had stayed home. I moved through the darkened dining room and turned on the lights in the kitchen. As they blinked to life, I heard a heavy knock at the front door.

Hurrying to open it, I recognized the face of Geoffrey, the restaurant's owner and my current boyfriend, bundled up in a thick scarf and hat.

"Kailani, what are you doing here?" he exclaimed, brushing snow off his boots in the vestibule.

"Someone has to be here to get things started," I answered testily.

"I don't think we can open today," Geoffrey said. "There's no way the delivery trucks can get through, and I don't think we'd have any customers even if they could."

"You mean I came all this way for nothing?" I whined.

Geoffrey smiled down at me. "Sorry. I just assumed you'd know not to come in on a day like this."

"Why did you come in, then?"

"To catch up on paperwork. Plus, snowstorms don't bother me."

"Ugh. They bother me. Well, I guess if you don't need me here, I'll head back home."

"Want me to stop by later?"

I didn't, but I nodded. Geoffrey and I hadn't been dating for long. He was already becoming a little too clingy.

He leaned over and kissed me on the cheek. "Be safe getting home. I'd call you a cab, but there isn't a single one on the streets."

"Believe me, I know."

I trudged home the same way I had come, the snow falling even harder now and blowing sideways, making it difficult for me to see.

When I finally made it to my apartment building, I clumped up the stairs in my heavy boots and stood inside my apartment, leaning against the door for several moments to catch my breath. It took me a while to peel off all my layers. I left them lying on the floor while I heated up milk on the stove for hot chocolate. As the milk warmed, I gazed at a canvas photo that hung in my front hall. It was a faraway view of the beach, taken from my parents' backyard, overlooking the black sand and the curling waves of the azure Pacific Ocean.

"We've got to go home," I said aloud to my cat, Meli, as she stepped daintily around me. This wasn't the first time I had expressed this sentiment to Meli, but this time she stopped and looked up at me. She blinked and twitched her ears.

It was the sign I needed.

I watched the snow continue to fall for several hours from the warmth and safety of my apartment. Meli and I curled up on the couch while I tried to read a book, but I couldn't concentrate. My thoughts returned again and again to palm trees and warm, caressing trade winds, to the faces of my mother and father, of my sister and her little girl.

Geoffrey eventually stopped by, bringing with him an icy blast of air as I opened the door to the hallway.

He laughed. "Looks like this storm may never end."

I invited him into the warmth of the apartment. "Take off your stuff. Want some hot chocolate?" I called over my shoulder as I walked into the kitchen.

"Sure," he answered, struggling with one of his boots.

I joined him in the living room a few minutes later. He was trying to stroke Meli's chin, but she apparently wanted none of that. Her ears flattened back and she squirmed out of his reach.

I handed him the mug of hot chocolate and sat down opposite him. "Geoffrey, I have news," I told him warily, knowing he probably wouldn't be as happy as I was.

"What is it?"

"I'm going back to Hawaii." I waited for his reaction.

"That's nice. It'll do you good to get out of this weather for a while."

He obviously wasn't getting it. "No, not for a while. I'm *moving* back. For good."

I was right. He was not happy. In fact, he looked stricken, his eyes wide and his mouth agape. "What do you mean, for good?" he asked, choking on his hot chocolate.

"I mean, I just can't stand it here any longer. I'm never going to get used to the weather, I miss my parents, and my niece is growing up without her auntie. It's time to go back. This is something I've been thinking about for a long time.

"I'll miss you, Geoffrey, but this is what's best for me," I added, trying to soften the blow.

He looked like he was struggling for words.

"But . . . but . . . what will you do?"

"I'll do the same thing I do here, Geoffrey. Sous-chefs are not unique to DC."

"Okay, but what will I do? Without you, I mean?"

I felt sorry for him. He looked crestfallen.

"Geoffrey," I said gently, "there are lots of women in Washington who are looking for someone as wonderful and kind and handsome and successful as you are. I have to do what my heart is telling me to do, and that's to go back to Hawaii."

He nodded slowly, his eyes downcast. "Is there anything I can say to keep you here?"

"I'm afraid not."

"When are you leaving?"

"I don't know. I just made the decision this morning."

He sighed and leaned back against the couch cushions, holding his mug on his lap and staring into space.

"Geoffrey? You okay?" I asked.

He set his mug on the coffee table and pushed himself up from the sofa. "I guess I should get going, then. Will you keep working at the restaurant until you leave?"

I was surprised that he wanted to leave already, but I didn't mention it.

"Of course. I'll give you plenty of time to find another fabulous sous-chef."

I watched Geoffrey as he walked down the hallway of my apartment building. His shoulders were stooped and his gait slow. He looked like a forlorn little boy. Poor Geoffrey. At the end of the hallway, right by the elevator, he turned around and made a pleading motion with his hands and walked back toward me.

Uh-oh.

"Kailani, how can you just throw away all the time we've spent together?"

I was a little taken aback, but I suppose I shouldn't have been. Such dramatic statements were normal with him. "Geoffrey, we haven't really spent too much time together. We haven't been dating very long."

"But doesn't that time mean something to you?"

"Yes, of course it does. I've enjoyed getting to know you and we've had fun together. But it's time for me to go home. And I'm afraid a long-distance relationship just isn't possible. It's too far away."

"There's got to be a way, Kailani. I just can't stand the thought of losing you."

"I'm sorry, Geoffrey. I've got to go. I'll see you at work tomorrow." I closed the door gently and stood there until I heard the *ding* of the elevator.

I waited a few hours before calling my mother since there was a five-hour time difference between DC and Hawaii.

She and my father were both thrilled by my news, as I knew they would be. They had a million questions for me, like when I would be coming home, where I would be looking for a new job, and whether I could live with them for a while.

"I don't know!" I laughed. "I'm going to start putting out some feelers right away for jobs in restaurants and resorts along the Kohala

Coast. Someone must need a sous-chef. Or even a head chef. But I'll be home soon, don't worry. I can't stand another day of this winter weather."

I hung up, promising to keep them posted about my job hunt. Suddenly, the winter seemed a little warmer.

Chapter 2

I was still working for Geoffrey a couple weeks later, still floundering through the endless winter weather and finding our relationship a bit awkward. He made excuses to be wherever I was, whether it was in the kitchen or the basement of the restaurant or while I was coming to work or leaving work to go home. I was actively looking for a job on the Big Island, and didn't want to return home without any employment prospects, but I was seriously beginning to consider going home without a job just to get away from Geoffrey. I had told all my friends and colleagues in DC and on the island of Hawaii that I was going back home; everyone wished me well.

One night I worked very late at the restaurant. I couldn't catch a cab, so I had to walk home. I walked briskly on the dark sidewalk, trying to stay warm. I slipped on a patch of ice at one point, dropping my bag. As I stooped down to pick it up, I noticed a man walking not too far behind me. He had a toque pulled low over his forehead. I walked a little faster after that, not wanting to be the only woman on the street late at night. I glanced over my shoulder and noticed that the man walked a little more quickly too. A shiver of apprehension crept up the back of my neck. I ducked into a tiny twenty-four-hour grocery store and browsed for a few minutes, buying nothing, but giving the man plenty of time to walk past me and continue on his way.

When I went back outside, I looked left and right to make sure no one was following me. Seeing nobody, I kept walking, but it wasn't long before I noticed the same man walking slightly behind me and on the other side of the street. I wanted to run, but I couldn't because the sidewalks were too treacherous. All I could do was fumble for my cell phone and have it handy to call 911 if he came any closer. I looked over my shoulder again; he was crossing the street, walking a bit faster. I went faster too.

I took off my gloves and shoved them in my coat pocket so I could dial 911 quickly. I was almost in front of my building, pulling my phone out of my other pocket when I heard footsteps directly behind me. The man grabbed my elbow and I let out a cry.

"Kailani, it's me."

"Geoffrey! You scared me to death! What on earth are you doing?"

"I was just following you to make sure you made it home okay," he said, still gripping my elbow.

"You've never done that before," I said, my voice grating in irritation. "Why start now?"

"I was just concerned about you, that's all."

"Thank you, but I'm fine. Don't ever do that again. You really scared me."

"I'm sorry."

I shook his hand off my elbow and walked away. As I unlocked the door to my apartment building, I saw him out of the corner of my eye, watching me. I shivered, but not from the cold. Now I really couldn't wait to leave Washington. And Geoffrey.

Once I was inside my apartment I kicked off my boots and leaned down to stroke Meli, who came to greet me. My heart was still pounding from my encounter with Geoffrey. I leafed through the mail as I walked into the living room. The red light on my answering machine was blinking.

"Kailani? This is Dr. Barbara Merriweather-Jorgensen. I live on the west coast of the Big Island and I have heard through the grapevine that you are a sous-chef looking for a job here on the Kohala Coast. My family and I are in the district of North Kohala and I am looking for a personal chef to manage our kitchen and cook for us. I understand that you are a very capable young woman with local ties, and I think you might be perfect for the job. If you're interested in finding out more about this opportunity, give me a call." She went on to give me her email address and asked that I send her my résumé.

Was this the phone call I'd been waiting for? I was intrigued, but I wasn't so sure about the job title. I didn't know any personal chefs and I didn't know what responsibilities such a job entailed.

After sending her my résumé, I called Dr. Merriweather-Jorgensen back. I was soon talking to a receptionist at Orchid Isle Wellness.

"Ms. Merriweather-Jorgensen has left for our Kona office and won't be back today," the woman noted in a quiet, smooth voice.

"Oh. She's not a doctor?" I asked, surprised.

"She is a practitioner of acupuncture and Oriental medicine."

"Oh," I repeated. "Well, I'll try her again tomorrow."

I went online and searched for Barbara Merriweather-Jorgensen. I found out that she was a partner in a "wellness practice." Besides her work in acupuncture and Oriental medicine, the clinic also offered dermatology, massage therapy, internal medicine, personal training, and nutrition services at several locations on the island of Hawaii.

I thought of nothing else at work the following day as I tried to avoid Geoffrey, waiting to get home to call Ms. Merriweather-Jorgensen again. I reached her that night.

"Thank you for sending me your résumé. I've contacted your references and they speak *very highly* of you. So now that the formalities are out of the way, let me tell you more about the job. There are four of us. Besides me, there is my husband and our two children. You would be expected to prepare breakfast and dinner six days a week, plus provide school lunches for the children and luncheon for anyone who might be in the house on any given day. On Sundays, we require only dinner. In addition, you would be expected to prepare food for any entertaining that my husband and I do. You would, of course, have a suite of rooms in the house. You get vacation whenever we do, and obviously we would make arrangements for you to get time off if you need or want it. We pay a very good salary, naturally."

I listened breathlessly. It sounded like a huge commitment.

"Is this something you're interested in? Or would you like a day or two to think about it?"

I swallowed. I didn't want to make a decision right then, but I didn't want to lose this opportunity. "I am interested, yes," I heard myself say.

"That's *wonderful!* When can you start?"

We agreed that I would start in three weeks.

"If I may ask," I said. "Where did you get my name?"

"All my clients and colleagues know I'm looking for a personal chef. One man lives in Punalu'u and said the talk of the town is a young sous-chef, trained at the Culinary Institute of America, who wants to come home. I got your information that way."

So my parents and sister had been spreading the news!

We talked about more particulars for several minutes, then I told her I would see her soon.

She laughed lightly. "Fair warning: You may have a hard time at first. My husband and my kids prefer heavy American and European-style meals, and my goal is to get them to eat healthier."

"I'll do my best," I promised.

I was going home.

Chapter 3

Over the next two and a half weeks I packed, shipped the big things I didn't want to sell, and said my good-byes. Geoffrey still couldn't believe I was going.

"I didn't think you'd go through with it," he said, half-smiling. "Washington is such an exciting place to live. I was sure you'd decide to stay."

I shook my head, returning his small smile. "I know, but I really miss the Big Island. I miss my parents and the rest of my family. I miss the *weather*. I miss seeing the ocean when I drive down the road."

"I guess I can't blame you for that." He gave me a hug as I stood stiffly. "I'll miss you, Kailani."

"I'll miss you too, Geoffrey," I lied. "Take care." I waved to him as I turned around and walked back to my apartment for the last time.

Early the next morning I was on a plane heading for Kona. It was a long flight, with two long layovers, and I finally arrived on the Big Island that night at eight o'clock. I was exhausted, still on Washington time, but I got my second wind as soon as I saw my family waiting for me by baggage claim. My parents and sister hugged me while my niece, Haliaka, jumped up and down, clapping her hands and laughing. I looked around me, breathing in the warm tropical air, and felt an enveloping sense of peace and belonging.

Though it cost me a small fortune, I had checked four bags. My father and sister helped me get them to the car while my mother held Haliaka's hand.

"All your other things arrived yesterday," Mom said as we drove home in the darkness. "We put everything in the guest room for you."

"When do you start work?" Dad asked.

"Later this week, but the day after tomorrow I'm going up to Ms. Merriweather-Jorgensen's house to have a look at the kitchen and my rooms."

"The place must be pretty nice if they can afford a personal chef," my sister piped up. "Do you think we can come and see it?"

"Probably. But not until I've worked there awhile."

We all chatted happily on the way home, which was an hour south of the airport. When I stepped out of the car at my parents' house, I was wrapped in the same nostalgic feeling I always got when I returned home for a visit. The fragrance of flowers lightly scented the air, combining with the homey smell of the bread my parents baked for their bakery in outdoor ovens. The soft winds caressed my face and blew a few strands of my hair as I stood looking out over the blackness of the Pacific Ocean. I could hardly wait to see its bright blue waters in the morning.

I wasn't disappointed the following day when I woke up late, sitting up in bed to see the waves stretching out far below the guest-bedroom window. My parents' home was not on the shore, but on a slope that commanded sweeping views of the wooded hillside, black-sand beach, and the vast ocean beyond. The sun had risen high in the sky behind the house, but the yard was still in shadow. I could hear the birds as they sang riotously in the swaying trees outside the window. It was so good to be home.

I spent the day catching up with my parents and friends as I helped in the bakery, which had sold out of everything by mid-afternoon. Apparently my parents had told everyone they knew that I would be home, because neighbors, old friends, and acquaintances from nearby towns stopped by in a steady stream all day. It was wonderful to see everyone; it almost felt like I had never left.

The highlight of the day was when Liko, an old friend going all the way back to elementary school, dropped in to see me and to pick up a few *malasadas* for his family.

"Liko!" I yelled, running around the counter to give him a big hug. "You haven't changed at all!" He was medium height, barrel chested, with brown skin and long black hair. His arm and calves were wreathed in Polynesian tattoos. "How have you been?"

He grinned. "Pretty good. It's great to see you, K! How long you staying?"

"Forever!"

He beamed. "You got a job on the island?"

I nodded happily.

"Where you going to work?"

"Up the Kohala Coast, as a personal chef."

He whistled. "Sounds great!"

"What have you been doing?"

"Got laid off from the elementary school. State didn't have enough money to pay Hawaiian-language teachers any longer. I'm looking for work."

"I'm sorry to hear that. I'll let you know if I hear of anything," I promised.

"Thanks." He waved and left the shop.

Shortly after Liko left my parents decided to close the bakery for the rest of the day, since all the goodies were gone. They put me to work readying loaves to be baked and sold the next day.

The following morning I woke up early, still groggy with jet lag, and drove up the Kohala Coast to the Jorgensens' home. The drive was beautiful. It was warm, but I didn't want to use the air-conditioning in the car. I drove with the windows down, enjoying the feeling of the wind and sun on my skin. Looking out over the coast, I caught a glimpse of a whale tail slapping the surface of the water, likely a male performing part of his wintertime courtship ritual.

It took under three hours to drive to the outskirts of the small town where the Jorgensens lived. I was unprepared for the sight that met my eyes as I turned *makai* toward their home and drove downhill toward the ocean.

It was the only home in sight. From above the house on the road, all I could see were its expansive roofs, glinting brown in the sunlight. There appeared to be two or three levels; the house was probably built on a downhill gradient.

I finally reached a fork in the road. I could either veer to the left into a long driveway or right onto a small track toward the ocean. I took the left fork and drove through two enormous brown gates emblazoned with giant iron palm trees. The driveway, with its neat split-rail fences, wound through lush tropical gardens of palm trees, *monstera*, Hawaiian snowbush, Song of India, and ti trees. I glimpsed midnight jasmine, red ginger, and hibiscus. Marveling at the growth that was possible with a sprinkler system on the west coast of the Big Island, I pulled in front of a four-stall garage and got out of the car.

The house was on my right. I walked to the front door through a breezeway that straddled a huge rectangular koi pond. A pergola laden with hanging jade covered the breezeway; large orange, white, and black koi fish swam lazily in its shade. To my left and one level below me I could glimpse the pool, surrounded by chaise lounges. I raised my hand to grasp the huge ring that I supposed was the door knocker when the door swung noiselessly open.

"You must be Kailani," said the young woman who stood in the doorway. "I'm Akela, one of the housekeepers. Come on in."

Akela stood back, holding the door open as I stepped into the cool foyer. I took off my shoes and left them by the front door, as was the custom in Hawaii, then turned around and followed her down a short hallway that was open to the garden along the back of the house. The coolness of the tumbled marble floor felt good on my bare feet. When we reached the end of the hallway, the house opened up suddenly and I was treated to a magnificent view of the aquamarine Pacific Ocean and the island of Maui rising from the horizon.

"Mr. and Mrs. Jorgensen are out right now, so I'll be happy to show you around," said Akela with a smile.

I couldn't take my eyes off the view. Akela laughed. "Isn't that amazing? Everyone has that reaction when they first come in here."

"This is incredible! The water is so close!"

"The original owners of the house actually had to pay a fine because they built too close to the water."

"I can believe it."

"Come on, I'll show you your suite first."

I followed Akela through a large living area, then into the kitchen, which looked well-equipped but a bit small for such a large house. Akela turned to me and said, "You can have a look in here in just a sec. First, let me show you where your bedroom is."

We went through a door at the end of the kitchen and into a spacious den furnished with tropical rattan furniture. Akela pointed to two doors against the side wall of the room.

"The door on the right is the bathroom and the door on the left is your bedroom."

We walked across the den and she opened the bedroom door. It too was furnished in understated tropical prints and had a beautiful rattan four-poster bed, dresser, and nightstand. A large window looked out over lush gardens that sloped toward a *pali*, a small cliff of jagged black lava rock that protected the house from the rising tides. The Pacific sparkled in the warm sunshine.

"Why don't you take a look around the kitchen now?" she asked. "I'll be back in fifteen or twenty minutes to show you the rest of the house."

After I thanked her and she left, I made my way back to the kitchen and started getting acquainted with my new workspace. The room was rectangular and long, but narrow. The appliances were restaurant-quality, with stainless-steel finishes and touch-pad controls. The counters, made of black granite, were shining and immaculate. Two oblong windows gave anyone in the kitchen a breathtaking view, similar to the one in my bedroom.

The ocean was below me and about 150 feet away. The white waves curled as they broke close to shore, dashing rhythmically against the base of the *pali*.

I finally tore myself away from the view and started looking through the cabinets and drawers. I found everything from gleaming pots and pans to hand-thrown pottery to serving vessels and ceramic dishes for everyday use. There was one drawer full of fun kitchen gadgets, like an immersion blender and a tofu press. I couldn't wait to start using some of those toys!

Akela poked her head in the kitchen. "What do you think?"

"Everything I could ever need is in here!"

"You ready to see the rest of the house?"

She led me out of the kitchen and toward the back of the house, away from the water.

We walked along the corridor that was open to the gardens on the *mauka* side of the house and to the large living area on the *makai* side. A soft breeze blew down the hall, ushering in the scent of *kiele* flowers. We passed a wine cellar, which Akela informed me was quite extensive, then she walked through a wide doorway on our right and we were in a large office, again facing the front of the house and the ocean.

"This is Mr. Jorgensen's office," Akela said with a sweep of her arm.

It looked like the entire office had been paneled with koa wood. The walls, cabinets, and desk were the rich burled caramel color of the rare and precious wood, gleaming in the midday sunlight. A sitting area consisting of three rattan chairs and a round glass-topped table completed the contemporary look of the office. Two huge shadow boxes hung on the walls. One held a latte-colored T-shirt with a *Kaimana* logo on the breast and the other contained an aloha shirt patterned with tropical vines and flowers, also with the *Kaimana* logo on the sleeve.

"Does Mr. Jorgensen surf?" I asked, knowing that clothes with the *Kaimana* logo were popular among island surfers.

"He loves it."

"He must like *Kaimana* stuff," I noted with a smile.

She raised her eyebrows at me. "Likes it? He owns it."

I was surprised. "Mr. Jorgensen owns the *Kaimana* Company?"

She nodded. "Founder, president, and owner. He's out surfing now, I'm sure."

No wonder the house was so amazing. *Kaimana* was a favorite among surfers, who were known for their fierce brand loyalty.

I followed Akela out of the office and onto the lanai, where we stood facing the water.

"How do you get any work done here?" I asked.

"It isn't easy," Akela said with a laugh.

I followed her along the lanai, which seemed to run the entire length of the house, to a large covered seating area. It contained a dining table and ten chairs, a huge daybed with batik coverings and pillows, a comfortable-looking sofa and matching armchairs, several occasional tables, lots of large potted tropical plants, and a small wet bar.

"Is this where the family eats dinner?"

"Most nights, yes. Once in a while they eat in a small dining room on the other side of the kitchen."

"Have the Jorgensens always had a personal chef?"

"As long as I've been here. The last one left about a month ago."

"Why did she leave?" I knew I was being nosy, but I couldn't help asking.

"He. And it was because he hated working for Mrs. Jorgensen. But you didn't hear that from me." Akela grinned.

"Uh-oh."

"I wouldn't worry about it. You'll probably get along with her much better than he did."

"I hope so."

I followed Akela down the length of the lanai. She stopped at an open doorway and gestured inside. "This is Justine's room. She's the Jorgensens' daughter and she's a sweetheart. You'll like her. You probably don't really need to know where her room is, but I figured you ought to know your way around the house."

I nodded, looking in and noting more beautiful koa furnishings and light pink, girly accents. Akela continued to the end of the lanai and turned a corner. This side of the lanai overlooked the pool, guest-house, and more gardens. She stopped and indicated another open doorway. "This is Marcus's room. He's the Jorgensens' son. Your typical teenage boy. Again, you probably don't need to know all this, but this is just to give you an idea." I peeked in the doorway. More koa furniture, this time decorated in navy blue. Clearly a masculine bedroom.

My tour continued; near the door where I had entered the house there was a massive spiral staircase. Upstairs was the master suite, which occupied the entire top floor of the home.

"I shouldn't really be showing you this," said Akela conspiratori-ally as we climbed the stairs, "but you've got to see it."

It was a magnificent space with an airy bedroom, his-and-her bath-rooms, two huge sitting rooms that doubled as closets, and a sauna. The entire suite overlooked the ocean, just as the rooms downstairs did. At the bottom of the spiral staircase, the lowest level of the home contained a huge family room, bigger than any I had ever seen, and more storage space than I could have imagined. The family room led directly to a lush ground-floor courtyard and a sparkling pool. We walked out to the pool and Akela indicated the guesthouse nearby.

"The guesthouse has two suites, each with its own bedroom and living room. The suites also share a workout room, a common den, and a huge common kitchen. Whenever guests stay here, they're in-vited for meals in the main house. They could cook in the kitchen in the guesthouse, but they usually don't."

"Are there guests here often?"

"Yes. One of the doctors who works with Mrs. Jorgensen stays here all the time. He lives on O'ahu, so he only goes home once or twice a week. You'll meet him soon, I'm sure."

"When will I meet the Jorgensens?"

"Mrs. Jorgensen will be here in a little while. She wants you to stay until she gets here. You'll meet Mr. Jorgensen eventually. Well, that's the end of the tour. I need to get back to work," she said with a smile.

"Akela, do the Jorgensens have any pets?"

"No. Why?"

"It's just that I have this cat, Meli, who moved from Washington with me. I was wondering if I'm allowed to have her here."

"I don't know. No one has ever had pets here. You'll have to ask."

"Thanks."

Akela returned to her duties and I found my way back to the kitchen, where I found a pad of paper and a pencil. I started making notes of things I wanted to ask Mrs. Jorgensen. I wandered out onto the lanai to find the small dining room Akela had mentioned earlier. It was indeed tucked right next to the kitchen, though there was no way to get to it directly from inside the house, making it a cozy and intimate space.

So far, I loved this job.

Chapter 4

I was checking cupboards in the kitchen again, taking stock of the pantry staples that were already there, when I heard voices coming through the living area. A high-pitched laugh was accompanied by lower, quieter tones.

A petite woman with long curly blond hair appeared in the kitchen. She walked over to me briskly on her very high heels, holding out her hand.

"You must be Kailani," she said with a wide smile. "I'm Barbie Merriweather-Jorgensen and this is my colleague, Dr. Douglas Fitzgibbons."

I shook hands with them in turn, then faced Mrs. Merriweather-Jorgensen. "I'm just acquainting myself with your kitchen. It looks like I have everything I'll need to get started whenever you're ready."

She beamed. "Wonderful! Can you start now? We're *rav*enous!"

I was suddenly a little nervous, but I smiled and answered, "Of course. What can I get you?"

"Oh, surprise us. Just something light, though, since we both have to get back to work." She motioned Dr. Fitzgibbons onto the lanai. I looked around and took a deep breath. I had seen chicken broth and dry soba noodles in one of the cupboards, so I reached for those. Normally I would have made my own chicken stock, but there wasn't time for that now. I searched in the refrigerator for vegetables and found carrots, mushrooms, and scallions. I threw together a quick soup, added some bread I had found, and lunch was ready in no time. I arranged the food with napkins and utensils on a large lacquered tray and carried it out of the kitchen carefully.

I found them seated across from each other at the large dining table farther down the lanai.

"I hope chicken and soba-noodle soup is okay for lunch," I told them.

"Sounds de*lic*ious!" gushed Mrs. Merriweather-Jorgensen.

Dr. Fitzgibbons made an *mmm* sound and nodded his agreement.

They still needed drinks, so I went back to the kitchen for iced tea and took it to them. Mrs. Merriweather-Jorgensen was putting down her spoon.

"Kailani, this soup is out*standi*ng!" she effused.

"Great!" the doctor agreed.

"Thanks," I said, putting down the drinks. I returned to the kitchen, where I cleaned up from lunch and waited to collect the soup bowls from the table.

It wasn't long before the pair came into the kitchen again. "Kailani, thank you for the *won*derful lunch! I won't be home in time for dinner, and Lars and the children can fend for themselves. Can you start with breakfast the day after tomorrow? You can move your things in tomorrow."

"Sure." I paused. "Do you have any objection to me having a cat here?"

She looked doubtful. "You have a cat?"

"Yes. She's a small cat. I would keep her confined to my rooms. Her name is Meli."

"Is that a Hawaiian name?"

"Yes. It means *honey*."

"Well, I guess we can give it a try. Bring her here and we'll see how it works out. But if she smells, she'll have to go," Mrs. Merriweather-Jorgensen said, wrinkling her nose.

"Thank you," I said, sighing with relief. She didn't seem too keen on the idea of having a cat in the house, but if I could keep Meli in my suite, it should work out.

I left after quickly cleaning up the remaining lunch dishes, then went back to my parents' house to make sure everything was packed.

They had finished up their baking for the day and were tending to the late-afternoon swarm of customers who came in to pick up a dessert or a loaf of bread to have with dinner. I helped the last patrons who straggled in at closing time and then returned to my mother's kitchen, where I never tired of watching her cook.

For dinner Dad had picked up a fish from a place down the road. The fisherman and his wife sold his fresh catch from a small porch off the side of their house; it's where my parents bought all their fresh fish. Mom cleaned it and roasted it whole, adding lemon slices and herbs. She never used a recipe; she just knew what tasted good and did all her cooking "by feel," as she described it.

I went outside and picked a couple papayas for dessert, and the three of us had dinner with my sister and Haliaka. As always, it was fun and noisy and delicious.

I packed most of my things in the car after dinner. Haliaka bounced around, asking me all kinds of questions about my new job.

"Will you live there?"

"Is the house nice?"

"Is it near the water?"

"What will you cook for the people?"

"Can I visit you there?"

"Are there any kids?"

"Do they like you?"

I answered her queries dutifully and finally, laughing, I told her to go find Tutu and think of some questions to ask her. I knew my mother would indulge Haliaka's constant queries.

The next day I helped my parents with the morning baking, then set out with my full car and a cat carrier on the front seat, Meli meowing inside. She did not like cars.

When we arrived at the Jorgensens' house, I took Meli out first. I lugged her carrier to the front door. Once again, Akela was there to open it before I could even knock. She stepped back to let me carry Meli through the door and down the hall.

I let Meli out on the floor of my bedroom. She crouched low to the ground, sniffing and moving very slowly as she checked out her new home. Her ears were back, the classic sign of an anxious cat, but I knew she would eventually get used to living at the Jorgensen house. She didn't really have a choice.

I returned to the car for more of my things, this time accompanied by Akela. Together we took one suitcase full of clothes and three crates full of cookbooks to my rooms. There was a built-in bookcase in my den, so we placed the cookbooks in there. Meli walked over and wound between my legs while I was putting the books away. She seemed to be adjusting well already.

I hadn't planned to make any meals that day because I was supposed to start with breakfast the following morning. No one showed up wanting lunch, so I spent part of the afternoon unpacking all my things and getting them set up in my suite. I sat down in the den for a while with a pad and paper, jotting down ideas for menus. Since I hadn't met anyone in the household except for Akela and Mrs. Jorgensen, I didn't know what the family's tastes were. I did recall Mrs. Jorgensen telling me that her family liked heavy meals and that she was trying to get them to eat healthier, so I focused on lean meats, fish, and vegetables.

Once I had double-checked for ingredients in the kitchen and finalized my grocery list, I set out in my car for the nearest market, which was not far up the main road. I had never been inside this particular market, but it was typical of those in small towns on the island of Hawaii: lots of Asian ingredients, produce from local farms, a limited dairy selection, a nice meat and poultry section, and lots of fresh fish. Mrs. Jorgensen had set up accounts with all the nearby markets, so I didn't have to pay for the groceries myself. I also picked up a free local paper that I knew would list farmers' markets in the North Kohala district.

I unpacked the groceries back at the house. It was quiet in the kitchen. I watched the waves crashing down below on the lava rock as I put things in the cupboards. Suddenly someone coughed behind me. I spun around, startled.

A young girl was standing in the doorway to the kitchen. She was about nine years old, tall and skinny with a deep tan and dark brown hair pulled into a ponytail. She wore bright pink shorts and a white tank top. She was barefoot.

"Are you the new chef?" she asked with a tentative smile.

"Yes. My name is Kailani. You must be Justine."

"Yes."

"It's nice to meet you, Justine. Did you just get home from school?" She nodded.

"I'll bet you're looking for a snack."

She smiled and nodded again.

"I brought some papaya with me from my mom and dad's house. Would you like some?" Justine wrinkled her nose in response. "How about an orange? I brought some of those too." Another nose-wrinkle.

"Do we have any chips?"

I knew Mrs. Jorgensen wanted her kids to eat healthy, but there *were* chips in the cupboard, along with cheese popcorn, candy bars, and barbeque-flavored onion rings. I suppressed a shudder. "Yes. Would you like them, or would you rather have some pretzels?"

"Chips." She walked over to the cupboard and pulled out a bag of potato chips. Taking the bag with her, she disappeared around the corner with a wave. "See you later!"

I went to my rooms in search of Meli. She was batting the dust motes that floated in the sunlight slanting into the bedroom. I sat down in the armchair in the den and she left her game to curl up on my lap. It wasn't long before I heard someone rummaging around in the kitchen. Meli rocketed off my lap and ran into the bedroom while I checked out the noise.

There was a young teenage boy with his hand in the chip cupboard. He obviously didn't expect me to appear, because he jumped when I poked my head in the kitchen.

"Don't do that! Who are you, anyways?" he demanded.

"I'm the new chef. I'm Kailani," I said with a smile, hoping he turned out to be nicer than my first impression of him.

"Oh. Is there any Coke?"

"I haven't found any. There's water and tea in the fridge."

"I want Coke. Can you get some at the store?"

"I don't know. I have to check with your mom first to see if that's okay with her."

"Ugh." He rolled his eyes and left.

And that's how I met Marcus.

Early that evening I made myself a salad for dinner and ate slowly on the lanai, watching the sun sink lower toward the horizon in the west. The sky was a brilliant tapestry of orange and yellow and burnished gold streaks before turning several shades of pink, then lavender, and finally a deep indigo that signaled the nearby bugs and *coqui* frogs to start their nighttime chorus. I was a little surprised that I hadn't seen any of the family for dinner, but maybe they were out. The rest of the house was very quiet. I went back to my room and opened a book.

It wasn't long before I heard faint voices coming from the lanai. I went through the kitchen and listened.

"She wouldn't buy Coke," a surly voice said. Obviously Marcus.

"She tried to get me to eat something healthy after school," a high-pitched girl's voice whined. Justine.

"Well then, hurry up and eat your burgers before the food sergeant comes out here and replaces them with celery," said a man's voice. *That must be Mr. Jorgensen. Lovely,* I thought sarcastically.

Food sergeant. Is that what they already thought of me around here? I groaned inwardly.

I spent the night tossing and turning, suddenly nervous about breakfast. What could I serve that Mr. Jorgensen and the kids would eat? Meli, curled next to my feet, glared at me whenever I moved, her eyes reflected in the moonlight coming through the blinds.

I was up before the sun and decided to make oatmeal with cream and sliced bananas. I found a kitchen torch and set it up to caramelize the brown sugar on top of the bananas for each family member as they appeared for breakfast.

Justine and Marcus rushed into the kitchen at 6:30, clearly in a hurry to get to school on time. They dropped their backpacks on the kitchen floor. The oatmeal was ready, so I quickly torched the sugar and bananas and served each child at the lanai dining table.

"Wow!" cried Justine. "This is really good! Can we have it again tomorrow?" I nodded, pleased that I had made at least one person happy. Marcus, who had been wolfing down his breakfast, looked up at Justine but continued eating in silence. I returned to the kitchen, where I made their lunches and set them on the counter. I gave them salads in plastic containers with dressing in separate small jars. They each got a slice of my mom's bread and a handful of strawberries too. I didn't know what they usually ate, but I supposed if they didn't like what I packed they would let me know after school.

The kids clattered into the kitchen and grabbed their lunches, then their backpacks, and were on their way out when a man appeared in the doorway.

He was stocky and clean-shaven with shaggy hair, wearing board shorts and a *Kaimana* T-shirt. His boyish looks made him appear younger than he probably was. His blond hair had the shine that came from spending lots of time in the sun and water and his eyes were a piercing blue. He kissed Justine before she headed out and told Marcus to have a good day.

He then held out his hand to me politely. "I'm Lars Jorgensen," he said.

"Kailani Kanaka," I answered.

"Nice to meet you. Have you found your way around the kitchen?"

"I'm starting to get my bearings."

"Barbie said you're from Washington."

"That's right. I was the sous-chef in a restaurant there."

"Why did you come to Hawaii?"

Apparently he hadn't noticed my Hawaiian features. I had long straight black hair and dark eyes thanks to my Japanese-American mother, and olive skin and a broad nose thanks to my Hawaiian father.

"My family lives near Punalu'u," I told him. "I was ready to come home." He seemed surprised that I was a local.

He rubbed his hands together. "I'm starving. Got anything good for breakfast?"

"I made the kids oatmeal and caramelized some sliced bananas with brown sugar on the top. Does that sound okay?"

"Sounds great. Got coffee?"

I filled a large mug for him and he helped himself to cream and sugar while I handled the kitchen torch.

"That's cool!" he said as he watched me.

I smiled at him.

"Has Barbie eaten yet?" he asked.

"No. I haven't seen her this morning."

He grimaced and took his oatmeal out to the table. I took him a glass of juice and a slice of toast made with my parents' bread as he opened the newspaper and began to read. He grunted when I set the plate and glass down next to him. I supposed that was his way of saying "thanks."

It wasn't long before Mrs. Jorgensen came into the kitchen. "Good morning, Kailani!" she sang. "What's for breakfast?"

I recited the menu. Looking pleased, Mrs. Jorgensen went out to the lanai, where she sat across from Mr. Jorgensen, opened her own paper, and waited for her breakfast. I felt strange when I took her tray to her. It was completely silent at the table except for the rustling of newspaper pages and the wind whistling down the length of the lanai. Neither husband nor wife looked up as I set the tray on the table and quickly returned to the kitchen.

Before long Mr. Jorgensen brought his dishes and utensils into the kitchen. "Thanks. That was great," he remarked, then left.

I didn't see Mrs. Jorgensen again that morning. When I looked out onto the lanai a bit later, her dishes were at her place. I cleared them and readied the kitchen for the next meal. I still didn't know who would be eating lunch, but I wanted to be ready with something just in case someone was hungry.

It was early afternoon when Mr. Jorgensen came into the kitchen again. "Is there anything for lunch?" he asked.

"I have a spinach salad with strawberries, red onions, and toasted almonds," I offered. He didn't say anything right away.

"Any other choices?" he finally asked.

"I have chicken and soba-noodle soup." There was some left from yesterday's lunch.

He sighed. "All right. I guess I'll have the soup."

"Is there something special you'd like me to make for tomorrow's lunch?" I asked.

"How about a burger? With macaroni salad?"

"Would you like a veggie burger? I make a great veggie burger with mushrooms."

He raised his eyebrows. That apparently wasn't what he had in mind. "Don't trouble yourself," he answered. "A regular burger would be fine."

I prepared the soup for him and carried it to his office with a piece of bread and a glass of tea. He was on the phone and mouthed the word "thanks" when I set the tray down.

Mrs. Jorgensen and Dr. Fitzgibbons were waiting for me when I returned to the kitchen. They both chose the spinach salad for lunch and waited for me to serve it on the lanai. As I walked toward the table with their tray, I passed Akela. She raised her eyebrows and whispered "Yikes!"

I had no idea what she was talking about. I was back in the kitchen, rummaging in the refrigerator, when Akela tapped me on the shoulder. I jumped and gave a little yelp. She put her finger to her lips.

"Has Mr. Jorgensen seen them?" she asked in a low voice.

"Seen who?"

"Mrs. Jorgensen and Dr. Doug."

"I have no idea. Why?"

"Because he hates Dr. Doug."

"Oh."

"Don't you want to know why?"

I didn't care, but I answered dutifully, "Why?"

"Because Mrs. Jorgensen and Dr. Doug are sleeping together."

It was none of my business, but I couldn't help being drawn into conversation. "You're kidding!"

"Nope," Akela replied. "Been going on for a while now."

"And she brings him to the house?"

"Right under Mr. Jorgensen's nose," Akela replied, shaking her head.

"Does he know?"

"He must. How could he not realize what's going on?"

"How do you know all this?"

"It doesn't take a genius to figure it out," she replied, rolling her eyes.

So maybe she wasn't really sure. Maybe she was just assuming the worst of Mrs. Jorgensen and Dr. Fitzgibbons.

"We shouldn't be talking about it while they're out there," I cautioned. She shrugged and went off to her own tasks.

I felt a little guilty having gossiped about the Jorgensens. My only impression of Mrs. Jorgensen so far was of a friendly, enthusiastic woman. My impression of Mr. Jorgensen was a little fuzzy—after all, he *had* referred to me as a food sergeant—but he had been pleasant and polite enough since then.

Is there something going on that Mrs. Jorgensen is trying to hide? I walked out to the lanai and glanced toward the dining table. Mrs. Jorgensen and Dr. Fitzgibbons sat comfortably across from each other, chatting amiably. It was quite different from the scene at breakfast, where Mr. and Mrs. Jorgensen had sat across from each other, silent and preoccupied.

I hurried back into the kitchen to wait for them to leave so I could clear the table. Mr. Jorgensen came in.

"Is there anything else for lunch? I'm still hungry."

"I can bring you some pretzels and a honey-mustard dip if you'd like," I suggested.

"Sounds good." He turned and went out to the lanai. But a second later he turned around and stalked past the kitchen doorway, his mouth set in a grim line. "I'll be in my office," he told me brusquely.

He must have seen them, I thought anxiously. *He must know.*

I hurriedly put a large handful of pretzels on a plate and mixed together a small bowl of honey mustard, then took it quietly to his office. He was on the phone again, talking in a low voice, and he motioned me to leave the plate on his desk. I complied and left the room quickly and quietly. I noticed when I went back to the kitchen that Mrs. Jorgensen and Dr. Fitzgibbons were walking out the front door together, probably to go back to work. I heard Mr. Jorgensen slam the phone down. I was suddenly nervous and edgy.

Just then Akela walked by the kitchen doorway. She arched her eyebrows at me. "Double yikes," she whispered. I nodded.

It wasn't long before the kids came home from school. As they had the day before, they came to the kitchen in search of snacks. I had made a large plate of vegetables that I arranged in a starburst pattern, and there was a bowl of fruit salad. I offered those, then when the kids declined I offered pretzels. They both shook their heads. I told them to help themselves to whatever they could find, knowing they would opt for the chips and cookies in the cupboard. My plan was to wait until they had eaten every unhealthy snack in the cupboard and then offer only healthy snacks after school. If they were hungry, I reasoned, they would eat what I made. I made a mental note to discuss the issue with Mrs. Jorgensen next time I saw her.

"Is there any Coke?" asked Marcus.

"Not yet. I haven't had a chance to ask your mother about it. But I made a *lilikoi* puree and added it to the iced tea. It tastes really good."

He scowled. "What is *lilikoi*, anyways?"

"Passion fruit. You're from Hawaii and you don't know what *lilikoi* is?" I asked in surprise.

"I'm from California, not Hawaii. And it sounds gross."

This might be my chance to engage him, to get him to smile, I thought.

"Oh? You're from California? When did you move to Hawaii?"

"We're from San Diego. We moved here five years ago because my dad wanted to move his company here."

"Do you ever go back to San Diego?"

"Sometimes."

He clearly did not want to talk anymore. He took a bag of mini-Oreos and left.

Justine watched him go. "He hates living in Hawaii," she said, shaking her head in a very grown-up way. "He wants to move back to California."

"Why?"

"He hardly has any friends here."

"Why not?"

"He doesn't want any," she answered. She seemed wise beyond her years.

"That's sad."

"I know. I'm his friend, though."

"I'm glad to hear that."

Justine, suddenly melancholy, turned and walked slowly out of the kitchen. She even forgot to take a snack.

Chapter 5

The entire family was at dinner that evening. I hoped Mrs. Jorgensen would address everyone, tell them she wanted them to eat healthier and that she had enlisted my help in her quest. I didn't want to continue to be at odds with Mr. Jorgensen and the kids over the food I prepared. For dinner I made sea bass and served it with garlicky broccolini and brown-rice pilaf. I chose sea bass because it was a happy medium between healthy and rich. Mrs. Jorgensen loved it, as I knew she would. She seemed quite happy with everything I had made. So far. The kids both protested, but Mrs. Jorgensen insisted that they eat half of what was on their plates. Mr. Jorgensen dutifully made a good example, but he clearly would have preferred lasagna or a steak. He told me as much after dinner.

"Kailani, the fish was good, though it wouldn't have been my first choice. My wife told us at dinner that she has asked for your help in trying to get us to eat healthier, so at least I now understand why you've been serving us foods we're not used to." He made a pleading motion with his hands. "But can I still have that burger for lunch tomorrow? I'll even forget about the macaroni salad. But don't tell her."

I relented. "Okay. Maybe I can make you a pasta salad that has vinaigrette instead of mayonnaise."

"I'll try anything," he said with a smile.

Later that evening I had opened my bedroom window to the sound of the surf when I thought I heard heated whispering outdoors. I peered through the blinds to see who was outside, but no one was there. It was then I realized the voices were being carried on the wind from the master-bedroom lanai, above and to the left of my room. I strained to hear what was going on.

"Why do you bring him here?" Mr. Jorgensen's voice hissed.

"Because he's a colleague and a friend. And he hates hotels. They're so impersonal. You're the one who insisted on coming to live here."

"A colleague and a friend? Is that all?"

"Of course."

"You're lying."

"If you don't believe me, then why did you ask?"

"To see if you had the guts to tell me the truth!" Mr. Jorgensen's voice rose.

"Shh!"

Their voices lowered immediately and I couldn't hear anymore. It was clear that Mr. Jorgensen suspected an affair between Mrs. Jorgensen and Dr. Fitzgibbons, but she hadn't admitted it. I suddenly felt sorry for Mr. Jorgensen.

The next morning when the kids came into the kitchen they were tired and cranky. I greeted them brightly and got stares and mumbles in return. They ate the breakfast I made them and grabbed their lunches as Mr. Jorgensen appeared in the kitchen to tell them good-bye. Marcus called to me over his shoulder as he left for school, "I hope this is better than yesterday's lunch."

He was going to be disappointed.

Mr. Jorgensen told me not to bother with that burger that he had ordered for lunch. Something had come up unexpectedly and he was catching a flight to the mainland and would be there for a couple days.

Mrs. Jorgensen informed me that neither she nor Dr. Fitzgibbons were coming home for lunch either, so I had much of the day to myself. I spent part of the day tidying up my suite of rooms, then decided to go kayaking in the afternoon.

I had strapped my kayak to the roof of the car when I moved to the Jorgensens' house and it was stored in the garage. This was my first chance to use it. Carrying the kayak over my head, I wound my way down to the water in front of the house. A short, steep path had been worn into the lava near the *pali*, and I managed to lug my kayak down the path.

The lava at the shore was jagged and rough. I always marveled at the way lava looked soft and ropy from a distance, when up close it could be as sharp as broken glass. Small pulverized bits of the charcoal-colored rock led down to the water, which was crashing lazily against the shoreline. It was a perfect day for being on the water.

I put in between two swells and rowed quickly to get over the waves and away from the shore. Once I was out a short distance, I started paddling north, parallel to the coast, taking my time and enjoying the view. Maui was sixty miles ahead of me and to the left. I felt tiny. I watched the land slip by and savored the quiet lapping of the waves and the bright sunshine. My kayak dipped and rose with the waves and the effect was so mesmerizing I almost forgot to paddle. As I drifted closer to shore, I could see a faraway figure walking slowly down the main road to the Jorgensen house. It looked like Marcus.

My heart went out to him. He looked so small and alone on his way home from school. I wished he weren't so unapproachable and prickly, because I would be happy to be his friend. Justine skipped along behind him, swinging her backpack and taking time to stop every now and then to pluck flowers from the side of the road.

I didn't hurry back to the house because I had left food in the kitchen for the kids' snack. I was enjoying the freedom of being on the water, the warm trade winds whipping my hair. Eventually I turned back and headed down the coastline. The wind was kicking up the waves a bit so I couldn't relax much, but it felt good to be working hard. And it was certainly easier than fighting the bitterly cold wind in Washington. Close to the *pali*, I again waited for a lull in the waves and eased over to the rocky shoreline between two crests. I scrambled out of the kayak and onto land, hauling my boat up behind me before a wave could come and smash me into the rocks.

I made my way back up to the house, put the kayak back in the garage, and walked to the front door, marveling again at the vibrant turquoise jade vines hanging from the pergola above me. I wished I could see them from my bedroom window.

After I had changed my clothes, I found Marcus waiting for me in the kitchen when I went in to prepare dinner. Maybe this was my chance to reintroduce myself.

"Hi, Marcus. What's up?"

"Nuthin'. What's for dinner?"

"Pork tenderloin. You like pork, don't you?"

"I guess. Are you going to ruin it with vegetables?"

I laughed. "Yes, but maybe you'll like them."

"Doubt it."

"Did you get a snack?"

"No. I couldn't find anything good. There aren't any chips."

"I know. Your mom asked me to stop buying them. There's a rice-cracker mix in the cupboard. Have you ever tried it?"

"No. It sounds gross."

I pulled the mix from the cupboard and gave it to him. It was a crispy, crunchy mix of rice crackers, bits of dried seaweed, sesame seeds, and lots of spices. He looked askance at the bag.

"Just try it," I urged. "I can't believe you live on the Big Island and you've never tried this stuff."

He took a fistful of mix from the bag and ate a few pieces. I watched him, then asked, "What do you think?"

He shrugged. "It's not bad." He ate another fistful. "It's actually pretty good." He smiled. I felt a small thrill of victory.

"Go on. Take the bag," I urged him.

"Thanks. I still don't want vegetables tonight, though."

"Let's take one food at a time," I said with a grin. "I didn't steer you wrong with the rice crackers, did I?"

That evening it was just the two kids at the long dining table on the lanai. Mr. Jorgensen wouldn't be back for another day or two, and Mrs. Jorgensen was still at work. I served Marcus and Justine their dinner.

"Why don't you sit and eat with us?" Justine suggested.

"That would be nice. Thanks," I replied.

I got a plate for myself from the kitchen and sat down with the kids. "What grades are you in?" I asked. This would be a good chance to get to know them better.

"I'm in fourth grade," Justine said, wiping her mouth.

"I'm in ninth," Marcus said.

"Do you like school?"

"Yes!" Justine cried.

"No," Marcus said glumly.

"Ninth grade can be hard," I told him sympathetically. "The work gets much harder all of a sudden, plus there are all the pressures of high school."

He nodded. I changed the subject.

"What do you think of those veggies?"

"I like them," Justine told me. "I've never had this green stuff before."

She was referring to the grilled bok choy with a soy glaze.

"Do you like them, Marcus?" she asked.

"Yeah. They're actually pretty good," he admitted. I smiled at him.

"It's all in the way they're presented," I said. "Grilled bok choy looks pretty cool, doesn't it?"

They both nodded, their mouths full.

"So what do you guys do after dinner?" I asked.

"I text with my friends," Justine said happily.

"Homework," Marcus answered.

"What do you do if you need help?"

"If Dad or Mom is here, I ask one of them for help. Sometimes Dr. Doug helps me with math."

"I don't want to brag, but I'm not too bad at math myself," I told him, grinning. "If you need help and no one is around, you can always ask me."

"Okay. Thanks."

With that, dinner came to an end and the kids left for their bedrooms. A while later, after I had cleaned up from dinner, I found Marcus at the dining table, books and folders scattered around him.

"Kailani, can you help me with math?" he asked.

"Sure," I answered. I hadn't expected him to ask me for help so soon.

We spent the next half hour doing algebraic equations under the soft lights on the lanai. He seemed to be having some trouble understanding, and made slow progress. When he was done, he gathered up his supplies and turned to thank me.

"You're a good math teacher," he said with a small smile. "Sorry I'm not a great student."

"You are a good student," I assured him. "You just need a little extra help, that's all. But don't worry. It may take a while, but you'll be surprised one day when all of a sudden you just get it. That's how algebra works."

"My mom wants me to have a math tutor."

"Do you think having a tutor would help?"

He lifted his shoulders slightly. "I don't know."

The wheels in my mind were turning. Liko needed a job, Marcus needed a tutor. I knew Liko taught Hawaiian language and culture, but I remembered him being a pretty sharp student in math too. He was also just the type of guy who could draw Marcus out of his shell, and it would be helping them both at the same time. I made a mental note to ask Mrs. Jorgensen if she would be interested in hiring Liko as Marcus's tutor.

Later on that evening I heard noises in the kitchen. I went in to see if someone needed anything and was surprised to see Mrs. Jorgensen, still in her white coat, and Dr. Fitzgibbons rummaging through the refrigerator. They turned around, startled, when I coughed quietly.

"Hi, Kailani! We're *starving*! What did you make the kids for dinner?" she asked.

"Pork tenderloin with soy-glazed bok choy and roasted fingerling potatoes. Want some?"

"*Defi*nitely!"

I made up plates of food for the two of them and they ate in the small dining room next to the kitchen. They lingered over a bottle of wine, talking quietly. I could hear them from the kitchen. When I took a platter of sliced fruit out to them for dessert, they were gazing at each other with more than friendship in their eyes. It was not the time to discuss Liko's tutoring qualifications with Mrs. Jorgensen.

Their dinner together was none of my business, but I wondered uneasily how Mr. Jorgensen would feel about it.

Marcus told me the next morning that his father had called him late the previous night to tell him that he was on his way home. He expected to be home in time for lunch. I thanked Marcus for letting me know, and after the kids left for school I went to the grocery store to pick up the ingredients I would need to make a thick, juicy burger to welcome Mr. Jorgensen home. I got grass-fed beef, red onion, cheese, freshly baked rolls, and sliced pickles.

Back at the house, I prepared a macaroni salad with tomatoes, chickpeas, cucumber, feta, and a red-wine vinaigrette. After seeing the looks Mrs. Jorgensen and Dr. Fitzgibbons had given each other at dinner the previous night, I again felt sorry for Mr. Jorgensen and wanted to serve him something he would enjoy.

When he did arrive, he saw me, nodded a greeting, and went straight to his office. Shortly after that, I took his lunch to him on a tray. He was on the phone when I entered. He swiveled around in his chair, his face lighting up when he saw what I had made for him.

Later that afternoon, he came to find me in the kitchen. "That burger was great! I haven't had one that good in a long time."

"Thanks. Now can I make a tofu stir-fry for dinner?"

He made a face. "If that's the price I have to pay for the burger, then I guess so."

I smiled and turned back to my cooking when he left. That night I did, indeed, serve a stir-fry of tofu and vegetables to Mr. Jorgensen and the kids. Mrs. Jorgensen came home just as the rest of the family was finishing their meal.

"Kailani, is there any dinner left?" she called from the lanai.

I took a plate to her and she sat down with the rest of the family. It wasn't long before Mr. Jorgensen and the kids left the table. When I went out to check on Mrs. Jorgensen, she waved me into a chair.

"They all left me and Dr. Fitzgibbons is working late," she said with a pout. "Come keep me company."

I sat down across from her and waited for her to speak. I didn't know what to say.

"This stir-fry is really good, Kailani. I love the meals you've been making. The kids and Lars may not love them, but they'll learn."

This was my chance. "Speaking of learning, Mrs. Jorgensen—"

"Please, call me Barbie," she interrupted.

"Okay. Speaking of learning, Barbie, Marcus mentioned that you would like him to have a tutor to help him with his math."

She nodded, a forkful of tofu halfway to her mouth. "He needs help and I don't have time to sit down and teach him. Why do you ask? Do you know someone we could hire?"

"As a matter of fact, I have a friend who's looking for work right now. He was laid off from the public school system because of cutbacks. He was teaching Hawaiian culture and language classes, but he's a whiz at math too. I've known him since we were kids."

"What's his name?"

"Liko."

"Can you give me his contact info?"

I went into the kitchen and came back out with Liko's name and phone number written on a piece of paper. Barbie tucked it into her jacket pocket, promising to call him the next day.

But she didn't get the chance.

Chapter 6

Before I went to bed that night, I found the scuppers from my kayak on a small table in the den. I remembered leaving them there after I came back from kayaking the day before. I tiptoed through the dark, quiet house to put them back in the kayak. I was coming back through the front door from the garage when I thought I heard voices. I stood still for several seconds, listening.

Yes, there were voices coming from the master bedroom upstairs. Angry voices. Though I shouldn't have, I stood still for a little longer, straining my ears. I was becoming more like Akela every day.

"How could you do this to the rest of us?" Lars asked. "And with that freeloader?"

"I have told you a thousand times, Doug is not a freeloader! He just sleeps here on the nights he doesn't go to O'ahu!"

"I don't think he's doing much sleeping," Lars spat.

"Shut up, Lars!"

"Why do we even stay married?" When there was no answer, he continued. "I mean it, Barbie. Why do we stay married when you're sleeping with someone else?"

"I'm not even talking to you right now," she said vehemently, and that ended their conversation. I suddenly felt guilty and stole quietly back to my rooms behind the kitchen. I tried sleeping, but sleep was elusive that night. I tossed and turned for what seemed like hours, trying to rid my mind of the ugly conversation I had heard. When I finally got up, it was still dark out. I needed a brisk walk to clear my head. I slipped out the front door and walked up the long driveway. I strode a short distance along the main road, then turned around and headed back to the house when I figured it was time to start getting breakfast ready.

It wasn't until I got to the end of the driveway that I heard an ear-splitting scream. I started running in the direction of the noise in the early-morning semidarkness.

I followed the screams to the pool, where they were joined by a chorus of shouts and barked commands. Lars, yelling for someone to call the police. Two gardeners, running toward the house and gesturing wildly. Barbie, screaming unintelligibly. Akela, shrieking that she didn't know what was going on. Justine, standing away from the others and crying as Marcus tried to shield her with his body.

He was protecting her from the sight of a body lying face up on the lanai, its matted hair shiny and wet-looking. Dark droplets were sprinkled around the body, like angry raindrops. It was Dr. Fitzgibbons.

I quickly grabbed each of the kids by the wrists and pulled them into the house. I couldn't believe no one else had thought to do it.

Once we were in Marcus's room I quickly shut the door to the lanai and turned around to face the kids. Marcus still had his arm around Justine and she was crying uncontrollably into his shoulder. I didn't want to intrude, so I sat down in a chair in the corner of the room and waited for Justine to catch her breath. Marcus was so good to her: He put his arm around her and didn't shrug her off or make a face or do any of the things teenaged brothers do sometimes.

Eventually she calmed down. She looked up at Marcus, her face tearstained, her eyes puffy. "What do you think happened?" she sniffled. Marcus looked at me over the top of her head.

"I don't know," he said quietly, hugging her tighter.

"Dr. Doug was really nice," she continued.

Marcus nodded silently.

"Is there anything I can do for you?" I asked.

They both shook their heads.

"Why don't you come into the kitchen with me and I'll fix you something for breakfast?" I suggested.

"I'm not hungry," Justine said, beginning to cry again.

"Me neither," said Marcus.

Food was my way of making sense of things, of introducing some order into an otherwise chaotic situation. If the kids didn't want me to cook for them, I was a bit lost.

I stood up and peered through Marcus's closed blinds. Dr. Fitzgibbons's body, dressed only in lounge pants, still lay on the ground, lifeless. Barbie was bent over, her hands on her knees. It looked like she was trying to catch her breath. Lars was standing by the body, arms akimbo, his lips white and pressed together tightly. Akela stood in the corner, her eyes wide with shock. A gardener came around the corner onto the lanai and whispered something to Lars. He listened, then spoke aloud to Barbie. I couldn't hear what he said.

Barbie lifted her tearstained face to look at Lars. "How could you do this?" she shrieked.

"Do what?" he demanded, his voice raised.

"How could you *kill him*?"

"I didn't kill him!" Lars shouted. Barbie ignored him, burying her face once again in her hands, sobbing.

I was shocked to hear their exchange. I could feel the color draining from my face as I considered the possibility that Dr. Fitzgibbons had died at the hands of someone he knew.

I wondered if I should take it upon myself to get the kids off to school. Part of me knew it was a good idea to get them away from the scene outdoors, but part of me knew they would never be able to concentrate with the image of Dr. Fitzgibbons in their heads. In the end, I decided to stay in Marcus's room with them, opting not to send them to school. The police would be there soon and I assumed they would want to talk to everyone who was present around the time of Dr. Fitzgibbons's death, whenever that had been.

Indeed, it wasn't long before the police arrived. They ordered Lars, Barbie, and the household staff out of the way before they surrounded the lanai with yellow crime-scene tape and covered the body with a white sheet. Then they began their questioning. I watched the goings-on through the window. They started with Lars, leading him into the family room, and it was quite some time before they led him out again. Next it was Barbie's turn, then Akela, then the gardeners.

Eventually the police knocked on Marcus's bedroom door. I opened it.

The officer standing in the doorway started with me. "We'd like to ask you a few questions, miss." I followed him to the family room, where I sat at a round table with him and another officer.

I told them everything I knew: That I had gone for a walk and come upon the scene when I heard screaming coming from the pool area. No, I hadn't heard any sound coming from the lanai before the screaming began. No, I hadn't seen Dr. Fitzgibbons the previous night.

Since the police didn't ask, I didn't mention that I had heard part of an argument between Lars and Barbie that was about Dr. Fitzgibbons.

As the officer's questioning of me was drawing to a close, another officer appeared in the doorway, escorting Marcus and Lars. Apparently, Lars would be permitted to sit in on Marcus's questioning.

I returned to Marcus's room, where Justine was lying face down on his bed. No one else was around. I was surprised that Barbie hadn't come looking for her yet.

"Justine? Can I get you anything?"

"No," came the muffled reply. "I'm not hungry."

"I didn't mean just food. Do you need a tissue or a glass of water or something from your room?"

She pushed herself into a seated position and looked at me from puffy, hooded eyes.

"Can I have a drink of water?"

I got her a drink from Marcus's bathroom and sat on the bed with her while she drank it. She drained the glass and hiccupped. "Will the police want to talk to me next?"

"Probably. I think they've talked to everyone else already."

"Will Dad stay in there with me like he is with Marcus?"

"I don't know. But since they're letting your dad in with Marcus, I would think they'll let him in there with you too."

She sighed. I couldn't tell if it was a sigh of relief or something else. I wondered what was going through her mind.

I couldn't even make sense of what was going through my own mind. Who could have killed Dr. Fitzgibbons? Why was he killed? I tried not to think of the harsh words that had been spoken between Lars and Barbie last night. I wondered what Dr. Fitzgibbons's last thoughts had been. I wondered about the person who had spoken to him last.

Was it Lars? Did the two men argue about Barbie?

Or was it Barbie? Did she have a fight with Dr. Fitzgibbons?

I was letting my imagination run away with me. There wasn't even any proof that the doctor had been killed. Maybe he hit his head and lost consciousness before he died. Maybe he was drunk. Maybe he was sick. The possibilities were endless.

I squeezed Justine's hand and stood up as another police officer came into Marcus's room. This officer was a woman. She knelt down in front of the bed and spoke gently to Justine.

"I'd like to talk to you for a few minutes about Dr. Doug," she began.

"Okay," Justine said timidly.

"Would you come with me into the family room? Your dad is in there and he can sit with you while I ask you some quick questions."

Justine took the officer's hand and accompanied the woman out of the room. I hesitated a moment before going back to the kitchen to make breakfast for everyone. I wanted to be close by in case Marcus came back and needed someone to talk to, but on the other hand, I didn't want to seem too eager and force myself on him. I decided that if he wanted to talk to me, he knew where he could find me.

Once I was cooking again, some of the stress and horror of the morning was pushed to the back of my mind. I prepared a big buffet breakfast for everyone who was around, including Lars and Barbie and the kids, as well as Akela, the gardeners, and any of the police officers who might want something. That was one of the best things about cooking: I could lose myself in preparing meals, not stopping to worry about what was going on around me. It was exactly what I needed at that moment.

During the next hour I prepared a feast for breakfast. For once I didn't care about fat or calories or carbohydrates. I made huevos rancheros, sticky rice, fruit salad, and Portuguese sausage. I set everything out on the dining table on the lanai and went in search of people who were probably hungry. Eventually everyone but the police filed one-by-one and helped themselves to the meal. It was still fairly early in the morning.

Justine wandered into the kitchen after a while, looking lost.

"Did you get breakfast?"

She nodded, her shoulders drooping and her mouth turned down at the corners. "Would you like to help me in the kitchen today since you're not going to school? Cooking always helps me when I'm under stress or feeling sad."

"Okay," she said with a sigh.

I found an old apron of mine in my room and tied it behind her back. "What would you like to make?" I asked her.

She looked around, as if she didn't know her way around the kitchen. "I don't know," she answered. "What can we make?"

"Anything you'd like. We can get lunch started, or we can make something fun for dessert tonight, or we can make something special to give to your teacher."

"Hmmm. Let's make something for dessert."

"Okay. Do you have anything in mind or would you like to look through my cookbooks?"

"I want to see your cookbooks."

I led her into my den and Meli immediately got up from her sunny place on the floor, stretched, and came up to Justine, purring and rubbing her nose against her leg. Justine smiled tremulously as she ran her hand across Meli's sleek, warm back.

"I love your cat. Mom doesn't like cats very much."

"I keep her in my rooms so that she doesn't bother your mom. It's very nice of her to let me keep Meli here."

Justine nodded and took the first book I handed to her. I showed her where the dessert section was and she began thumbing slowly through the pages. Each of the recipes was accompanied by a picture, so she could have a look at the finished product.

After she had leafed through the pages, she looked up at me expectantly. "Do you have any more cookbooks?"

I laughed. "You'd be amazed at how many cookbooks I have. Lots of them are at my mom and dad's house, but I have quite a few on my shelves here too." I selected a few for her and returned to the kitchen while she perused the lists of goodies.

I was crouched down, looking for a Dutch oven, when Akela came in. "Kailani, there's someone here to see you."

"Who is it?"

"He didn't give his name. He's waiting at the end of the driveway. The police wouldn't let him come up to the house, so one of them came to escort you."

I followed Akela to the front door, where an officer stood waiting. He explained that he and his partner could not allow anyone on the property and said he would take me to see my visitor. We walked in silence to the end of the driveway. Another officer was stationed by the large gate, and on the other side of it a tall man in shorts and a T-shirt stood with his back to me. Even before he turned around I knew who it was.

"Geoffrey? What are you doing here?" I asked, incredulous. I had only emailed him a couple times since leaving Washington, and none of those emails had included an invitation to visit or the location of my new job. I opened the gate slowly.

He turned to look at me, a big grin spread across his face. "Surprise!" He came forward and gave me a big hug. I pushed myself away gently.

"I can't believe you're here! What made you decide to come all the way to Hawaii?"

"You! What else?" I stole a glance at the officers, who were politely looking in the other direction.

"Wow. I'm flattered. I wish you'd told me you were coming, because I could have met you at the airport or something." I faltered, searching for the right thing to say. I thought he had realized that I didn't want to see him anymore. That he wasn't part of my life in Hawaii the way he had been in Washington.

He stepped back a bit. "Is it okay that I'm here? I mean, do you mind? I just thought it would be a nice surprise."

"Oh, no," I assured him quickly. "It is a nice surprise. I just can't believe you came all this way, that's all. How did you know where to find me?"

"It's a long story," he said vaguely. I let that go for the moment.

"Why are the police here?" he asked.

"Someone died here last night."

His eyes widened. "Really? Who?"

"A doctor who was staying here."

"How did he die?"

"We don't know yet."

"Wow. That's too bad. Can I come in?" He didn't seem too ruffled by the news that someone had recently died just a few feet away.

"Uh, I don't think that's a good idea."

"Why not?"

Was he kidding? I thought incredulously.

"Because it's really not a good time, Geoffrey. There's obviously a lot going on here and I don't think Mr. and Mrs. Jorgensen—not to mention the police—want a stranger in the house."

"Oh. Okay. Can we go somewhere and talk?"

I shook my head. "Not now. I need to stay here in case someone needs me to answer any questions." The police hadn't actually told me to stay on the property, so I hoped the two officers standing nearby wouldn't say I was free to leave with Geoffrey.

"How about later?"

He obviously wasn't going to be shaken off easily. "All right," I acquiesced. "How about tonight? There's a place in Kona where we could meet."

"How about at the condo I'm renting? I could make dinner for you."

Uh-oh. Renting a condo? He must be planning to stay longer than I thought.

"You didn't come all the way to Hawaii to eat indoors, did you?" I asked with a weak laugh. Geoffrey was a great cook, but I preferred to be in a public place with him so he didn't get the wrong idea about my intentions.

"Let's meet at a restaurant on Ali'i Drive. It's right along the water." I gave him directions to the Kona Inn, a nostalgic restaurant with a long history of catering to locals and tourists alike. When I had told him where to meet me I added, "I can't get there until pretty late."

He beamed. "No problem! I'll see you then." He leaned in to kiss me and I turned my head just in time as his lips brushed my cheek. I turned around quickly to go back to the house.

I sneaked a looked over my shoulder a few seconds later. He was sauntering toward his rental car, whistling a nameless tune. The police officers were watching him leave.

Why did he have to come here? And how did he know where I was working? I would have to remember to ask him that at dinner. He was part of the life I had left behind. And while we had had fun while we dated, it was never serious, at least as far as I was concerned. I found myself almost hoping the police would need to talk to me that evening.

I went back to my den in search of Justine. She was playing with Meli, twirling a cat toy as she watched her new friend jump and pounce on it.

"Did you decide on something for dessert?" I asked.

"Chocolate cake," she answered with a smile.

"That sounds delicious. Let's check the kitchen for all the ingredients we'll need." She accompanied me back to the kitchen, where we gathered up the ingredients and got to work.

I helped her measure the dry ingredients into a large bowl, then we mixed the buttermilk, oil, eggs, and vanilla with an electric mixer. Justine laughed as she held the mixer in the bowl. Her giggles dispelled some of the pall that had shrouded the house since the discovery of Dr. Doug's body.

"I've never done this before!" she cried. "The mixer tickles my hand!"

I laughed with her as I poured the dry ingredients into her mixture, then we poured the batter into the pans we had prepared. While the cake baked, we set out what we needed for the frosting.

"This is fun! I wish Marcus could help us," Justine said.

"Do you want to ask him if he'd like to help with the frosting?"

"Yes!" She ran off, her apron strings flying behind her, in search of Marcus. She was gone only a few minutes.

"He doesn't want to help. He said he wants to be alone."

"That's okay," I said. "I bet he'll help eat it!"

Justine flashed me a wide smile. It was clear that some of her pain and fear had lifted thanks to the simple action of baking a cake. I was glad she had agreed with my suggestion, though I wished Marcus had come to join us in the kitchen. Maybe next time.

"Is there something you'd like to do for a little while? We can't frost the cake until it cools, and that's going to take some time," I said.

Justine cocked her head. "Can I make lunch for Dad?"

"Sure. Why don't you go ask him what he'd like?"

Justine ran off again and was back again quickly. "He said he'd like a salad. Dad never has salad!" She was breathless.

I grinned. "Let's make a big salad and set it out for everyone to have, just like I did at breakfast."

"Okay." She washed her hands again and helped me gather all the salad ingredients. "What's this?" she asked, pointing to a large light-brown vegetable that looked like a cross between a potato and a piece of ginger.

"That's jicama. We'll peel it and put it in the salad. It's crunchy." She shrugged.

We made the salad and put it in a huge bowl, then Justine helped me make a mango vinaigrette that we placed in a small pitcher. We placed sandwich fixings on a large tray and took everything out to the table.

I asked her to help me announce to everyone else that lunch was ready on the lanai. She went off in search of Marcus first, while I went to the pool to tell the officers they were welcome to eat lunch. They looked grateful but said they were too busy to stop and eat.

The police were focused on the droplets near the body. They were measuring the distance between the drops, between the drops and the house, and between the drops and the guesthouse.

I went back inside, where I found Lars on the lanai helping himself to salad and a few slices of sandwich meat. He smiled wanly at me, passing a hand over his unshaven face. Dark circles surrounded his eyes. "Thanks for giving Justine something to do this morning. She needed that."

"So did I. She's a very sweet girl. She made cake for dinner too, and we'll frost it this afternoon. But don't tell her I told you. I think she wants it to be a surprise."

He chuckled and turned to go back to his office, but Barbie appeared on the lanai as he was leaving. She looked terrible. Her long curly hair frizzed in all directions and she was dressed in a stained T-shirt and cutoff sweatpants. Her skin had a pallid cast; her eyes were puffy and bloodshot.

"Thanks for making lunch, Kailani. I know how hard it must be to cook with the tragedy that's occurred," she said.

"Cooking is like therapy for me, so I cook whenever I'm under stress. It works well for everyone," I answered with a small smile.

"Have the children eaten?"

"I don't know," Lars answered. He looked at me. "Kailani, have you seen Justine and Marcus?"

"No. Justine went looking for him a few minutes ago to tell him that lunch is ready." Just then, both kids walked through the doorway and onto the lanai.

"My darlings, you must eat something to keep up your strength," Barbie urged them, her bottom lip trembling. Marcus rolled his eyes.

"Don't worry about me, Mom. I'm fine."

"I made lunch," Justine announced to her mother. "Kailani helped me."

"Oh?" Barbie asked, obviously uninterested. Justine seemed to brush off her mother's indifference; she helped herself to a large serving of salad and drowned it with mango dressing. "C'mon, Marcus. Have some. It's good." Marcus took a helping of salad and several pieces of sandwich meat, then sat next to her.

Lars glowered at Barbie, his lips a thin white line. He took her arm and steered her away from the table, but his words were audible to the rest of us.

"Barbie, would you please pull yourself together? I know you're upset about your boyfriend, but you still have a family and your daughter is trying to talk to you."

Marcus stopped chewing and looked down at his plate. Justine looked at me out of the corner of her eye. I gave her what I hoped was a reassuring smile.

Barbie stared at Lars. Despite the warm trade winds dancing lightly around us, it suddenly seemed very cold. "Have you no heart?" she asked him shrilly.

"I used to." He turned and stalked back to his office. Barbie watched him go, her eyes flashing, then turned to the kids.

"Don't worry. Your father is just upset. I'm going back upstairs. Would you both come visit me this afternoon?" She turned without waiting for a reply.

Marcus and Justine looked at each other wordlessly. I didn't know what to say. I cleared my throat. "Justine, the cake should be cool by the time the lunch things have been cleared away. Would you still like to make the frosting with me?"

She stopped eating and tears began to roll down her cheeks. She shook her head as she ran from the lanai toward her room.

I looked helplessly at Marcus. He pushed his chair back. "I'll go talk to her," he said in a gruff voice. He didn't look at me. I wondered if he was holding back tears of his own—tears of anger? Or fear? The events of the morning were starting to take their toll.

Chapter 7

I was cleaning the kitchen and preparing to make the frosting for Justine's cake when the police came looking for me.

I accompanied an officer to the family room, where they had apparently been questioning members of the household staff again. I took them through my actions that morning, once more leaving out the argument I had heard between Barbie and Lars the night before.

"Do you know the nature of the relationship between Dr. Fitzgibbons and Mrs. Jorgensen?"

I hesitated. "I'm not sure."

"What do you understand to be their relationship?"

"Well, I have heard that they were having an affair."

"Who told you that?"

"Akela, the housekeeper."

"Do you know how long that had been going on?"

"No, sir."

"Have you observed any behavior between Dr. Fitzgibbons and Mrs. Jorgensen that would support that rumor?"

I recalled seeing them eating dinner together in the small dining room and being convinced their relationship went beyond being friends. I related the incident to the officer.

"Thanks. Stick around. We may want to talk to you again later."

"A friend asked me to go to dinner later tonight, after I've served dinner here. Should I stay?"

The officer shook his head curtly. "You're free to go out to dinner. Just tell the officer where you're going before you leave."

* * *

I went looking for Justine. I knocked softly on her bedroom door. "Justine? I'm going to start the frosting now and I was wondering if you've changed your mind about helping."

"No," came the muffled answer from the other side of the door. I went back to the kitchen and made the frosting myself. Then I finished dinner preparations and went to my bedroom for a short nap. I was tired from all the drama and not sleeping much the previous night.

The family straggled in for dinner at different times. Marcus and Justine ate together. Lars took a plate to his office after the children had disappeared to their rooms once again. Barbie dragged herself into the kitchen after Lars had returned to his work. She had obviously been crying.

"How are you doing, Barbie?" I asked.

"Not very well, I'm afraid."

"Can I get you something to eat?"

She nodded and turned around to go out to the lanai. I took her a tray with a small bowl of yogurt and honey and some sliced fruit and found her sitting at the dining table, her head resting on her arms. Her shoulders shook.

"Barbie?" I ventured softly. "Here. Eat this. It might make you feel a bit better."

She looked up at me, miserable, her tearstained face sallow and pasty. "Have the police talked to you?"

"Yes."

"Did they tell you anything? About how Doug died?"

"No."

"They didn't tell me anything, either. I guess they have to wait and see what the medical examiner says."

I nodded in silence. I fervently hoped Dr. Fitzgibbons had fallen, that he had hit his head on the ground and died that way. Accidentally. I turned and went back to the kitchen to wait for her to finish her meal. I felt a prick of guilt over leaving her alone with her pain, but it was uncomfortable sitting with her.

After a while I heard her chair scraping against the tiles. I waited a few more moments, then went to clear away her dishes. She had eaten almost nothing. I felt sorry for her.

I took my time washing the dishes, I think because I was putting off the moment I had to face Geoffrey and tell him that I did not want our relationship to continue. But I couldn't wait forever, so shortly after I cleaned up the kitchen I set out for Kona.

The sun had set, so there was no ocean vista to calm my mind as I drove. I found myself getting anxious and fidgety. My fingers tapped the steering wheel the whole way and I kept switching radio stations, not content to listen to any one song for more than a few seconds. My mind flitted from one scenario to another, worrying about how the conversation with Geoffrey was going to go.

But Geoffrey took the news better than I thought he would. We sat at a table overlooking the water, unable to see it, but listening to the waves crashing against the shore. The wind blew softly. It would have been the perfect setting for a date.

I told Geoffrey that I didn't think it would work out between us now that I was home. "We're just at different places in our lives," I told him gently. "I'm home, where I want to stay. Your family and your business are in Washington, and it wouldn't be fair of me to expect you to leave all that behind to stay here."

"I think I should be the one to decide whether I want to leave everything behind," he answered.

"But you'll regret the decision to stay here. I know you will. Then you'll resent me for making you leave Washington. And I'll feel guilty, and then we'll both be unhappy. I can see it now."

He sighed. "But what if I want to stay here?"

I looked at him, sitting across the table from me, his handsome face reflecting the candles on the table. "I just don't think I'm ready for anything serious right now. I just got back, started a new job— heck, maybe started on what could be a different career path. I'm just not ready for anything else. I don't feel that this is the right time to have someone else in my life. I'd feel selfish."

"Okay, Kailani. I think I understand. Can we still be friends? I rented the condo for a month, so I'd like to stay and see what the island is like. Maybe we could get together sometimes, you know, just as friends."

"That sounds good, Geoffrey."

After our meal, which we finished eating in relative silence, we parted ways in front of the Kona Inn. He kissed me lightly on the cheek.

"Give me a call sometime if you feel like getting a drink or something," he told me.

"I will," I promised.

I waved to him as we went our separate ways. I should have felt sad, but there was a lightness in my heart that I couldn't ignore. Geoffrey and I weren't meant to be more than friends.

There was one officer still on duty when I got back to the Jorgensens' house. He stood by the breezeway as I walked into the house.

"Any word?" I asked him, fully expecting him to ignore me.

"The medical examiner put a rush on this because he's not sure the doctor's death was an accident. There was evidence that his death involved foul play."

I was stunned. A chill went up my spine and my arms were suddenly covered in goose bumps. "They don't know that for sure, though, right?" I asked, hoping they were wrong.

"No, but they wouldn't put a rush on it if they weren't very suspicious. Goodnight, miss," he said abruptly. *Maybe he wasn't supposed to tell me as much as he did.*

I hurried along the hall to the lanai, then to my bedroom. I wanted to break into a run, but I forced myself to remain calm. When I got to my rooms, I locked myself in and made sure all the blinds were drawn. I scooped Meli up, hugging her to me while she tried to escape, bewildered by my behavior. She did eventually curl up with me in my den chair while I watched television for a while. There was really nothing on worth watching, but at least I felt like I had company.

My mind kept returning to Marcus and Justine. I was worried about them. I felt a certain protectiveness toward them because they sometimes seemed so alone in the world, but I didn't want them to suspect that Dr. Fitzgibbons may have died from something other than a simple accident.

I wondered if Barbie and Lars were aware of this development. I could imagine Barbie, crying alone in the master suite upstairs and Lars, sitting alone in his office, brooding.

Lars. He would be viewed with suspicion, I was sure. He had known that Barbie and Dr. Fitzgibbons were more than just coworkers, and told Barbie as much. I didn't want to think that he had been involved in Dr. Fitzgibbons's death. I wouldn't speculate in that direction.

I thought again of the kids. Barbie and Lars and the police wouldn't be able to keep the secret of Dr. Fitzgibbons's death from them forever. I couldn't imagine the fear they would suffer upon learning that murder had visited their home.

I shook my head forcefully. I had to stop thinking such terrible thoughts. Nothing had been confirmed. Maybe the medical examiner was wrong.

Chapter 8

But the medical examiner's suspicions were borne out when the autopsy was performed on Dr. Fitzgibbons.

He had been murdered.

It took a couple days for the results to be finalized, but once they were the police returned to the house in full force to begin shifting the focus of their investigations. Dr. Fitzgibbons, they informed us tersely, had died from blunt-force trauma to the back of the head, not drowning. He had apparently been standing near the pool when he was hit from behind. We were all called into the family room again for additional questioning, and Marcus and Justine were questioned again when they got home from school. The police called the gardeners in one by one and kept each one in the family room for a long time, according to Akela. Then the police talked to her and to me.

The questions were more grueling this time, probing for more personal information. The police wanted to know what I knew, what I had heard or seen, which would shed light on the relationship between Barbie and Lars. As much as I didn't want to, I had to tell them about the argument I heard between them the night I had to go outside with the scuppers for my kayak.

They also wanted to know if I knew anything about the affair between Barbie and Dr. Fitzgibbons and whether Lars had ever confronted Dr. Fitzgibbons about it. I told them that I had only seen Barbie and Dr. Fitzgibbons have meals together, and it seemed to me that they were extremely close, but I had never seen any direct evidence of a romantic link between them. I had no idea if Lars and Dr. Fitzgibbons had ever had a showdown over Barbie, but I thought it unlikely based on what little I knew about Lars. He seemed to be a man who would keep things inside.

Would he keep something inside until it burst out in the form of violence?

I had to confess to myself that even though I lived in the house, I didn't really know Lars or Barbie well at all. I saw them for meals and I saw them interact with Marcus and Justine occasionally, but I didn't really *know* them. I didn't discuss my thoughts with the police, since it was pure speculation on my part and they knew their jobs better than I did.

But I looked over my shoulder constantly over the long days that followed as the police continued poking around the house and asking questions of everyone who was present during the night of the murder.

A dark presence had invaded the Jorgensens' house. It was always quiet, but not in a peaceful way. It was quiet in a wary, watching way. Barbie and Lars continued to work every day, and Lars had received permission from the authorities to continue to travel off-island for his business. He was often gone for a day or two at a time, returning at various times and always looking haggard and worn.

Marcus and Justine too had been quieter lately, spending more time in their rooms and eating quickly at dinnertime. I never saw them with Barbie or Lars, but I assumed the family spoke together about everything that had happened in their home. I hoped Barbie and Lars had reassured the children that everything was going to be okay.

But was it? The police seemed no closer to figuring out who had killed Dr. Fitzgibbons. Fear was my constant companion and if I was scared, I couldn't imagine what Marcus and Justine were going through. I found myself listening intently for any sound and checking and rechecking my door at night, making sure it was locked.

As the days passed, there was no further violence and the police made no arrests in the case. It seemed more and more likely that the doctor's death had been a random occurrence, perhaps committed by someone who was surprised during a burglary. I hoped that was true, because it was exhausting to be frightened all the time. And the more I got to know the family, the less likely it appeared that either Lars or Barbie was even capable of committing such a heinous act. They were both intelligent people who didn't seem inclined to resorting to violence to solve problems. Yelling, yes, but not violence.

A few weeks after Dr. Fitzgibbons's death, the kids brought home their report cards. Barbie was working late that night and Lars was home to have dinner with his children. Knowing the three of them would be eating together, I worked hard that day to make an extra-special dinner.

I served a salad of soba noodles and grilled mahimahi with a balsamic vinegar and sesame-oil dressing, followed by a light spring vegetable risotto, followed by a dessert of Greek yogurt *panna cotta* topped with crystallized ginger and dried papaya. While I was clearing away their dessert dishes, I saw out of the corner of my eye that Marcus had a sheet of paper on his lap. He drew it out and showed it to his father.

Lars examined the paper while I stacked the dishes on a tray to take back to the kitchen. He frowned. I left the room, but could hear him talking to Marcus as I walked away.

"Marcus, your math grade is terrible. What's going on?"

"I don't know. Maybe I can't concentrate because Mom's boyfriend was murdered at our house?" Marcus answered in a surly voice.

"*Marcus!*" Lars shouted.

Their voices dropped immediately and I couldn't hear any more. I wondered what they were saying.

I found out later that night. I was cleaning the kitchen and preparing for breakfast the next morning when Marcus walked in.

"How's it going, Marcus?"

"It sucks."

"Can I get you anything?"

"Yeah. An A in math."

I laughed. "I would if I could, believe me. But a few weeks ago I gave your mom the name of a teacher friend of mine who's been laid off. He'd make a great tutor. I don't know if she ever called him, because . . ."

"Because why?"

"Because Dr. Fitzgibbons died the next morning and I think the tutor kind of got put on the back burner."

"Well, it's back on the front burner now."

"Would you like me to ask your mom if she ever called my friend?"

"Yeah, okay."

Marcus helped himself to a bowl of rice crackers and a glass of juice I had made that afternoon and returned to his room.

I talked to Barbie the next morning before she left for work.

"Oh, Kailani," she whined in answer to my query, "could you call him for me? I meant to, and then the tragedy with Doug happened, and I just haven't gotten back to it. If he wants to come here so I can meet him, make the arrangements for sometime Sunday and I'll plan to be here."

I called Liko right after Barbie left.

"K! Good to hear from you!"

"Hey, Liko, have you found a job yet?"

"No. Still looking."

"I have something you might be interested in."

"Really? What you got?"

"My boss's son, Marcus, needs a math tutor. Things have been pretty crazy around here lately and I think he needs some help getting focused. I thought you'd be perfect for the job."

"That's great! Have you talked to his mom and dad about it?"

"Yes. I talked to his mother this morning, and she asked me to call you and get you up here on Sunday so they can meet you."

"I'll be there! Hey—why have things been so crazy? Everything all right with you?"

I smiled wryly to myself. "Get here a little early on Sunday and I'll tell you all about it."

We decided on a time, I gave him directions to the Jorgensens' and then hung up. I was very pleased that Marcus was at last going to be getting some help with his math. And maybe make a friend in the process. Liko would be great for him.

The rest of the week passed quickly. Barbie worked late each night and Lars left for business meetings in Peru. The children were mostly on their own in the evenings. I ate meals with them and even got them to play a board game with me one night. I always made sure the alarm system was armed, thinking it would help to allay some of our fears. We didn't talk about being afraid in the house, but I suspected worry and apprehension were never far from the kids' minds. Anxiety was certainly a part of my daily life.

On Sunday Lars returned from his trip early in the morning and Barbie didn't have to go into the office. The family members were scattered in different spots around the house. Barbie had been careful to avoid the courtyard around the pool since Dr. Fitzgibbons's death, but she lay out in the sun for a short while that afternoon. Lars took Justine down to the water in their two-seater kayak. Marcus had a science project due the following day, so he was in his room working.

Liko arrived a little early for his appointment with Barbie and Lars, so I showed him the view from the lanai and the kitchen before we went into my rooms.

"This house—it's amazing," he began.

"This is how the other half lives, I guess," I said with a smile.

"Hard to believe. So, tell me why it's been so crazy around here."

I took a deep breath and explained, in a quiet voice, all that had been going on, including the murder of Dr. Doug, the affair between Barbie and Doug that had been going on right under Lars's nose, and how the kids didn't see their parents very often.

"So you can see why Marcus needs a friend around here," I finished.

"Definitely. Poor kid. And to be a teenager . . ." he trailed off, shaking his head. "Who killed the doctor?"

"I wish I knew. Then I would sleep better. I feel like everyone is a suspect until the police find out who did it."

Liko raised his eyebrows at me. "And you think I should work for these people?"

"Marcus needs someone, Liko. I hope you'll take the job if they offer it to you."

"I definitely need the work," he replied with a grimace.

We went down to the family room to wait for Barbie and Lars. When they both arrived, I introduced them to Liko and returned to my room. I was sure they would hire Liko as Marcus's tutor, but I was waiting for the official word.

They hired him on the spot. Barbie and Lars didn't seem to agree on much these days, but they did agree that Marcus needed a tutor and that Liko seemed to be the perfect candidate. Since Liko lived over two hours away, they decided that Liko would stay in the guesthouse.

Liko was excited to get started. He seemed to have forgotten his earlier apprehension about working in a house where a man had been killed. He hadn't met Marcus yet, either, so Barbie and Lars asked Liko to stay for dinner that evening so he could meet his new student.

I served dinner and quietly slipped away. I knew Liko would find me after dinner and tell me how it went with Marcus.

And sure enough, just as I was going to clear away the dinner dishes, Liko came into the kitchen to offer his help and to talk. I listened to him as we washed dishes and cleaned up the kitchen.

"So how'd it go?"

"You shoulda told me Barbie is so hot," he replied in a loud whisper.

"That's not why you were invited here, Liko," I told him, rolling my eyes. "How did it go with Marcus?"

"That Marcus—he's a smart kid. I can tell. But he's so quiet. He's gotta come out of his shell."

I nodded in agreement. "I think he's pretty shaken up by all that's been happening around here."

"I'm sure you're right, K."

"Do you think you can help him?"

"Oh, yeah. I'll spend a little time with him, help him with his math, take him surfing sometimes—you know."

"Is math the biggest problem?"

He cocked his head. "I don't know. His biggest problem might be that he's a teenage boy." He chuckled, shaking his head. "Brah, those days could be *rough.*"

I thought back to when Liko was in high school. He could be a clown—he laughed a lot—but he had a serious side too, and there were days when he could be quiet and aloof. Not unlike Marcus.

"I think it's great that you'll be around for him."

"Thanks for thinking of me, K." Liko pecked me on the cheek and turned to go. "See you tomorrow!"

The next day Liko moved some of his things into the guesthouse before Marcus got home from school. I helped him move in a set of weights, his surfboard, diving equipment, a snorkel mask and fins, a kayak, a basketball, two tennis racquets, a few articles of clothing, and a dopp kit. *Just like a man,* I thought with a smile. It was obvious how he planned to spend his days while Marcus was in school.

That afternoon Liko was waiting on the lanai by the time Marcus left the kitchen with a snack and a drink. I could hear them talking together at the table as Marcus joined him to start his homework. They were still working when I went out to set the table for dinner.

"Should we move, K?" asked Liko.

"No, I'll just put the place settings at the other end of the table."

I assumed Barbie would be working until later in the evening, so I didn't set a place for her. I did set a place for Lars, since he had poked his head in the kitchen earlier and asked what time he should be ready for dinner.

To my surprise, Barbie did come home in time for dinner. She asked me to set a place for her and one for Liko too, so the family could get to know him better. I hurriedly set two more places and served dinner when they were all seated. Justine and Marcus sat on either side of Liko. He seemed to be making a great impression.

Over the meal of grilled salmon with wilted spinach, roasted asparagus, and pea and mint salad, I could hear Liko answering questions about himself. And me.

"I was a Hawaiian language and culture teacher at a school in Punalu'u."

"I grew up there. Near Kailani."

"Her parents have the greatest bakery on the Big Island. They make *ono* bread and desserts."

I heard his deep laugh. "*Ono* means 'great'."

"I like to surf, kayak, dive, snorkel. On weekends I'm on an outrigger team. We have races all around the islands."

"Yeah! You can come watch anytime you want. That would be great!"

"No, I'm not married. No girlfriend, even."

"The tattoos are Samoan. My family comes from Samoa. I have lots of aunties and uncles still there, so I try to get there often to visit them."

I smiled to myself in the kitchen. It seemed that Liko would get along just fine at the Jorgensen house.

That night Liko came to visit me in my den after Marcus's homework was done.

"Sounded like dinner went well," I told him.

"Yeah. Nice family. Dad doesn't say much."

"No, he and Marcus are the quiet ones."

Meli came and rubbed her face against Liko's hand. "Want to go kayaking tomorrow?" he asked.

"I should be able to. There isn't much prep for tomorrow's lunch and dinner."

Liko and I spent three arduous but fun hours kayaking the next day before Marcus and Justine came home from school. I was in the kitchen fixing them a snack when my cell phone rang. I looked at the screen.

Geoffrey.

What did he want? I hadn't talked to him since our dinner at the Kona Inn. I hesitated a moment before answering, but I knew he would just call back if I ignored him. Besides, maybe he was calling to tell me he was going back to Washington.

"Hi, Geoffrey. What's up?"

"Hi, Kailani. I was wondering if you're available to get a drink tonight." So he wasn't calling me to say good-bye.

"I'm sorry, Geoffrey. I'm helping plan a party that the Jorgensens are throwing, and I promised I would be around tonight to help," I fibbed.

"Oh." He sounded hurt. "Well then, how about tomorrow night?"

I knew he would just keep asking and asking until I agreed, so against my better judgment I said I would.

"Great! Where would you like to meet?"

I didn't feel like driving all the way to Kona Town to meet with him, so I decided to pick someplace close to the Jorgensens. Maybe he wouldn't call me again if he thought I would make him drive a long distance every time he wanted to get together.

"There's a place just up the road from here," I answered. "It's a little place, but the locals love it. Does that sound okay?"

"Sure," he said eagerly.

I gave him directions, thinking suddenly that perhaps asking him to drive up north had been a bad idea. What if he drank too much? What if he asked if he could stay with me? Then what would I do?

I pushed those thoughts from my mind and concentrated on getting the kids their snacks. I took a tray of veggies and hummus to the dining table where Liko and Marcus were already pulling out notebooks and pencils to start math homework.

"How was school, brah?" Liko asked Marcus.

"Okay, I guess."

Marcus looked up at me as I was bearing my tray of veggies. "Gross. Vegetables again? Why don't we ever get chips anymore?"

"Your mom doesn't want me buying that stuff. You know that. I'll tell you what. Why don't you go to the farmers' market with me sometime? You can pick out whatever vegetables you want and I'll make something with them. Deal?"

He rolled his eyes. "I guess."

I smiled at him and returned to the kitchen. I was chopping vegetables to make a soup for dinner when Lars came into the kitchen. "Rabbit food?"

"No, soup."

"Do you know how to make lasagna?"

I grinned. "Yes, but when Barbie hired me she said no foods like that."

He groaned. "I miss my heavy Italian meals. And my burgers."

"Would you like to try vegetable lasagna? I have a great recipe."

"Only if you're refusing to make a real lasagna with actual sausage."

I laughed. "You'll like my version."

He sighed and turned to go. "Hey, I think your friend Liko seems to be working out."

"Liko is good with kids. I'm sure he'll help Justine if she needs it too."

He returned to his office.

That night Barbie joined the family for dinner again, though Lars was called away to a meeting on O'ahu. As I walked to and from the dining table on the lanai I could hear her questioning Liko.

"Have you ever had a massage?"

"No, can't say that I have."

"You should really come into the office sometime. We have a massage therapist who gives a great deep-tissue massage."

"Sounds painful."

She giggled in her high-pitched voice. "Oh, no. It's very freeing and rejuvenating. You'd love it."

Was she *flirting* with him? Just weeks after her lover's death? And in front of her children? I was thankful Lars wasn't around to hear her.

Marcus spoke up. "What would he need a massage for?"

"A massage is very good for loosening up after kayaking. And for post–weight training. And I know Liko does those things, right?"

Liko nodded.

When had she seen Liko kayaking? Or lifting weights?

I didn't get a chance to ask him about it right away because I had to go meet Geoffrey. I got to the bar in Hawi Town right on time. Geoffrey was already waiting for me.

"I see you found the place okay," I greeted him.

"Yup. No trouble at all. I left Kona a few hours ago just in case, so I've been in Hawi for a while. Just looking around. There are some really nice shops here."

"Yes."

"What would you like to drink?" he asked.

"Just a beer."

"I think I'll have one too." He called the bartender over and ordered. We took our drinks to a small table in the corner of the bar.

"So. How's work going?" he asked.

"Fine. I love working for the Jorgensens."

"I hear you have a friend tutoring there now."

I looked at him in surprise. "How did you know Liko is working there?"

"Liko? I didn't know his name. I found out because I paid a visit to your parents' bakery and I heard them talking about you." He smiled proudly.

"How did you know it was my parents' bakery?" I was feeling a little trapped. What other information was Geoffrey trying to dig up in his free time?

"I knew the name of it. You mentioned it once, and you told me it's the only bakery in the town where you're from, so it was easy to find. That's how I figured out where you were working too."

"Did you tell them who you are?"

"No. I just talked to them for a while. Told them I was from the East Coast. They showed me the ovens they use to bake the bread. Great setup they have there. And their house is nice. Pretty cool how the bakery is attached to it."

I was finding this conversation decidedly unnerving. "You should have introduced yourself. I'm sure they would have appreciated knowing they were talking to my old boyfriend." I put a slight emphasis on the word *old*.

"I thought it was kind of fun being a mysterious stranger," he answered with a grin. "They had no idea!"

"Geoffrey, don't you think that's a little weird?"

"What's a little weird?"

"To go to my parents' business and pretend you just stumbled upon the bakery out of sheer luck?"

"That's not weird. It's fun. Don't be so uptight."

I sighed loudly. "I would appreciate it if you don't go there again."

"But their bread is really good. I'd like to get some more."

"Good. I'll give you the names of a few stores in Kona where it's sold."

"But I'll have to pay more at a store."

"Geoffrey," I snapped, "just don't go back, okay? It gives me the creeps."

"Okay," he said quietly, looking hurt. But it didn't last long. "What's Liko like?"

I looked at him askance. "He's funny and smart. His family are native Hawaiians. He and I have been good friends since we were kids. He's tutoring Marcus, the boy in the house where I work. But you already knew that."

"Were you ever more than friends?"

I squinted at Geoffrey and shook my head. "No. Why?"

"Just wondering." The silence settled between us for a couple minutes.

"How about now?"

"What are you talking about?" I asked.

"Is there anything going on between you and Liko now?"

"No!" I said a little too loudly. A couple patrons at nearby tables looked at us. I lowered my voice. "Geoffrey, that's really none of your business."

"I just want to make sure you're safe, that's all."

"I'm perfectly safe. I've known Liko for years. Much longer than I've known you. I think I should be going now. Speaking of going, when are you headed back to Washington?" I stood up to leave, putting money on the table for my beer.

"I haven't decided."

"I'm sure they need you at the restaurant."

"They're fine without me. Should I follow you home to make sure you get there okay?"

I shot him a freezing look. "No. I know the way and I'll be fine. Goodnight, Geoffrey."

"G'night."

I walked briskly to my car, which was parked a little way down the main road of Hawi Town. I looked back over my shoulder when I reached the car. Sure enough, Geoffrey was standing outside the bar, watching me go. I shuddered. What did I ever see in him?

Chapter 9

When I got home I flopped down on the couch in my den and reached for Meli. I was stroking her soft fur when there was a knock at my door. For a brief moment I was afraid it was Geoffrey, having followed me from the bar, then I bolted upright, my mind racing back to the morning Dr. Doug was found dead, but I gathered up enough courage to open the door a crack. Liko was standing there.

"Come on in," I said with a sigh of relief.

"How was your date with Geoffrey?"

I grimaced. "He gives me the creeps, Liko. He knew all about you and he had been to my parents' bakery, and it was all so bizarre. I can't believe we used to date."

Liko arched his eyebrows at me. "Sounds like he still thinks you're dating."

I shook my head. "How could he? I couldn't have been clearer that I don't want him doing things like visiting my parents and following me anywhere."

Liko pressed his lips together tightly. "Trust me. He doesn't think you two are finished. You want me to make it clear to him?" His eyes glittered brightly.

"No. Don't do anything. I can handle him myself. Hopefully he's going back to Washington soon and I'll never have to see him again."

"You know where to find me if you change your mind, little sistah," he said with a big smile, cracking his knuckles.

I shook my head as I hugged him goodnight. "Thanks, Liko."

I was thinking about Dr. Doug's death again as I drifted off to sleep that night. The more I thought about it, the more I was convinced that his murder had been committed by a thwarted burglar. I almost hoped that was the case, since it would mean such violence would likely never happen again and the rest of us would be safe.

The next morning Barbie didn't go into work at the usual early hour. She said she had an appointment at home, so she ate breakfast with the kids and Liko before school. The kids left in semidarkness, but Barbie and Liko stayed at the dining table, talking as the sun rose over the Kohala Mountains behind the house, painting the sky with strokes of purple, then pink, then orange, finally brightening to a brilliant blue. They lingered over coffee and fresh fruit and toast, laughing and chatting like old friends. I didn't join them, but I could see and hear them as I was sitting in a chair with a cup of coffee on the lanai right outside the kitchen. Lars sat down with them for a short time to have a quick bowl of cereal, then left, saying he was going surfing.

"You surf?" asked Liko. He must not have realized that Lars owned a surfing clothing company.

Lars grinned. "Every chance I get. You?"

"I love it!"

"You want to come with me? I'm going over to Honoli'i."

"Yeah, brah! Let me get my stuff." Liko pushed back from the table and left at a slow jog back to the guesthouse. Barbie looked annoyed.

"Will you be back before the kids get home from school?" she asked Lars acidly.

"Yes. I have work to do right after lunch. We'll be back by early afternoon." He turned and left.

Barbie wandered to the kitchen to refill her coffee mug. "I don't understand why people love surfing," she said with a sigh as she pulled up a chair next to mine. "What's the attraction?"

I smiled. "It's the adrenaline rush. And the challenge. Surfers are always looking for higher waves, longer barrels. It's fun."

"You surf?" she asked with surprise.

"I used to surf a lot. Now I prefer kayaking."

"Lars likes both. And anything else that keeps him out in the water." She paused. "I'll see you for dinner, Kailani." I didn't know whether her appointment had been canceled, but she left shortly afterward for work.

I decided to head out to a local market to see what fresh fish I could cook that evening for the family. As I drove my car up to the main road, I saw a slight movement out of the corner of my eye. I hit the brakes and got out of the car. I walked slowly over to the low, thick trees by the side of the road and the bushes moved suddenly. I jumped back in a fright.

"Marcus! You scared me! Why aren't you in school?"

"You won't tell my parents, will you?"

"I don't know yet. What are you doing out here?"

He kicked the dirt. "I just didn't feel like going, that's all."

"There must be a reason. What's going on?"

"I don't know. Nothing, I guess. I just didn't get on the bus this morning."

"Did Justine go to school?"

"Yeah. I made her promise not to tell."

"You shouldn't do that to her. It puts her in a tough spot."

"Oh, yeah? What about my tough spot?" he asked.

I was confused. "What do you mean?"

"I mean, I hate school and I hate living here and I hate every-thing."

I didn't know what to say. I wished Liko were there to help, to take charge of this troubled young boy.

"Marcus, I'm just heading over to the fish market. Want to go? You can help me pick out something for dinner. We can talk on the way."

"I hate fish."

I smiled. "Have you ever tried *monchong*?"

He shook his head. "Never heard of it."

"Let's see if they have any at the market and I promise you'll love it."

He sighed. "Might as well. Are you going to take me to school?"

"If you want me to. But you'll have to explain what's going on if you don't want me to tell your parents about this."

He scowled. "Okay."

He got into the car beside me and we drove to the fish market. He remained silent until we walked in.

"It stinks in here."

"That's the smell of the ocean and very fresh food—I love it."

He walked around, looking at all the offerings from the sea. I walked straight to the cooler where I had seen *monchong* previously. There was a fresh supply of it, gray-brown and glistening. I picked out two fish and pointed them out to the woman behind the counter. She smiled and said "Very nice choice."

Marcus came over to stand next to me. "Do you have to take the scales off and everything?"

"Yes. It's not as bad as you think."

He looked at me doubtfully. I scanned the counter of chilled *poke* under glass. "I'll also take a half pound of your spicy ahi," I told the woman. I turned to Marcus.

"That'll be my lunch. Do you like *poke*?"

"Never had it."

"You can try some of mine. It's so good."

"It's raw fish, isn't it? Aren't you afraid of getting sick?"

"Not when it's this fresh and gorgeous. Look at it—it's firm and red, exactly the way it's supposed to look."

"We're supposed to be having a *poke* sale for school."

"Like a fund raiser?"

"Yeah. I'm not doing it, though."

"Why not?"

He shrugged. "Don't know how to make *poke*."

"I'll help you."

He hesitated. "I don't know."

"Do you have some friends who'd like to help us?"

"Nah. Well, maybe one. My friend James."

"Invite him over and we'll make *poke*. It'll be fun."

"I gotta think about it."

I paid for the fish and our lunch, grabbed two sets of chopsticks from the counter by the register, and we left. I drove to an overlook north of Hawi Town and pulled in.

"Now, try this," I instructed Marcus, handing him the plastic container of *poke* and a set of chopsticks.

"Do I have to?" he whined.

"Yes. Hurry up, because I'm starving!"

"Okay, okay." He fumbled with the chopsticks. "How do you use these things, anyways?"

I showed him how to place his fingers so the chopsticks would stay in place, then he clumsily maneuvered them to pick up one small piece of the fish. He squeezed his eyes shut and put it in his mouth. He started to chew slowly.

"Well? What do you think?"

He continued chewing, then swallowed and said, "I don't know. Can I have another piece?"

"Sure."

He took another piece, a little bigger, and ate it. "This doesn't taste like fish. It's not bad."

I grinned. "That's the great thing about *poke*. The fish doesn't have a strong flavor, so you're able to taste the seasonings. All you taste of the fish is a delicious freshness."

He had a third piece, then handed me the container. "It's pretty good," he admitted.

"Why don't you finish it? I can get some more for myself on the way back to the house."

"No, it's yours. I'll eat the lunch you made this morning." He pulled the small padded cooler out of his backpack.

I settled back in the driver's seat, admiring the sweeping view of the Pacific and waiting for him to get his lunch out. Once he started eating the cheese sandwich I had made for him, I asked my first question.

"So, what were you doing in the trees beside the road?"

"Nothing. Really. I was just waiting in there until the bus came and dropped Justine off. Then I was going to walk into the house with her."

"You were just going to hang out there all day?"

"Yeah. Where else was I supposed to go?"

"How about school?"

"The kids in my classes are all jerks."

"What about James?"

"He's not a jerk, but he's not in any of my classes."

"How do you know him?"

"He lives up the road. He rides my bus."

"So the kids are all jerks. Any other reason you didn't go to school today?"

He was silent for a full minute. "I don't know," he finally said with a sigh. "I just don't care about it."

"Does it have anything to do with Dr. Doug?" I asked gently.

He only hesitated for a moment. "Maybe. I'm sick of the cops asking questions, I'm sick of my parents not talking to each other, I'm sick of living here. I want to go back to California. I had lots of friends there. I was one of the cool kids. Here I'm just a loser *haole* with rich parents."

I changed the subject. "What's the *poke* sale for?"

He shrugged. "The school. There's not enough money in the budget for lots of things, so the school has to raise its own money."

I nodded. Not enough money for lots of things—like a job for Liko, like Hawaiian-culture classes. "So why not get involved? Join clubs, meet people. Maybe the kids in school just need to get to know you better."

He shrugged again. "Maybe."

"Anything else going on?"

"Nah. That's pretty much it."

"What do you think of Liko?"

He hesitated again. "He's cool. He's a good math teacher and my parents like him. He even helps Justine sometimes."

"I'm glad. He likes being a tutor. Maybe you and he could go surfing or kayaking together sometime."

He nodded. "That'd be cool."

"You want me to take you back to school?"

"I don't know. Okay."

I smiled and handed him the container with the remainder of the *poke*. "Here. Finish this. I'm full."

He accepted it with a "thanks" and finished it. "That's pretty good, actually," he said with a shy smile.

"Told you."

I dropped him off at school and watched him walk inside, his backpack hanging off one shoulder. I felt sorry for him. Being a teenager could be so hard, and he had the added stress of Dr. Doug's death weighing on his mind. As unnerving as it was to think of an unknown person creeping around on the Jorgensens' property, I hoped again for the millionth time that Dr. Doug's death had been committed by a stranger. Anything was better than believing Dr. Doug had been killed by Lars or Barbie.

I returned home and was skinning and cleaning the fish when Lars and Liko came in, laughing about something.

"Hi Kailani," Lars said, still chuckling. "Got anything for a late lunch? We're starving."

I made them plates of sliced tomatoes with a balsamic drizzle and grilled cheese *panini*. They talked as they ate together on the lanai, acting like they had been friends for years.

When the kids came home, Marcus caught my eye and I winked

at him. His secret was safe with me. Justine looked at me out of the corner of her eye and I smiled at her. Marcus must have told her that I knew he had tried to skip school.

"Did you ask James about helping make *poke*?" I asked him.

"Yeah. He said he'll do it with us."

"Great! When's the sale?"

"The day after tomorrow. It starts first thing in the morning."

"Okay. I'll make sure we have everything we need tomorrow, except for the fish. We can grab James really early the day of the sale and run over to the fish market to pick up fresh ahi, then we'll come back here and mix it up."

Marcus smiled. "Okay."

Justine piped up. "Can I help?"

I looked at Marcus. "All right," he said, "but don't say anything stupid while James is here."

She scowled at him. "I won't."

I spent the rest of the afternoon preparing the *monchong*. After I was done I made grilled portobello mushrooms and a Greek salad to complete the meal.

Liko, Marcus, and Justine dug into their dinner with surprising gusto. They seemed to enjoy the fish even more than I thought they would.

While they were eating, Barbie came home from the office and joined the rest of them at the table. I hadn't seen Lars since lunch.

"How are the lessons going, Liko?" I heard Barbie ask.

"Great! Right, Marcus?"

"Yeah. I've gotten a couple good grades this week."

"Liko, it's all thanks to your help," Barbie said sweetly.

I couldn't see Marcus from where I stood, but I had a feeling he was rolling his eyes. As good as Liko was, Marcus had something to do with his better grades too.

Marcus and Liko did homework in the family room after dinner, since it was too windy on the lanai. They worked late into the evening on Marcus's science project. Justine seemed content to be in the room with them, listening to music on her headphones. I took them all some popcorn right before Justine went to bed.

Lars poked his head in while I was in the family room. "Liko, surf's up tomorrow at Pohoiki. Want to go?"

"Sure!" Liko answered with a big smile.

"Can I go sometime, Dad?" Marcus asked.

"Sure! Maybe over the weekend."

Marcus smiled happily and got back to work. He and Liko bent their heads over a science textbook and spoke together in low voices. Lars looked at me and nodded. He seemed to have made a new friend too.

Chapter 10

The next morning I made sure I had on hand all the ingredients we would need to make a spicy ahi *poke*. Marcus went to school—I walked to the bus stop with him and Justine and watched them both get on the bus—since I had told him that I wouldn't help with the *poke* fund raiser if he skipped again.

Liko came looking for me as soon as I got back. "K? Can I talk to you in your room?"

"Sure, Liko. Is everything okay?"

He shrugged. "I guess so." He helped himself to a cup of coffee and followed me into my den. He seemed to be in a pensive mood.

"Is this about Marcus?" I asked quickly. "Because I talked to him about yesterday and—"

"What about yesterday?" Liko looked at me quizzically.

Apparently this wasn't about Marcus skipping school. "Oh. Never mind. What do you want to talk about?"

Liko took a deep breath and leaned in toward me. "K, it's just that Barbie is coming on to me. What do I do?"

Uh-oh. I stared at him. I couldn't believe what I was hearing. First Doug, now Liko. What was she thinking?

"Are you sure?" I already knew the answer.

He smirked at me. "K, I'm not *pupule*. I know when I'm being hit on."

"Okay, okay, Liko. I just can't believe she'd do that to her family after all everyone has been through. What are you going to do about it?"

"I really like her, K. But I know it's the wrong thing to do. I'm really torn."

"If you know it's the wrong thing to do, then there's your answer.

Don't do anything stupid," I urged him. "And don't forget that Lars is your friend too. And your boss."

He hung his head. "I know. I know. But things aren't good between them."

"Things will be much worse if you and Barbie . . ." I trailed off.

"I know," he repeated. "I'll see you later. Lars and I are going up to Pohoiki today."

I was dismayed that Liko would even consider a relationship with Barbie. I was also worried about the kids, about the family, and my job, if the Jorgensens' marriage crumbled. I was preparing dinner that afternoon when Marcus came into the kitchen. "Have you seen Liko?" he asked.

"He's surfing at Pohoiki with your dad. Anything I can help you with?"

"Nah. I have a question for him about my math test."

"How'd you do on it?"

"I got an A," he said with a wide smile. "But I got one wrong and I need him to explain it to me."

"Nice job! I'll tell him you're looking for him when I see him."

Liko was home in time for dinner. He and Lars joined the kids on the lanai for homemade pizza. It was a big hit. Lars and Liko regaled the kids during dinner with stories of their surfing prowess. As I refilled glasses of *lilikoi* iced tea, I saw Marcus's eyes shining with excitement. "Are you still planning to go surfing this weekend?" he asked. "I want to go."

"Sure thing, son," said Lars.

I was glad Marcus had something to look forward to. Time with his dad would be good for him.

At 5:00 the next morning my alarm went off. I texted Marcus.

You up?

Yes. Be right there.

I waited for him in the kitchen, then we went out to my car in the darkness and headed for the fish market. On the way we picked up James so he could help choose the fish for our *poke*. Both boys were tired, but they seemed to be excited. They wrinkled their noses when we walked into the fish market. We weren't the only ones there; there were two fishermen talking to the owner, and one chef waiting patiently for his fish to be wrapped. When it was our turn, I told the boys to ask the owner for two very large pieces of sashimi-grade ahi. If we needed more, we could always return to the market before school started.

We took the fish back to the house and went straight to the kitchen. We had also bought some *masago*. The boys weren't thrilled with the idea of putting roe into the *poke* with the raw ahi, but I convinced them that it would add a beautiful texture and flavor to the *poke*. Justine came into the kitchen just as we were starting, so she helped us. We sliced the deep red ahi into small cubes and coated them with sesame oil, added Japanese mayonnaise, Hawaiian salt, scallions, onion, wasabi oil, and the brilliant orange *masago*.

Marcus stood back and snapped a photo of the *poke* when we were done. He showed it to me with a smile. "This looks so cool!" he said, beaming. James looked over my shoulder and nodded.

"You need to try it now," I told them. "A good chef never lets anything leave the kitchen without tasting it first."

James went first and pronounced it delicious. His family ate a lot of *poke*, he told me, and our homemade version was better than he had ever tasted. I was thrilled.

Next it was Marcus's turn. He looked at me, then James, then took a big chunk of the ahi and popped it in his mouth. He chewed and smiled.

"*Ewww*," said Justine.

"You should try it, Justine," he urged. "It's really good."

"No, thanks. I don't eat raw fish."

He shrugged. "Your loss. Kailani, can you drive us to school so we don't have to carry the *poke* on the bus?"

"Sure."

Just then Lars walked into the kitchen. "Is there any coffee, Kailani?" He stopped and looked at the large bowls of *poke* sitting on the counter. "What's all this?"

"There's a *poke* fund raiser at school today. Kailani helped me and James make *poke* to sell. It's really good. Want to try some?"

Lars looked at his son dubiously. "Isn't that raw fish?"

Marcus grinned. "Yeah, but try it. It's good." He handed Lars a fork. "You're really supposed to eat it with chopsticks."

"All right. I'll just try a small piece." He chose a tiny piece of ahi and closed his eyes tightly as he put the fish in his mouth. We all waited expectantly for his reaction.

He nodded as he chewed. "This isn't bad at all. I expected something much different." He looked at Marcus appreciatively. "You made this?"

Marcus smiled proudly. "Kailani helped us make it. We used her recipe."

"I didn't know you were interested in cooking," Lars marveled. He helped himself to another piece. "This is actually very good. You taking all of this to school?"

"Yeah."

"Maybe you can make some more for dinner," Lars suggested. Then he poured himself a cup of coffee, wished the kids a good day, and went off whistling to his office.

Marcus wore a wide smile. "Can we make more after school?"

I nodded. "I'll go pick up more fish after I drop you all off."

We set off, the kids talking happily in the backseat. It was nice to see Marcus happy and excited about going to school. I would have to tell Liko—he would be thrilled for Marcus.

My thoughts darkened as they turned to Liko. I wondered whether he would give in to Barbie's charms or do the right thing and continue as nothing more than Marcus's tutor. Barbie could be captivating, but I had also seen that she was capable of willingly causing great pain to her family. And Liko, who didn't have a girlfriend, could easily give in. Barbie was pretty, petite, lively, and gregarious—just the combination that Liko would find attractive. I decided to talk to him about Barbie again that evening.

But Barbie had other plans. She came home early, in time for dinner with the family, with an announcement. Orchid Isle Wellness had won a coveted award, an "*Ono*" Island Favorite. The wellness center had been voted by residents and visitors to be the best provider of wellness services on the Big Island and this meant the Jorgensens would be hosting a celebration.

Lars took her by the elbow and drew her to the small dining room near the kitchen. They probably didn't realize I could hear their entire conversation.

"Barbie, you shouldn't be throwing a big party so soon after Doug's death. It's in poor taste. We don't even know who killed him yet."

She scoffed. "You think I don't know you did it?" she hissed. "You think I don't know how jealous you were of Doug? Of my relationship with him?"

"*What?*" he spluttered.

"You're just lucky I've protected you. So far. We're having this party, Lars."

"What are you talking about?" he whispered loudly. "I didn't kill Doug! I couldn't care less what you were doing with him! I just couldn't stand to see the kids being hurt. You're nothing but a selfish—"

"Dad!" Marcus's voice could be heard coming from the other end of the lanai. "Dad! Want some *poke* for dinner? I made more after school."

"We'll continue this later," Lars said curtly.

"We certainly will."

I ducked into my room until I figured Lars and Barbie were both gone, since I didn't want them to think I had heard their argument. I hoped they would both eat the *poke*. I knew Justine wouldn't, but it was important to Marcus that his parents enjoy the meal he had made.

And they did. Lars came into the kitchen after dinner and thanked me for helping Marcus make the *poke*. Barbie followed him several minutes later, exclaiming that Marcus had made the best *poke* she'd had in a long time. I was thrilled for him.

Barbie stayed in the kitchen for quite a long time, discussing her plans for the award celebration.

"We'll be inviting everyone from the office. Let's see . . . that's Lars and me, the other doctors and their significant others, the massage therapists, the receptionists, the nutritionist, the office manager. Let's plan for forty people. I'd rather have too much food than not enough. Can you come up with a menu for me?"

I nodded, reaching for a pen and paper.

"I'd like to serve a mix of healthy and decadent snacks," she began. "You know, crudités, bruschetta, yogurt dips. And then a selection of savory, rich hors d'oeuvres for the people who prefer that sort of thing, and of course, small desserts."

I wrote furiously, trying to keep up with her wishes. "I'll put a list of pupus together and you can let me know if it looks okay," I told her.

She wrinkled her nose. "Pupus," she repeated. "I never liked that word." She waved a hand in the air. "English works just fine for me."

I ignored her slight jab and told her I would have a list for her in the morning.

Marcus came to see me that evening as I sat on the lanai on a large daybed with a book and a cup of tea. "I just wanted to thank you for helping me and James. We sold out of our *poke* at school today and almost nobody else did. We raised a lot of money for the school too." He smiled at me shyly.

"I was happy to help, Marcus. You're a talented cook. Anytime you want to help me make a meal or want help doing it yourself, let me know."

He nodded and walked away. Liko wandered by just a short while later. "I hear the *poke* you and Marcus made was a big success."

"That's what he told me. I hope he gains some confidence from this and starts to make some more friends. He made another batch for dinner. There's some in the fridge if you want it."

"I ate already, but thanks. I just wanted to tell you that I think you're helping him just as much as the tutoring is."

"Thanks, Liko." He wandered off and I was left alone with my book again. I clicked off the lamp glowing next to me, set the book aside, and spent the next few minutes being mesmerized by the moonlight rippling on the waves. I let my mind empty of worries about the Jorgensens and allowed the serenity of the evening to seep into my mind.

It was getting late. I wasn't tired yet, so I walked slowly down the length of the lanai, unable to take my eyes off the moonlit black water, listening to the insects nearby and the waves *shooshing* into the rocky shoreline just a short distance away.

At the end of the lanai I turned *mauka* and walked slowly past Marcus's room and toward the front of the house. As I turned the corner toward the front door, I stopped short when I saw someone stealing out the door and whisking down the breezeway under the veils of hanging jade. I froze and flattened my body against the wall, my heart pounding and my breath caught in my throat. Was it all going to happen again? Was tragedy going to strike this house once more? Was I watching a murderer steal away in the night?

As the figure stepped onto the path between the breezeway and the guesthouse, soft light from one of the landscaping lamps illuminated the person's face.

Barbie.

I watched as she made her way to the side of the guesthouse that was facing me. I remained on the lanai, hidden in the shadows. Barbie knocked quietly on the door, glancing around behind her as she waited for admittance. The door swung open and Liko appeared in the doorway. She ducked under his arm and the door closed behind her.

I groaned inwardly and pleaded silently with Liko, as if he could hear me. *Don't do it! Don't destroy this family!* My heart broke for Lars and the children as my anger toward Liko and Barbie increased quickly from a simmer to a rolling boil with each furtive step I took toward the front door.

I crept silently into the front hall, hoping everyone was asleep and my footsteps would be unheard. But they weren't. Lars appeared in his office doorway as I slipped past.

"Kailani? Why are you sneaking around?"

I resented the implied accusation and forgot about feeling sorry for Lars. "I wasn't sneaking anywhere. I went out for a walk and I didn't want to make any noise going back to my room."

"Oh. Goodnight, then."

"Goodnight."

I went straight to my room. I didn't want to be around when Lars went up to the master bedroom and discovered that Barbie was missing.

But I knew it when it happened. Not long after I curled up in my den with a good cookbook, I heard the front door slam. Lars must have gone off in search of his wayward wife.

I couldn't concentrate on my book any longer. I went to the kitchen for a drink of water and was startled when I heard Justine's voice.

"Kailani? Can I have some water too?"

I examined her face closely. She looked exhausted. "Of course," I answered. "Is everything all right?"

Standing there in her pink pajamas, her hair in a ponytail, she suddenly looked very little and vulnerable. Her face crumpled.

"I can't sleep," she whimpered. "I'm so tired, but I'm afraid to sleep. I haven't been able to sleep since Dr. Doug died."

I pulled her to me. Her small body sank against mine and she began to cry. "All I want is to stop being scared."

I held her at arm's length and looked in her bloodshot eyes. "Justine, don't you worry. The person who killed Dr. Doug was a stranger, someone who will never come back to this house because he knows the police are looking for him. He was probably just a petty thief who thought he could get lots of good things from such a magnificent house. And Dr. Doug surprised him, that's all. That thief is scared to death to ever come back here. It's nothing you need to worry about."

"Are you sure?" she sniffled. A glimmer of hope shone in her eyes.

"Of course I'm sure," I told her, hoping my voice sounded confident. "I want you to go back to your room and get some sleep now. You're perfectly safe in this house—I promise. Do you think your dad or your mom or Liko would ever let anything happen to you or Marcus?"

"No."

"See? There's nothing to worry about. Now scoot and get some sleep."

She smiled at me and hugged me around my waist. "Okay. Thanks."

She drank her water and scampered down the length of the lanai. I had a feeling she would sleep well that night.

And as long as I believed my own words, maybe I could sleep well too. And I fell asleep rather quickly after that. I didn't hear whether Lars or Barbie came back into the house.

The next morning, I was making breakfast when Lars appeared in the doorway. He looked exhausted, his eyes ringed by dark circles, his mouth thin and pinched.

"Can I get you some coffee?" I asked.

He rubbed his hair with one hand. "Sure," he mumbled. "Have the kids left for school yet?"

"No. I expect them to come in for breakfast in just a few minutes."

"Could you tell them I had to leave early for a meeting and I said to have a good day?"

"Sure."

He left and I could hear him closing his office door quietly behind him. I relayed his message when the kids came in to eat. Justine looked rested, her eyes bright. Neither she nor Marcus seemed to realize their mother had disappeared during the night. After they left for school, I knocked tentatively on Lars's office door. "It's Kailani."

"Come in."

"Would you like something to eat, Lars?"

He was sitting in his swivel chair, looking at the framed shirts on the wall behind his desk. He spun around slowly to face me.

"No, thanks. I'm not hungry."

I turned to go, but he called me back. "Kailani, I know now why you were being so quiet when you came in last night. I'm sorry I accused you of being sneaky. You knew that Barbie went out." It was a statement, not a question.

My heart went out to him. "Yes," I answered quietly.

Suddenly he pounded his fist on the desk. "If I just knew where she went . . ."

I was shocked. And torn. He didn't know where she had gone. *Should I tell him what I knew? But what if he—not a stranger in the night—really had killed Dr. Doug? What if he harmed Liko? What if he harmed Barbie? She might be behaving badly, but she didn't deserve that.*

I decided not to tell him where Barbie had been.

I returned to the kitchen and was preparing a plate for Barbie when she appeared in the doorway, looking fresh and perky as always.

"Good morning, Kailani! Have you got that list of hors d'oeuvres for me?"

I had forgotten all about the list. "I'm working on it. I thought I might try a couple new things today to see if they would work at the party," I lied.

"Great!" she answered brightly. She helped herself to the plate I had prepared for her and took it to the lanai.

Liko came into the kitchen shortly after Barbie left. "Hey, K! Got anything to eat?"

I looked daggers at him. "Find something yourself."

He looked hurt. "What's the matter?"

"As if you don't know."

"You know?" he whispered.

I nodded, scowling.

"Just let me tell you how it happened."

"Spare me the details."

"I'm sorry, K. Does anyone else know?"

"If you mean Lars, no. I haven't told him. Yet."

"Please don't say anything. I don't want him to be hurt."

"You're considering his feelings now? Now that it's too late?"

"He's my friend."

"I wonder if he would feel the same way if he knew how you spent last night."

"Have you seen Barbie?"

"She's on the lanai."

He headed toward the back of the house, away from the lanai. Maybe he was already having regrets. I hoped so.

Barbie came into the kitchen shortly after. "Have you seen Liko this morning, by any chance?"

I was standing at the counter with my back to her. I didn't turn around. "He came in here a while ago and I don't know where he went after that."

I spent that day cooking to chase away my stress. I made an elaborate meal for dinner, as well as chicken stock and vegetable stock to freeze and several desserts that could also be frozen and served at Barbie's party. I drew up the list of additional foods for the party and made two new appetizers for her to try.

When they came home from school, Marcus and Justine were happy to see that I had spent the entire day cooking. I had replenished the supplies of homemade snacks that they liked.

Not one to be deceived, Justine spoke up. "What's the matter, Kailani? Are you okay?"

I smiled fondly at her. "Everything is going to be fine, Justine. Don't worry about me. I just felt a little stressed out, that's all."

She returned my grin, but I noticed Marcus looking at me with concern. He took a snack and looked over his shoulder and gave me a brief, worried look as he left the kitchen.

That night after dinner, Marcus and Liko sat on the lanai doing math homework when the doorbell rang. Justine ran to answer it.

A moment later there was a tap on my shoulder as I stood doing dishes. I jumped, startled. Geoffrey stood behind me, grinning from ear to ear.

"Geoffrey! You scared me! What are you doing here?" I sounded as annoyed as I felt.

"I was just in the area and I thought I'd stop by and see what you're doing."

"I'm working," I told him curtly.

"Want to take a break and go for a walk?"

"I really can't, Geoffrey."

"C'mon, take a walk with me. I won't keep you out long."

I sighed. "Geoffrey, I really don't have time. Why are you so far from Kona, anyway?"

He winked at me. "Okay, you caught me. I just wanted to see you."

I took a deep breath and put my hands on the counter. "Geoffrey . . ." I began slowly. "I thought I had made it clear that we are not dating anymore."

"But why not? I came all the way to Hawaii to show you that I'm willing to go where you want to be. That should count for something," he whined. "And you're not dating anyone else, right? So deep down you must miss me."

I knew then that Geoffrey wasn't going to go away. I needed to do something to make him leave, so I lied to him.

It was a decision I would live to regret.

Chapter 11

"Actually, I *am* dating," I said breezily.

He looked at me intently, his eyebrows raised and his mouth hanging open. "You didn't tell me that," he said in an accusing tone. "Who is it?"

I had to think fast. "Liko."

"That Hawaiian guy? Kailani, you can do better than him. He barely has a job."

"He works here. He tutors Marcus. And the only reason he doesn't have a job in the school system is that the state doesn't have the money right now for the subject he teaches."

"Which is?"

"Hawaiian language and culture."

"Seems like the state would find the money if that's something they wanted the kids to learn."

"It doesn't work that way, Geoffrey."

"How long have you two been seeing each other?"

"Since around the time I came back from Washington." My lie was growing.

"Didn't take you long, did it?" he sneered.

"Geoffrey, please. I don't really want to discuss it."

"Why did you lie to me when I asked you if you were dating him?" I had forgotten our conversation that night in Hawi.

"I just didn't think it was any of your business. And I still feel that way. I really don't want to talk about it." I had to change the subject.

"I'd like to meet him."

"That's not a good idea."

"We'll see."

I shuddered. I didn't know what to expect from Geoffrey anymore. He made me uncomfortable and nervous. "Geoffrey, I think you should go now."

He gave me a hard look. "Okay, but you're not getting rid of me that easily. I intend to find out more about this Liko of yours." He frowned and turned to leave. My first thought was that I needed to find Liko and apologize for creating this mess.

He and Marcus had apparently finished doing homework, because neither of them was on the lanai. I found him in the workout room in the guesthouse. He looked angry.

"Liko, we need to talk about something."

He scoffed. "You talking to me again? What do you want? No lectures, please."

"I'm not here to lecture you. I'm sorry about that. I was just thinking of Lars and the kids, that's all. We can talk about it later if you want, but I'm here to tell you that I told a lie about you and I want you to be aware of it in case it comes up."

He looked at me, obviously puzzled. He said nothing though, and I continued after hesitating a moment.

"Geoffrey was just here. He scares me a little. He wants to get back together and I told him no. He was insisting, so I told him you and I were dating. I'm really sorry," I finished lamely.

He cocked his head and smiled at me kindly. "That's okay. From what you've told me about him, the guy's a little crazy. I'm glad you told him that. Maybe now he'll leave you alone."

"I just wanted you to know in case he ever approaches you and asks if it's true."

"I'd actually love it if that guy came up to me and asked me about you. I'd let him have it. What's wrong with him, anyway?"

"He's possessive and jealous. I never saw that side of him in Washington." I thought uneasily of the time Geoffrey followed me home from the restaurant, but mentally brushed it aside.

"Just watch yourself, K."

"I will, Liko. And *mahalo* for helping me."

"You're welcome, little sistah."

I didn't sleep well that night. I woke up cranky and still tired. I blamed Geoffrey for my restlessness and vowed to come clean with him the next time I saw him—and I was sure there would be a next time. I couldn't stand being caught in the middle of a lie of my own making. Barbie was in a hurry when she came in for breakfast, so I wrapped a muffin for her and poured her coffee in a travel mug. She seemed to be in a foul mood too. I wondered if it had anything to do with Liko.

But when Liko appeared for breakfast after the kids left for school, he appeared happy and carefree, quite a change from the day before.

"Lars and I are going to the beach to see if there are any good swells," he announced. I gave him a sideways look and he read my mind. "Lars isn't going to find out about me and Barbie, so don't worry," he said quietly. I hoped he was right.

I had the day to myself since no one was home. Dinner was already prepared; I had been marinating two large pieces of butterfish for two days in a mixture of sake, mirin, miso paste, and sugar. I knew Barbie and Lars would like it, but I was hoping for a thumbs-up from Marcus and Justine. They were being great about all the gastronomic introductions I was making, and I wanted to prove to them once again that fish could be heavenly. I decided to head down to Kona to do some shopping.

I drove south with the windows open, the wind whipping my hair and the radio on. I seemed to be leaving some of my bad mood behind me and my spirits rose as I drove into Kona. I had arranged to meet my mom and my sister for lunch, and I was looking forward to seeing them. I had errands to run first, though.

I was cutting through an alley near the library when I saw Geoffrey from a short distance away. His back was turned to me, but I recognized him immediately by his stance and by his blindingly white skin, a rarity in Kona. I turned quickly so he wouldn't see me, but he caught a glimpse of my retreating back and called out to me.

"Kailani! What are you doing here?" He jogged up to me, a wide smile lighting up his face. "Were you looking for me?" he asked hopefully.

"Actually, I was just going to run into the library for a minute to borrow a book," I said. "What are you doing?"

"I was just at the library too."

Was he ever leaving?"

"Well, I've got to run. Bye," I said after an awkward silence.

"Wait!" he called, walking after me. "How about lunch?"

I shook my head. "Can't. I already have lunch plans."

"With Liko?" he sneered.

"No, as a matter of fact."

"Then who?"

"Geoffrey, it's none of your business. I'm leaving. Please don't follow me."

I walked away, not looking back. I prayed he wasn't behind me. As I turned the corner onto a main street, I glanced over my shoulder. He was standing where I had left him, watching me. I shivered.

It took some effort, but I threw off my nervousness at seeing Geoffrey when I met my mom and sister for lunch. This was the first time I had seen my family since I started my job, so it was a happy reunion. My mom and sister wanted to know all about the Jorgensens and their home. Carefully avoiding all the drama that had occurred since I had begun my job as personal chef, I regaled them with descriptions of the magnificent house on the water. My sister couldn't wait to see it.

"When can we visit?" she asked.

"Probably anytime is okay, but let me ask Mr. or Mrs. Jorgensen first. I've been so busy that I haven't even had time to think of having visitors."

They told me about my dad, who was working at the bakery, and all my old friends who continued to visit in hopes of hearing about me and my new job.

"Speaking of old friends, how's Liko?" my sister asked.

"Oh, he's fine," I answered, hoping to change the subject quickly.

My sister looked at me conspiratorially. "I hear he's found himself a new girlfriend," she said slyly. "Anything you want to tell us?"

I looked at her in surprise. "No," I answered slowly. "Where did you hear that?"

"Is it true? Are you and Liko dating? That's so exciting!" my mother exclaimed, smiling.

"No, it's not true. I'm not dating anyone," I told them firmly. "And neither is Liko."

"But a guy stopped in the bakery and said he had met you recently and that you were dating some Hawaiian tutor who lived with the Jorgensens."

Geoffrey. "Who was this guy?" I asked, even though I already knew the answer.

My sister shrugged. "Some guy who said he knew you from a place in Hawi Town. I think he's interested in you too."

"What did he look like?"

"Tall, *haole*, blond hair, pale white skin."

Definitely Geoffrey. I didn't want to alarm my mom and sister by telling them who Geoffrey was or why he was asking about me, but I wanted them to know that they should ignore him.

"I know who you're talking about, and he's weird. A little *pupule*, if you know what I mean. His name is Geoffrey. Don't pay any attention to him." I smiled broadly to indicate that he didn't concern me at all.

"So you're not dating Liko?" my sister asked with a frown.

I laughed. "Sorry to disappoint you, but no."

My mom finally changed the subject, asking about Marcus and Justine.

"They're good kids," I replied. "Marcus is a typical teenage boy, a little withdrawn and moody, but he's coming around a little with Liko tutoring him. Justine is a sweetheart. Their parents don't have much time for them."

"How does everyone like your cooking?" my mom wanted to know.

"They're definitely making progress. Barbie likes everything I make, but Lars and the kids like heavy meals. They've been harder to please. But I got Marcus to eat *poke*, and he really liked it. I even helped him make some for his school and he had fun."

Far too soon, it was time for me to head back to the Jorgensens' house, and for my mom and sister to return home too. We said our good-byes, promising to see each other again soon.

I drove north again, watching the sun as it began its descent toward the ocean, thankful once again that I was back at home on the Big Island.

When I got back, Liko and Lars were in the kitchen rummaging for snacks. They turned around when I walked in.

"Kailani, we're starving," Lars said by way of greeting.

I showed them where I kept the kids' after-school snacks and they helped themselves, taking the food to Lars's office. Liko gave me a quick glance over his shoulder as he followed Lars down the hallway.

I was torn. Liko had been my good friend for many years. He was unwaveringly complicit in my lie about us to Geoffrey. I had helped him get a job working for the Jorgensens. And yet, I disapproved of his behavior with Barbie. I was beginning to really like the family, and I hated to see them hurt because of Liko's indiscretion.

But of course, the indiscretion didn't belong just to Liko. Barbie played a big role too. She seemed to be a shameless flirt—and worse than that, she went far beyond flirting with the men she ensnared. First Doug, now Liko. And who knew how many others there had been? I felt another pang of sympathy for Lars.

My stress level was beginning to increase again. It had receded for a couple of hours as I sat chatting with my mother and my sister at lunchtime, but now that I was back in the Jorgensens' house I was feeling anxious again.

As usual, I soothed myself by cooking, preparing a huge salad for dinner along with an elaborate fresh-fruit-and-meringue dessert to go with the butterfish I had been marinating. At least the Jorgensens' appetites were benefitting from all my stress.

That night after dinner I sat on the lanai again, nursing a glass of wine, when I thought I heard low voices. I walked quietly in the direction of the sound and was dismayed when I saw Liko and Barbie lying on a blanket in the grass under the awning of a large *hala* tree. A nearby landscaping lamp gave off just enough light for me to see their bodies entwined in the darkness. I was seized with a sudden urge to throw up. My heart ached for the rest of the family and for the mess Liko was making. He didn't seem to understand or care that he was hurting Lars and the two children. And me.

I turned and practically ran to my room. Meli obliged as I stroked her soft fur until I had calmed down. I wondered if Lars could see the two lovebirds from the upstairs master suite, but I knew Liko and Barbie had chosen their spot carefully, as the leaves of the *hala* tree would block any view from above. And apparently they weren't worried about Lars spotting them from the lanai. He was always in his office, anyway.

Once again, I couldn't sleep. When I got up in the morning to fix breakfast, I was angry at both Liko and Barbie. It troubled me that they could carry on an affair in the very house where the rest of the family was sleeping and, most likely, oblivious to their activities.

I couldn't very well accuse Liko of indiscretions when I had asked him to go along with my lie to Geoffrey, though I felt his dishonesty was far greater than mine. And I couldn't approach Barbie about her behavior if I wanted to keep my job. I needed to keep my opinions to myself, as hard as that would be.

When Barbie came in for breakfast later, I found it hard to look at her directly. When she spoke to me, my answers were terse and clipped.

"How are you coming on that list of foods for the party, Kailani?"

"Good. Here." I took the list I had completed out of a drawer and handed it to her. She perused it with a look of interest.

"These sound *won*derful!" she gushed. "Did I try a couple of these already?"

"Yes."

"What's for breakfast?"

"Muffins from my parents' bakery and fresh fruit."

"Ooh! *Yum*my!"

Barbie's cheerfulness was starting to grate on my nerves.

"I'll bring a tray out to the lanai for you." It wasn't a very subtle attempt to get her to leave the kitchen.

She looked at me, a bit deflated. "Is everything all right, Kailani?"

"Yeah."

She studied me through narrowed eyes for a moment. I did my best to ignore her, and she left the kitchen. Had she figured out what I knew? I would have to do a better job of hiding my feelings or she might simply decide she didn't want me around anymore.

I poured her a cup of coffee and put it on a tray along with sliced papaya with a lime wedge and a wheat muffin studded with chunks of ripe orange mango. She thanked me quietly and I returned to the kitchen.

Liko came in next. "What's up, K?" he asked, smiling broadly.

I gave him a brief, pained stare, pleading silently with him to understand what he was doing to the Jorgensens. But he didn't seem to notice, or he didn't care.

He took his breakfast to the lanai and sat down across from Barbie. I stayed in the kitchen, not wanting to see the looks exchanged between them, the knowing smiles they would share. I couldn't wait for the kids to leave for school so they wouldn't have to witness their mother so obviously holding court with yet another man who wasn't their father.

Marcus and Justine hurried in a minute later, grabbing muffins and yogurt drinks for breakfast. They would eat on their way to the bus, they told me. They came from the back of the house, so they had apparently been spared the sight of their mother with Marcus's tutor.

I heard Lars join Liko and Barbie at the table. Things were barely civil between Lars and Barbie these days; Lars seemed to know where he stood with his wife, but obviously hadn't yet figured out that Liko was the man who had captured his wife's attentions. I could hear Lars and Liko laughing together about something.

After breakfast, Barbie returned to the kitchen. "Kailani, I'm going to be sending out invitations for the party today. I'm not giving people much notice—just one week. Can you have everything ready by then?"

"Sure," I answered, attempting to show her that my earlier rude behavior had passed. "I'll start shopping today."

"Good. This is going to be a great party." She turned and left for work.

I spent much of that day in the markets in Hawi and up in Waimea. I hadn't been to Waimea in a long time, and it was fun rediscovering all my favorite markets and shops in the up-country ranching town. I got all the nonperishables I would need for Barbie's party, then treated myself to an afternoon snack at one of the several organic restaurants that called Waimea home.

As I walked to my car, I thought I heard a familiar voice. I turned and was surprised to see Barbie walking arm in arm with a tall man in a white coat. I didn't want her to see me, so I ducked into the nearest shop, where I could see them from the front window. They looked as if they were in the throes of puppy love. They stopped next to a small sports car and she kissed him on tiptoe while he bent down to meet her lips halfway. They lingered there for another minute, then he got into the car and drove away with a wave in her direction.

I wondered whether the man—whoever he was—knew Barbie was married to one man and sleeping with another. If he was one of her colleagues, surely he knew she was married. He probably didn't know about Liko, though, and I wondered with an ironic pang of sadness whether Liko knew about him.

Barbie turned around and walked back into a nearby building without a backward glance. I was sure she hadn't seen me. I drove slowly past the building on my way out of Waimea. A sign outside said it was Orchid Isle Wellness.

I drove back to the Jorgensens in an uncomfortable cloud. I didn't like secrets, and now I was the keeper of too many. I had lied to Geoffrey about Liko and me, I was hiding the truth from Lars about Barbie and Liko, and now I would be hiding the truth from both Lars and Liko about this other man. My stomach was in knots and I wasn't sure if cooking would alleviate the stress this time. *Maybe I should just come clean with everyone. But I don't want to be the one to break the news to Lars and Liko that Barbie is cheating on both of them.*

I pulled my car into the drive in front of the Jorgensens' house. I lugged all the bags of groceries with me under the pergola and glanced up at the hanging jade, dripping down in all its perfect turquoise glory. As beautiful as the plant was, it was considered an aggressive member of the landscape. *Barbie is the same way*, I thought ruefully. She is beautiful and tempting, but also aggressively flirtatious and over-reaching. *Does she sleep with every man she meets?*

I was surprised to run directly into Lars as I opened the front door. He laughed and offered to lighten my load of bags a bit. I gratefully handed him two heavy sacks and followed him into the kitchen.

"Kailani, I'm going to take the kids out to dinner tonight," he told me as we set the bags down on the counters. "You have the evening off."

"Thanks. That'll give me time to work on the details for Barbie's party."

"About that party . . ."

"Hmm?"

He hesitated. "Nothing." He shook his head slightly and left.

I was glad Lars was taking Marcus and Justine to dinner, not because it gave me the evening off, but because it was so nice to see him spending time with his kids. When dinnertime came, I scrambled an egg for myself and ate it with a side of homemade salsa and a slice of my parents' bread, toasted and buttered. As I enjoyed the simple meal on the lanai, I thought again of the man whom I'd seen kissing Barbie earlier. Who was he? Didn't he care that she was married? Didn't *she* care? And why did she work so hard to destroy her family?

I could come up with no answers. I was glad Liko didn't come looking for dinner, because I wanted to be alone. Maybe he had even gone with Lars and the kids, though Lars hadn't mentioned it.

I was in my den, looking through cookbooks for one more show-stopping dessert recipe for Barbie's party, when I heard voices in the kitchen. I poked my head around the door to find Marcus and Justine helping themselves to drinks from the refrigerator.

"Hi, guys. How was dinner?"

I wasn't prepared for their response. Justine started crying and ran off toward the lanai and Marcus stared at me for a moment, anger flashing in his young eyes. "Dinner sucked," he said, then turned on his heel and followed Justine, calling her name.

I was stunned. What had happened during dinner? Had they fought with Lars? Had they gotten in trouble for something? I stood, staring at nothing out the kitchen doorway, when Lars came down the hall from the front door. I hadn't even heard him coming.

I looked at him, confused, but if he noticed, he ignored the question in my eyes. "Where did the kids go?" he asked brusquely.

I blinked. "I just saw them go toward their rooms."

He nodded and left, going in the same direction the kids had gone. *What was happening?*

I couldn't concentrate on dessert recipes anymore. I poured myself a glass of wine and took it out to the lanai. After quite a long time, Lars walked by, his shoulders drooping and his head down. He hadn't seen me.

"Can I get you anything, Lars?" He jumped, looking startled. "I mean, is everything okay?" I asked.

"Oh. Hi, Kailani. Sorry, I didn't see you there. No, everything is not okay. I'll be back in a minute."

He left, but returned several minutes later with a bottle of wine and a large glass. He sat down heavily at the dining table. I felt funny talking to him from the daybed, so I took my wine to the table and sat down opposite him. I didn't know what to say, so I waited for him to talk. He poured himself a large measure of the dark purple wine and took a long sip.

When he spoke, his words came as a surprise, even though I guess I should have expected them.

"I took the kids out to dinner to tell them that things are not working out between their mother and me," he announced flatly.

"I'm sorry to hear that," I murmured.

He sighed. "I should have stayed home to tell them," he said. "They were upset, and they were mad at me for telling them in public. I didn't even think about that. I just wanted to get away from the house for a while. Neither one of them is speaking to me. Like it's my fault this marriage isn't working out."

I didn't know what to say. He continued, "I didn't come right out and tell them that we're divorcing, but I think it was pretty clear."

"I'm sure they got the message," I said.

"Do you think it was wrong of me to do that?"

I was startled. I didn't know what to say. I thought carefully before I answered. "I think you probably put into words what they've known for a while now. I know for a fact that Marcus hasn't been oblivious to what's been going on, because he's mentioned it to me before. And I'm sure not much escapes Justine's notice."

Lars seemed surprised. "You think they know what's been going on?"

I nodded. "I think kids know more than adults give them credit for."

"You're probably right. But I wish they weren't mad at me. It's like they're blaming me for everything. I've tried. God knows I've tried. We even moved here from California to start fresh after I caught Barbie cheating on me. We moved here because I thought she just needed to get away from the temptation. But there are men here too. And she found them, just like I should have known she would."

He was revealing more to me than I was comfortable hearing, but perhaps getting this off his chest was helping him. So I remained silent. He poured himself another large glass of wine.

"I know I spend a lot of time working, but I've always tried to balance that with family. Maybe I haven't tried hard enough. And I know she's seeing someone else. I just don't know who it is." He took another long swig of wine.

She was seeing at least two other people, but I didn't tell him that.

"Do you want to know something? I don't even think Justine is my daughter. I think she's the daughter of someone Barbie worked with back in California. Justine doesn't know that, of course."

I was astonished. I was sure Lars wouldn't have shared that information with me if he had been stone cold sober, and I worried that he would regret it tomorrow. There were a thousand questions I wanted to ask him about why he suspected Justine wasn't his child, but it wasn't my place to ask.

Lars and I sat in silence for a bit longer, then I excused myself and went to my room. I didn't sleep well again that night—which was getting to be a habit. When the kids came into the kitchen in the morning, Justine hadn't even brushed her hair and Marcus's eyes wore a hooded look.

"Justine, can I braid your hair for you?" I offered. "It would look great."

She looked at me listlessly. "I guess." She walked over and presented the back of her head to me.

"You have to run and get a brush. Hurry so you don't miss the bus." I was pleased when she hustled down to her room and came back quickly with a brush.

I brushed her long, chestnut hair and put it in a French braid in time for her to catch the bus. She looked much better. I couldn't do much about Marcus's eyes, but I did remind him to have a great day and he smiled appreciatively.

I wanted to do something special for them. I didn't have a lot of money, but I had enough to take them into Hawi for ice cream after school. When they came home, I herded them into my car and we took off.

"Where are we going?" Marcus whined.

"Are we in trouble?" Justine asked.

I laughed. "We're going somewhere fun. It's a treat." For all of us, since I got ice cream as rarely as they did.

I pulled into a parking space right in front of the ice cream shop on the main road in Hawi Town.

"We're getting ice cream?" Marcus asked, his eyes lighting up.

"Yay!" screeched Justine from the backseat.

They followed me into the store and took their time deciding what they wanted. Finally, Marcus ended up with a two-scoop macadamia nut and coconut ice cream cone and Justine opted for a dragon-fruit sorbet, no doubt because of its gorgeous hot-pink color.

We took the cones with us and drove to Mahukona State Park, where we enjoyed the view from a picnic table near the boat ramp. I wanted them to feel comfortable talking to me; I ignored the twinge that reminded me that I knew the secret about Liko and their mother and I hadn't told anyone.

No one spoke, and finally I asked, "Where did you go for dinner with your dad last night?"

Marcus scowled and Justine glanced at him, pain showing in her eyes.

"A place in Waimea. It was okay," he answered.

"I didn't get a chance to ask you about it last night," I mentioned pointedly. "You know me. I'm always interested in what people are eating."

"Mom and Dad might be getting a divorce," Justine blurted out. Marcus shot her an angry look.

"As if you didn't know," he added, turning the angry look on me. I met his gaze and held it for a moment.

"What do you mean?"

"I mean, I heard Dad telling you some things last night that are private. You just brought us here to pump us for information!" he accused. Justine looked shocked. I wondered if Marcus had heard the entire conversation and specifically whether he had heard his father say that Justine might not be his child.

"Marcus, the reason I brought you here is to let you both know that yes, I do know why your dad took you to dinner last night and to tell you that you can talk to me anytime about it if you're feeling sad or scared or upset," I told him quietly. "The only information I'm pumping you for is what you had for dinner," I finished with a slight smile.

That broke the tension a bit. "I'm sorry," Marcus mumbled. "It's just—you know—it's not fair. Everything is always about them. They're always worrying about themselves and not us. We're upset too." And to my surprise, a tear trickled down his cheek. He suddenly looked much younger and more vulnerable. He wiped the tear away angrily. Justine leaned her head on his shoulder.

"You know, it always hurts when parents get divorced, but someday you'll realize that it was the best thing for the whole family. It won't always hurt the way it does today." I knew that might sound a little naïve, since I was the product of a long and stable marriage, but I felt it was what the kids needed to hear and I firmly believed it.

Marcus sighed and smiled at Justine. "We know that. But it's hard at first." Justine nodded, biting into her cone.

"Is there anything I can do to make you feel better?"

Marcus grinned. "Take us out for ice cream twice a week." Justine giggled.

I rolled my eyes at him. "Maybe not twice a week, but definitely sometimes. How does that sound?"

"Good," they answered in unison. We were all done with our cones, so we got back in the car and headed home. They seemed more relaxed when they went into the house together. I lingered behind, staying out of their conversation. The hanging jade rustled gently in the trade wind and I was reminded afresh of its similarity to Barbie. I shuddered.

That night Lars ate dinner with the kids and Barbie came home from work late. She was eating alone on the lanai when Liko and Marcus came into the kitchen looking for a snack. I gave them each a carob-dipped frozen banana and—after giving each other looks of uncertainty and groans of "why can't we have real chocolate?"— they slowly made their way to the long lanai table where they spread out Marcus's books and papers. I went out to see if Barbie needed anything else and saw the wink she gave Liko. I hoped Marcus missed it, though it seemed little escaped his notice. They settled down to work and Barbie slipped away and followed me back to the kitchen.

"That Liko is a wonder. He's so good with Marcus."

"Yes," was all I could think of to say. Listening to her talk about Liko made me feel uneasy.

"Do you think he'd be willing to stay on here at the house even after Marcus has finished school for the year?" I knew school ended in late spring. I had wondered what excuse she might find to keep Liko at the house over the summer, when there would be no homework for Marcus to do. I didn't have to wait long to find out.

"I really think it would be good for Marcus if Liko could stay here and give him math instruction over the summer. Marcus may not like the idea, but it's really for his own good. You know, so he doesn't fall behind in school. So many kids forget the math they've learned when they're on summer vacation."

"I don't know what Liko's summer plans are. You'll have to ask him," I answered. I knew exactly why she wanted Liko to stay, and it had nothing to do with math.

"Would you give Liko a message when he's done with Marcus?" she asked sweetly. "Would you ask him to come find me? I'd like to discuss his summer plans."

"Sure." Now I had to tell him. I had the uncomfortable feeling that I was facilitating their affair, but Barbie didn't seem to realize that I knew the extent of their relationship. I also didn't think she had seen me when she was kissing another man in Waimea. I was keeping two secrets for her and she didn't even know it. I could feel myself becoming angry and anxious.

It didn't help that Geoffrey chose that moment to call my cell phone. I picked up the call impatiently.

"Yes, Geoffrey?"

"Hi, Kailani. Haven't seen you in a few days. What are you doing tomorrow?"

"Working."

"Can you take a quick break and have lunch?"

"Not tomorrow, Geoffrey." *Not ever.* "I really have too much to do with this big party coming up."

"Oh? What's the party for?"

"Mrs. Jorgensen's wellness practice won an award and they're celebrating with a party."

"Sounds fun. When is it?"

"In a few days," I answered vaguely.

"Do you think it would be all right if I popped in?"

"For the party?"

"Yeah."

"No! You can't do that. You're a stranger."

"Not to you."

"You're a stranger to them. I can't go around inviting people to a party for someone else. C'mon, Geoffrey, you know that."

"I just want to see how the other half lives."

"They're just normal people having a normal party," I explained in growing frustration. "Geoffrey, I really have to go. Is that all you wanted?"

"Can you meet for a drink after the party's over?"

"No. I'm not meeting you for a drink. It's over, Geoffrey. How many ways do I have to say it?"

"It's because of that Liko, isn't it?"

"No, Geoffrey. It has nothing to do with Liko. You're not listening. I just don't want to see you anymore. Can't you understand that?"

"No, Kailani. I really can't," he said in a chilling voice. "I can't understand that. If you didn't want to be with me, why did you go out with me in Washington? Why have you led me on?"

"I haven't led you on, Geoffrey. I haven't done anything to encourage you since you came to Hawaii. In fact, I've done everything I can think of to *dis*courage you. You just don't get it."

"Oh, I get it all right. This is Liko's fault. He seduced you and you allowed it to happen and now you've spurned me. Even though I followed you all the way from Washington to make a new life with you."

I couldn't tell Geoffrey at this point that I had lied to him about Liko. He was unstable. There was no telling what he would do if he knew I had lied to him. I said the first thing that came to mind.

"Geoffrey, you're scaring me. I'm going to call the police if you contact me again." I hung up on him.

He called back almost immediately. I turned off the ringer and went into my room, closed and locked the door behind me, and scooped up Meli. I held her to my face, trembling. I knew I should tell Liko about my conversation with Geoffrey, but I was afraid he would find Geoffrey and dispense his own vigilante justice. As much as I wanted Geoffrey out of my life for good, the last thing I needed on my conscience was physical harm to him.

I took a sleeping pill so I could get some rest that night. With all the drama between Barbie and Lars, worrying about who killed Dr. Doug, my own problems with Geoffrey, my anxiety about the kids, and my guilt over keeping Barbie and Liko's secrets, it had been a while since I had slept well. I had a feeling the next several days would be challenging, between worrying about Geoffrey's intentions and preparing for Barbie's party.

My hunch proved right. For the next two days the household was in a frenzy of party preparations. Akela whirled around the house in a tornado of dust cloths and furniture polish, and the gardeners worked overtime to trim and prune the already-gorgeous flowers and trees on the property. Barbie oversaw the entire operation and even made herself useful a few times.

I busied myself in the kitchen, making everything that could be frozen ahead of time. Batch after batch of appetizers and *amuse-bouches* went into the Jorgensens' walk-in freezer in orderly rows. I made all the fruit purees for the alcoholic and nonalcoholic drinks and refrigerated them. I set out all the trays and platters I would need for serving. Since I was in charge of wines too, I spent some time on my laptop researching which wines would be best to serve with certain foods. I placed orders for fresh food at several local markets, made arrangements to have them delivered, and drove up to Waimea twice to pick up ingredients at specialty shops. My cookbooks were never far from my hands, and I don't think I took off my apron for those two days.

On the third day, I woke up to low-hanging clouds in an endless gray sky. The weather forecaster predicted light rain beginning late in the morning and continuing until nightfall. It was going to be one of those rare wet days on the west side of the Big Island. And though it would be nice to see the rain for a change, poor Justine had stayed home from school with a bad headache, probably brought on by the weather. I felt I needed a break from the constant party preparations, so I took my kayak out for a quick trip. I hoisted it up from its spot in the Jorgensens' garage and carried it down to the water.

I put in by the rocks below the house. The water was a bit choppier than usual, but visibility was still fine because the rain hadn't started falling yet.

I had been paddling for about ten minutes when I felt something bump against the bottom of the craft. I assumed I had paddled over the carapace of a *honu*. The sea turtles were plentiful around the rocks in front of the Jorgensens' home and I had seen them several times. I hadn't yet come across any while paddling, but I knew they were there. They were huge, beautiful, gentle creatures that were thrilling to see. I had seen tourists try to touch or feed them on many occasions, but doing so was actually a crime punishable by a huge fine. I craned my neck to get a look at the *honu*. I never would have paddled over it if I had seen it in the water.

But what I saw behind me wasn't a *honu*. It was a large dark gray triangle of skin circling the boat slowly.

It was a dorsal fin.

I had read enough newspaper stories of shark attacks to have a very basic knowledge of what to do. I wasn't sure I was actually being attacked by the shark, but I didn't want to wait to find out.

I felt another bump as the shark butted against the kayak a second time. The small boat tilted dangerously close to the surface of the water. My arms flailed out as I tried to use the paddle to regain my balance. My breath was coming faster. I needed to turn around and head back toward the shore.

I struggled with the paddle against the force of the waves and the mass of the shark's body. It appeared to be about five feet long, almost my height. I knew from what I had read that I should remain calm. I wondered briefly if the people who had written such advice had ever actually been attacked by a shark.

I tried taking a few deep breaths while the beast continued to nudge the boat with its snout. Somewhere in the back of my mind, I was reminded that drowning was far more common than shark attacks. To some ancient Hawaiians, sharks were guardian spirits called *aumakua*.

But at the moment, this shark was no guardian spirit. I was paddling furiously and finding it very hard to breathe deeply without hyperventilating.

A split second later the shark breached the surface of the water and opened its huge maw. Rows of sharp teeth erupted out of ragged-looking bright red gums. I heard a piercing scream that could only have come from me. I chanced a quick look back at the house to see if anyone had heard me, but I turned my attention immediately back to the shark, which had circled away from the kayak and was headed back in my direction, gaining speed.

Somehow, I remembered reading somewhere that it was important to be aggressive during a shark attack—to fight back at the shark's vulnerable spots and to use any available weapon. I clutched my paddle and maneuvered it to strike the monster when it got close enough to hit.

But as its huge mass bore down on me I lost my nerve. What if I made it mad? What if it charged and capsized the kayak and I was at the shark's mercy? I didn't want to die in the water. The thoughts charged through my racing brain as it bumped the kayak once more. I lurched sideways and clenched the side of the boat with both hands in a fierce grip. The shark swam away and began to circle around again, a deadly hunter stalking its prey. When it came to within four feet of the kayak, I grabbed my paddle like a bat and swung toward the shark's snout. I dimly remembered that its most vulnerable spots were its eyes and its gills, but I couldn't reach either with the paddle. I must have stunned it, though, because it stopped for just a moment. Then it charged again, ramming into the kayak with greater force. I raised the paddle to swing again, and this time I landed the edge of it along the side of the shark's face. I think I hit its eye. It slashed its tail in a huge arc in the water and twisted its massive body away from the kayak. I watched in horror as it flipped partially out of the water and charged at me again. I readied myself for another swipe at his head when I heard a scream. It distracted me and for just a second I turned my head in the direction of the sound. When I turned back, the shark was inches from the kayak. There was no way I had time to hit it again.

Instinct told me to lie down as flat as I could in the kayak to avoid being knocked into the water when the shark struck again. I held onto the edges of the boat as it rocked in the water like a cork, then sat up quickly when I realized the shark had circled away again. I gripped the paddle again, then swung with all my strength just as the shark neared the kayak one more time on its deadly quest.

I must have hit the shark squarely in the eye, because as it swam slowly alongside the kayak, a thin trail of blood wafted through the water behind it. I held my breath as I waited to see if the shark would swim away.

Thankfully, I must have hit the shark hard enough that it decided not to pursue. My chest heaved from the stress of exertion, and I righted my paddle to make my way back to shore as quickly as I could. I looked again at the rocky coast and saw the source of the scream I had heard.

Justine stood on the lava, waving her arms and jumping up and down. I was seized with terror, thinking she would tumble into the water and that the shark would return, this time for her. I started yelling to her.

"I'm okay, Justine! Please—no jumping! I don't want you to fall in!"

I don't know whether she could make out my words, but she stopped flailing around and waited for me to put in along the lava rocks.

"Kailani!" she screamed when I had jumped over the side of the craft and dragged it onto the shore. "I thought you were going to die!" She ran over to me and threw herself into my arms, sobbing.

Seeing her crying made my own tears start to flow. We hugged each other for several moments before she pulled away from me and looked me up and down carefully. "Did it get you? Are you all right?"

"Not a scratch, if you can believe it." I didn't want to scare her away from ever going in the water again, but it would probably be a while before she would be willing to set foot in the Pacific Ocean again after what she had just witnessed.

I knew it would be a long time before *I* ventured back in the water.

Justine's cries had attracted the attention of others from the house. As I hauled my kayak farther up the rocks, Lars and Liko came running from the direction of the house.

"K! Is everything all right?" Liko yelled.

"Justine, what happened?" Lars exclaimed as he ran up to us.

"Daddy, a shark attacked Kailani!" Justine started crying again.

Lars stopped short and stared at me, his mouth hanging open. Liko ran up to me and grabbed my arms. He turned me around so he could see for himself that I wasn't seriously hurt.

"Kailani, is that true?" Lars asked. "Are you okay?"

"I'm okay, just a little shaken up," I answered, then gave them a brief description of the attack and what I had done to scare off the shark. I turned to Liko. "Could you carry this kayak back to the house for me?"

He hoisted the kayak over his head and we all made our way slowly up the steep hill toward the house. Justine held my hand. She had stopped crying, but she still sniffled. I felt sorry for her. She must have been almost as scared as I was while the shark was attacking.

Lars stopped me at the front door. "Kailani, I'd like you to go get checked out by a doctor right away. I'm sure someone in Barbie's office can have a look at you. I'm going to call her and then I'm going to drive you over."

I tried telling him that I was okay, that I didn't need to see a doctor, but he insisted. I went to my room to shower and change my clothes and he was waiting for me in the kitchen when I emerged, feeling much better. He handed me a tall drink.

"I poured you some iced tea with whatever that fruit stuff was in the fridge. Drink it and we'll be on our way. Barbie is in Kona today, so we'll head down there."

"Really, Lars, you don't have to take me. If you're making me go to the doctor, at least let me drive myself."

He shook his head. "No way. You've been through quite a shock. I'm not letting you get behind the wheel of your car until a doctor has given the okay."

I sighed resignedly and got into the front seat of his car. He pulled onto the main highway and sped toward Kona. To my surprise, I fell asleep on the way and didn't awaken until we were pulling into the parking lot of Orchid Isle Wellness-Kona. Lars smiled when I woke up. "See? It's a good thing I drove!"

"I must have been more tired than I thought."

"Fighting off a shark would exhaust anyone."

"Have you ever seen a shark when you've been out surfing?"

"I've seen them, but always from a distance. Then the cry goes up and the beach closes until there's an all-clear from the county. It can be pretty scary, but the fact is that a shark is far more likely to be attacked *by* a human than to actually attack a human. You must have run into one that was out hunting."

I nodded in silence. The reality of my ordeal was finally starting to hit me and I was afraid I would get choked up if I tried to talk. Lars seemed to realize what was happening and patiently waited for me to compose myself before suggesting that we go inside.

The Orchid Isle Wellness office was a cocoon of serenity. I could feel some of my anxiety lifting as we sat in Barbie's office, waiting for her to finish with a client. She knew we were waiting for her and had asked the receptionist to tell us that she would be done shortly. Soft spa music piped through the latte-colored space and a beautiful scent drifted in the air. It smelled like jasmine mingled with lavender and a light, fruity fragrance. I closed my eyes and breathed deeply, trying very hard not to picture the shark's rows of teeth in my mind's eye. A samovar-shaped beverage dispenser sat in the corner, filled with ice and tea and sliced citrus fruits. I was thirsty, so I helped myself to a small glass. Lars said he didn't want any.

He sat in the chair next to mine, fidgeting with his hands, getting up to pace and then sitting down again, clearing his throat several times. It was then I realized that he was probably ill at ease in Barbie's office, where she spent so much of her time away from home, where she had met Dr. Fitzgibbons, and where, I knew, she had taken another lover.

"Lars, if you'd like to wait in the car, that's fine with me. I don't want you to stay here if it makes you uncomfortable."

"That's okay. I'll wait until she comes in and then I'll go out and wait in the car until you're done."

After that we waited in silence until Barbie appeared. When she saw me she crossed the room quickly and gave me a soft hug.

"What happened?" she exclaimed. "The receptionist talked to Lars on the phone and he said you were attacked by a shark!"

I nodded. "I'm okay. Lars thought I should be checked out, though."

She glanced over at him. "He absolutely did the right thing. I'm going to take you down the hall and have you dress in a gown and have one of the doctors look you over." She turned her attention to him.

"We've never seen any sharks in that area, have we?" He shook his head. "Did the children see the attack?"

"Unfortunately, yes," I answered ruefully. "At least Justine did. I screamed and she must have heard me and ran down to the shoreline.

She saw part of the attack. She was pretty shaken, but I know Lars talked to her about it. And I did too."

Barbie let out a long breath. "Poor thing. I'll have to make sure to find her when I get home and check on her myself."

Lars excused himself and told me he would be waiting outside. I followed Barbie to an exam room that was more antiseptic than the rest of the offices, with brighter light and shining instruments. I found I didn't like it as much as the other rooms.

Barbie chuckled when I mentioned it. "Nobody does, but the doctors need well-lit rooms to do their work. All the patients like to get out of these exam rooms as soon as possible and back into the comfort of the rest of the office."

She left me with a promise to come get me as soon as the doctor had completed his exam. I don't know why it never crossed my mind that I might be examined by the same person that I'd seen kissing Barbie up in Waimea, but I was shocked when he walked into the exam room.

He was at least six feet tall, with wavy brown hair and rimless glasses. He looked magnificent.

"I'm Dr. Rutledge. You live at Barbie's house, I understand," he began with a smile.

"Yes. I'm the Jorgensens' cook."

He smiled. "I wish I knew how to cook. About all I can do is throw something in a microwave and push the *start* button."

"I helped my parents cook from the time I was little, so I guess it was natural that I would end up as a chef."

"Then you'll be at Barbie's party the day after tomorrow," he said, as he looked carefully at my legs and feet.

"Yes. I'm hoping to be able to get right back to work or you'll all have nothing to eat but some frozen appetizers."

He smiled again, a beautiful, calm smile, and I could see why Barbie was attracted to him. But I still didn't agree with it.

He checked my arms and hands, noting where the scrapes and scratches were. "I'll give you an antibiotic cream to put on your hands and arms, just to be on the safe side. Now, let's check out your neurological system."

He performed a battery of tests aimed at finding out, he told me, whether I had suffered a concussion. I didn't remember banging my head, but he said it was just a precaution, in case I had hit my head and didn't even recall it due to the stress of the situation. He examined my eyes, telling me to look directly at his eyes. As I did, I noticed how large and liquid-brown they were. This man could be dangerous in a situation with a lot of women around, I suspected.

I must have passed the neurological tests, because he told me that I could go home and not to exert myself for the next twenty-four hours.

"That means someone's going to have to help you with the party preparations," he cautioned. "I don't want you doing it all yourself. I think I'll also write you a prescription for an antianxiety medication. Just in case you feel you need it. Follow the dosing instructions, but take it when you feel nervous or edgy."

I reluctantly agreed. I hated to take medicine, but having that prescription might not be such a bad thing. And I didn't have to use it if I didn't need it.

"And don't be surprised if your muscles are achy and tired for the next few days," he added. "You may feel all right, but your body has been through a lot and it will let you know when enough is enough." I thanked him and the exam was over.

Barbie walked with me to Lars's car, fussing over me, making sure I was all right. "Lars, I'll bring home dinner tonight so Kailani doesn't have to cook." I tried to protest, but they both agreed that I needed the rest of the day and evening off. I thanked them and Lars and I took the long drive back to the house. He didn't say much on the drive and seemed to be lost in his own thoughts. It was fine with me, because I leaned against the headrest and fell asleep again.

It was late in the afternoon when we got back to the house. I walked slowly into the house, my muscles starting to protest just as the doctor said they would.

Lars walked with me to my rooms, making sure I didn't need anything before leaving to go back to his office. He must have called Marcus and Justine on the way home or just before we left Kona, because they were waiting for us in the kitchen when we arrived, clamoring to know what the doctor had said and wanting assurances that I was okay. I smiled at them, trying to show them that I was just fine, but Lars instructed them to look in on me frequently so they could help me if I needed anything and to report back to him. That was exactly what Justine wanted to hear. She walked with me into my bedroom and fluttered around, helping me get comfortable in bed, running to get cookbooks that she thought I might like to read, and making sure Meli had enough to eat and drink. She got me a glass of tea from the kitchen and insisted that I eat something. I smiled and obliged her by eating a handful of almonds, even though I wasn't at all hungry. She left with concerned eyes and a promise to check in on me very soon.

And indeed she did. She checked on me at least every half hour, bringing other visitors with her several times, including Liko and Akela. Everyone wanted to hear about the shark attack, but my young nurse said she would tell them what happened and that I needed my rest.

On her fourth trip to see me, she excitedly handed me a gift bag. "Look what got delivered here! It's for you!"

"Who's it from?"

"I don't know. The delivery guy just dropped it off and left. Open it!"

The bag was light. I plunged my hand into the whorl of tissue paper and drew out a small gossamer bag. Justine took one look and let out a strangled sound as her hands flew to cover her mouth. Her eyes grew wider and wider as I untied the drawstring at the top of the bag and tipped the contents into my hand.

Chapter 12

It was a small collection of shark teeth. Each triangular, pointy tooth was a dull mottled gray or brown. I dropped them on my bedspread as if they were molten lava.

"Why would someone do that?" Justine asked in horror.

I didn't want her to know how shocked and rattled I really was, so I brushed it off as a silly practical joke. I laughed lightly. "Oh, I think this was someone's idea of a little joke."

"I don't think it's very funny."

"Well, I don't, either, but someone did. Didn't the delivery man say who sent the bag?"

She shook her head. "I should have asked him. I'm sorry."

"Don't be sorry. How were you supposed to know what was in the bag?" She shrugged.

"Should I get Dad?"

"No, I don't think we need to tell him about this. It's just a practical joke." I had a hunch it was more than that, so I hoped I sounded more confident than I felt. She seemed to brighten a little. "Mom said she'd get us burgers for dinner. Mom never lets us have burgers! I told her you'd rather have a salad. Is that okay?"

"That's fine. Thanks, Justine. And thanks for taking such good care of me." She beamed and skipped out, promising to return soon.

I picked up the shark teeth one by one and put them back in their small bag, then got up and put the bag in a cupboard under the bookshelves in my den. I never wanted to see them again. Who would have sent them?

As I crawled back into bed there was a light knock at the door and Liko opened it a crack. "K? Can I come in? I brought you some visitors."

"Sure." And before I knew what was happening, my room was filled with my parents, my sister, Haliaka, and Liko, all noisily questioning me and checking my limbs to satisfy themselves that I was unhurt. I was thrilled to see them.

"Auntie! I'm so glad the shark didn't bite you!" Haliaka yelled, climbing on the bed and throwing her arms around my neck.

I laughed, happy to be among my family again.

"When Liko called and said you had been attacked by a shark, I can't tell you what a horrible feeling that was," my mother said, tears sliding down her cheeks. My father stood next to her, blinking several times and looking away quickly.

"Don't cry, Tutu! Auntie's okay!" Haliaka exclaimed.

Just then Justine opened the door and peeked in. "Justine, come on in and meet my family," I encouraged her.

She came in timidly. I made all the introductions and Haliaka was thrilled to meet another young girl. She asked if she could see Justine's bedroom. Justine happily took Haliaka by the hand and they left, already friends.

Once the two kids had left the room, my parents and sisters wanted all the gory details of the attack. They had lots of questions.

"Why do you think the shark was out there?"

"Have you ever seen a shark out there?"

"You're never going in that kayak again, are you?"

"Do sharks usually attack at that time of day?"

I didn't have answers to any of their questions, except to say that I probably would go out in the kayak again, but not for a long time. I didn't mention the bag of shark teeth that I received shortly before they all arrived. I was keeping that secret until I could figure out who sent them and why. I fervently hoped that Justine wouldn't tell Haliaka, though my niece was probably too young to understand the macabre nature of such a "gift." And as long as Justine believed that it was nothing more than a practical joke, she had no reason to tell anyone else.

When Justine brought Haliaka back to my room, she also had a tray with my dinner on it. My parents said it was time for them to go. As much as I hated to see them leave, I was getting very tired. Haliaka didn't want to leave me or her new friend, but I convinced her that Justine could play with her next time she visited. That seemed to appease her, and they left after many hugs and kisses. After everyone left I took a sleeping pill so I could rest all night and not wake up worrying about the shark teeth.

Because the doctor had told me to take it easy the next day, I didn't even set my alarm. Liko had very kindly said he would make breakfast for the family in the morning. I didn't know what he had in mind, but I hoped it wouldn't be better than what I usually fixed for them.

It wasn't. I heard from Akela the next morning that Liko had served burned eggs, burned toast, and ice water for breakfast. The family couldn't wait for my return to the kitchen. It felt good.

With the party only a day away, I had to drag myself out of bed and continue the preparations. I told myself that I would sit down to rest whenever I got a chance, knowing very well that there would be no time for sitting. My muscles screamed in protest when I started moving around. I made my way slowly to the kitchen, then I called Akela and Liko and asked for their help with the preparations. Barbie had already told me the housekeeper would be able to help me. And though Liko would rather have been surfing and told me so many times in his good-natured way, he was willing to help too.

Since Barbie's celebration was to take place mostly on the lanai and around the pool, I had decided to use the guesthouse kitchen as a staging area for serving the food to the guests in the pool courtyard. The rest of the guests could be served from the kitchen in the main house.

The three of us spent the day carrying supplies back and forth between the kitchens, then stocking the guesthouse refrigerator and freezer with food and drinks. I moved a little slowly, but with everyone's help we were able to get the work done before dinner. I prepared some snacks and we sat around the table, talking.

"I'm so glad you're going to be here tomorrow night to help," I told Akela. "I don't know what I'd do without some extra hands."

"The Jorgensens' parties are usually smaller, so they don't need our help most of the time. Tomorrow night should be fun," she replied. "I helped out at one last year, though," Akela continued, her voice lowering. "It was a disaster."

"What happened?"

She clearly enjoyed being the bearer of gossip. "You should have seen it. Mr. Jorgensen caught Mrs. Jorgensen making a pass at one of the guests and he went through the roof. Not at the party, but as soon as everyone left."

This was making me uncomfortable. I stole a glance at Liko to see how he was reacting. He sat stone-faced, his eyes staring out over the Pacific.

"It was a doctor she works with. I don't even know his name. Mr. Jorgensen caught them in the wine cellar.

"She even flirted with the last chef they had here. I saw her do it lots of times. But he didn't like her. That's why he left." I hadn't known that. My heart went out to Lars who, it seemed, had been fighting a losing battle for some time.

I pushed my chair back and stood up slowly, the muscles in my legs and back resisting. "We shouldn't really be talking about this." I knew I sounded prudish, but I had to put a stop to all this talk about my employer. And hers. And I actually found myself feeling sorry for Liko, who hadn't said a word since the conversation started. Even though his relationship with Barbie was wrong, I could tell he had feelings for her and I knew the gossip was hurting him.

I spent a long time that evening chopping fruits and vegetables. It was mindless work that was good and bad: I was able to stop thinking about Barbie and the chaos she created around her, but I thought instead of the shark teeth. Who sent them? Who, besides the people in the house, knew about the shark attack in time to have the teeth delivered the same day? I could only think of one person who would have done such a thing: Geoffrey. I seethed when I thought of him. But how could he have known about the attack? I wondered if someone in the house had told him. My brain remained stuck on those thoughts while I prepared more food for Barbie's party.

I took one of the anxiety pills that night. I was glad I hadn't refused the doctor's offer of the prescription; I couldn't stop thinking about Geoffrey and the shark teeth, but I had to have a good night's sleep in order to function at the top of my game for the party. The pill worked and I slept like a log.

When I awoke the next morning, I felt rested and alert. Barbie appeared in the kitchen early to announce that she would be home from work early to "supervise." She apparently didn't realize that most of the work had already been done and she was only supervising the finishing touches. I was relieved to hear that she had hired a bartender so I wouldn't have to worry about mixing and pouring drinks. I had been a little apprehensive about it, since food—not drink—was my specialty.

I made a quick breakfast for the rest of the family. Marcus had a history project to work on and Justine was spending the day at a friend's house. Lars was holed up in his office, only coming out now and then for lunch and snacks. Since Marcus didn't need his help, Liko came to the kitchen to help me, along with Akela. I had them set out table linens, extra trays and platters, lots of glasses, and utensils.

The day passed very quickly. Barbie had asked me to skip making dinner for the family, since everyone would be eating party food all evening. When she came home from work, she checked on things in the kitchen and on the lanai, then hurried upstairs to change. When she came downstairs again she was dressed in a breathtaking cocktail dress, a curve-hugging, shimmery, champagne-colored creation with a lacy low V-neckline and short, tight sleeves. She moved gracefully on strappy gold sandals with four-inch heels. She looked beautiful. Lars wandered onto the lanai while Barbie was sneaking a radish.

"We have to get *that* dressed up?" he asked plaintively.

"Yes. You'd better hurry. People will be here soon and you can't look like that when they arrive." She nodded at him, indicating the long board shorts and T-shirt that was his regular work uniform.

He went upstairs and returned shortly, looking completely transformed. He had traded his surfer clothes for a gray suit complete with burgundy tie and white shirt.

"Thank you," Barbie said shortly as Lars presented himself for inspection. Then, "Wait!"

She pointed at his feet. I grinned.

He was barefoot.

"Get shoes on," she ordered him.

He rolled his eyes. "I'll get them on as soon as people start to get here. I want to be comfortable for as long as possible. Besides, we never wear shoes in the house. How can you wear those things, anyway?" he asked, looking down at her high heels.

"It's just different for women. Isn't it, Kailani?"

"Definitely for some women," I said noncommittally. I hated high heels. Lars turned and headed back for his office. Before I returned to the kitchen to make last-minute preparations, Liko appeared on the lanai. He took in Barbie's outfit and toned, trim body and smiled appreciatively. *Lecherously* was more like it.

She smiled back at him and traced her finger down his chest, seemingly oblivious to my presence. Even after the things Liko had heard about Barbie, I couldn't believe he was still drawn to her. I felt a tiny tightening in my chest, a dim awareness of trouble that I feared would visit this house again if their relationship continued. Could Lars take much more of the unfaithfulness going on right under his nose?

Soon the guests started arriving. I had just enough time to change into the uniform Barbie had requested of me: a soft white tank top and a khaki skirt, with low-heeled sandals. Not that any of us could ever compete with her, but she definitely wanted to make sure that the household staff remained inconspicuous. Akela was dressed just as I was.

For the next several hours I was very busy. I put Akela in charge of the kitchen in the guesthouse and serving food by the pool; I put Liko in charge of the main kitchen and serving food on the lanai. I spent my time going back and forth between the two serving areas, restocking, supervising, and making sure the party was going smoothly. Liko's long hair was pulled back in a neat ponytail for the event.

"Kailani, I think we're going to need more of those little shrimp and mango skewers," Akela told me on one of my passes through the crowd.

"I'll get them right now," I answered. I weaved my way back to the kitchen, where I was arranging the skewers on a platter when I heard a noise coming from under the kitchen window. I looked out into the gathering darkness and there was Barbie, giggling in the arms of Dr. Rutledge, who had examined me following the shark attack.

I was disgusted. How could Barbie behave this way at her own party? Wasn't she concerned that her children or Lars might discover her with another man? Didn't she care how Liko might feel if he saw her?

"Kailani?" I jumped.

"Sorry to bother you," said Lars, "but I'm looking for Barbie. Have you seen her?"

I didn't turn around. I didn't want to lie to him, and I didn't want to tell him the truth. "I think she went out for a breath of air. I'm sure she'll be back in just a minute."

"Okay. Will you tell her I need to speak to her if you see her before I do?"

"Yes."

I ventured another look outside when Lars had left. Barbie and Dr. Rutledge were still out there, kissing and cuddling under the darkening sky and the canopy of trees that hid them so well from everyone but me. I turned back to my work in anger. I couldn't believe what I had seen. I carried the platter out to Akela and caught her eye.

"What's the matter?" she asked in a low voice.

"Nothing. It's nothing."

"You okay?"

"I'm fine. Still feeling the effects of fighting off that shark, I guess," I said lamely. She looked at me with concern.

"You need some sleep."

"I'll get some as soon as tonight is over." I smiled at her and made my way out to the guesthouse, passing Marcus and Justine on my way. They were standing next to Lars, talking to a few of the guests. They waved at me. They both looked very nice, Marcus in a suit and Justine in a cute navy-blue organza dress with a wide black belt, but they seemed bored. When the guests moved away, they whispered something to Lars and came to find me.

"We're so bored," they complained, confirming my suspicions. "When is everyone leaving?"

"When the party's over," I answered with a smile.

"I want to go swimming," Justine said.

"I just want to go to bed," Marcus admitted. "I hate wearing a suit."

"I think every man here probably hates wearing a suit," I told him.

"Can we help you?" Justine asked.

"I'm afraid you'd better not," I warned. "I don't want to get in trouble if your parents think I asked you to help."

"But we'll tell them we wanted to help," she whined.

"Sorry. Just try to enjoy yourselves until the party's over. Have some food before it disappears. Marcus, there's *poke* on the table."

He set off in that direction with a smile. Justine followed him, her little feet teetering in her high heels. I hoped they wouldn't go in the kitchen and catch a glimpse of their mother outside. I wished suddenly that I had kept them out by the pool. I walked after them quickly.

Luckily, Barbie was on the lanai when I passed through. Liko was there too, watching her with an angry look on his face as he set a tray of hors d'oeuvres on the long dining table. I walked over to him and inclined my head toward the kitchen. He followed me.

"Everything all right, Liko?" I asked, reaching into the refrigerator for two more pineapples that were hollowed out and filled with chicken salad.

"K, I found out something."

"What?" I asked warily, knowing what he was going to say.

"I saw Barbie with another guy."

"I'm sorry, Liko. I saw them too," I blurted out.

"Why didn't you tell me?" He sounded hurt.

"It was just a little while ago, and I didn't see you until just now. To be honest, I don't know if I would have told you even if I had seen you."

"Why not? You know Barbie and I have a relationship."

I sighed. "Liko, why don't you come back here tonight when everyone is gone? I can't really talk about it right now. I have a thousand things to do."

He stayed in the kitchen after that, hiding out from the guests. Each time I went in there, I found him cleaning dishes, folding linens, wiping down counters, and doing much of the work I would have had to do later, after the guests left. *He must really be distraught.*

The last person to leave was Dr. Rutledge's wife. A frown marred her pretty face. "I can't find my husband anywhere," she told Lars. "Have you seen him?"

Lars shook his head. "Maybe there was an emergency at work?"

"What emergency?" she scoffed. "Some golfer with a twisted back? A tourist with a bad case of sunburn? No, this isn't the first time he's disappeared from a party."

Lars just looked at her, apparently at a loss for words.

"Do me a favor, will you?" she asked. "If you see him, tell him to find his own way home. And thanks for the party."

Shaking his head, Lars kicked off his shoes and helped himself to a heaping plate of food while I started to clear dishes, napkins, glasses, and utensils from various tables and surfaces across the huge space. I sent Liko to help Akela begin the cleanup process in the guesthouse kitchen and the courtyard surrounding the pool. It was going to be a long night.

I left the lanai briefly to take a stack of dirty dishes to the kitchen and Barbie was standing next to Lars when I returned. When I caught a snatch of their conversation, I ducked back into the short hallway by the kitchen and listened, feeling guilty but unable to tear myself away.

"Where were you earlier?" Lars asked her curtly.

"When?"

"When I went looking for you during the party. I couldn't find you anywhere."

"I was mingling. That's what people do at parties. Why were you looking for me?"

"I didn't know where you were."

"Well, I was around somewhere," Barbie answered breezily.

"You sure about that? I looked everywhere."

"Lars, if you have something to say, just say it."

"As a matter of fact, I do have something to say. Dr. Rutledge's wife couldn't find him, either. I thought you two might have been together."

"That's ridiculous."

"Is it? She couldn't find him, I couldn't find you. This house isn't so big that people can just go missing in it."

"Maybe I was in the bathroom! How am I supposed to know where I was at the exact time you went looking for me?" she retorted shrilly.

"I know you sleep around, Barbie. That's your business. This marriage has been a sham for years. But don't even think about misbehaving in this house, where the kids might see you. They deserve better from their own mother," he hissed at her.

"Let go of me, Lars," she warned in a low voice. Lars made a scoffing sound and I could hear him stalking toward the front of the house. I stayed where I was.

"He's gone," she whispered. "What a hothead."

I froze. I was so embarrassed that she had known I was there. I moved to step out onto the lanai, preparing to apologize, when I heard Liko's voice, low and quiet. I stepped back quickly. She hadn't seen me, after all.

"Barbie, why were you with that other guy?"

She sighed. "Liko, I'm just not the sort of woman to be tied down. Lars has never understood. In fact, if he finds out about you and me, he'll fire you on the spot. I'm afraid he and I are just going to have to come to some kind of agreement."

"What about me?"

"What do you mean?"

"Are we still going to see each other?"

I could hear soft noises, but I didn't stay to hear what else they might have to say to each other. I couldn't stand it anymore. Liko was making a fool of himself. Couldn't he see that?

Not wanting to run into Liko or Barbie on the lanai, I went all the way around to the back of the house, down the huge circular staircase, and through the family room. Marcus was in there, watching television.

"Hi, Marcus. Glad the party's over?"

He nodded sleepily, not paying much attention to me or the television. I hurried out to the pool area and guesthouse to see how the cleaning was going.

"We're just about done out here," Akela said in response to my question. She looked around, as if suddenly realizing Liko was missing. "I wonder where Liko went. How are you coming with cleaning up the lanai?"

"I hit a speed bump," I answered. "Barbie is out there and she's deep in conversation—or something—and I don't want to disturb her. Or them."

Akela's eyes widened. "Who's she with?" she asked eagerly. A little too eagerly. I immediately regretted having told her about Barbie.

"I don't know," I lied. "I just didn't want to go out there and make a lot of noise with dishes and utensils and stuff if she's trying to have a conversation."

"Do you need help cleaning up the kitchen?"

"No, Liko actually did a lot for me earlier. Go to bed and get some sleep. You've earned it. And thanks for all your help tonight." She looked grateful to be done. Giving me a little wave, she turned and walked toward the family room.

I returned to the kitchen the way I had come. Marcus had apparently gone to bed and the family room and lanai were deserted. I finished the cleaning and went to my room. My muscles ached. I was too wound up to sleep, so I sat in the den watching an old black-and-white movie on television when someone knocked on my door. I froze for a moment, my mind suddenly filling with images of Geoffrey and of Dr. Doug's body. I opened it cautiously, wondering who would want to see me so late in the evening.

It was Liko. He looked at me sheepishly as I stood aside to let him in. "Sorry I didn't help you finish the cleaning up," he said. "There was something I had to do."

"Yeah, I already know what you had to do."

His eyebrows shot up. "How did you find out?"

"I saw you and Barbie. You'd better be very careful, Liko. One of these days Lars is going to see you two."

"We're careful. You won't tell him, will you?"

"I should, but I can't bring myself to do it. You're my friend and I don't want to see you lose your job. What are you going to do if he finds out?"

"He won't find out."

"How could you want to be with her after you *knew* she was with Dr. Rutledge?"

"I don't know, K," he answered, rubbing his hand over his eyes. "It's like she has this spell over me. Over him too, I guess. There's just something about her . . ." he trailed off.

"But doesn't that bother you?"

"Sure it does."

"Did you ask her about it?"

"No. We don't talk about those things."

"I just don't want to see you get hurt."

"Don't worry, K. If I do, I have no one to blame but myself." Then he changed the subject. "Hey, have you heard from Geoffrey?"

I shook my head. "Maybe he's finally gotten the message."

He arched his eyebrows and looked at me intently. "I doubt it, K. You stay clear of him and let me know if he comes around or tries to bother you."

"Thanks, Liko. I appreciate it."

After Liko left I climbed into bed and finally was able to fall asleep. I was so exhausted from the party preparations and serving and running around that I slept soundly and woke up late the next morning. I had left breakfast in the refrigerator for anyone who was up before me, but it looked like no one had been in the kitchen. I made a big pot of coffee and padded out to the lanai, which was so quiet and peaceful after the previous night's noise and activity. I breathed the salt air deeply and stretched, then settled down at the long table. I didn't want to read a newspaper or a cookbook or a novel. I just wanted to relax and stare out at the bright blue Pacific Ocean as it undulated in the sunshine.

I sipped my coffee and let my eyes roam over the view, from Maui in the distance to the waves crashing into the lava rock below the house. Then I glimpsed something white against the black rocks. I squinted so I could see it better, but I wasn't able to see it very well. Probably a dead fish that had washed up onto shore.

Above me I could hear a chair being moved around. There was silence for a few minutes, then a shout. It was Barbie. I couldn't hear what she was saying.

I figured it out a moment later, when she came clattering down the stairs and raced out onto the lanai, where I was still enjoying the view. But my quiet time had ended.

"Hurry, Kailani! There's someone down on the rocks! Come with me!"

"What? Who? How can you tell?"

"I could see from my room."

"I don't see anything from here," I noted.

"See that white thing?" she asked, pointing at the dead fish I had seen a few minutes earlier.

"That fish?"

"No! It's a person! I can see the arm from upstairs! We have to call the police!"

"I'll do it, Barbie. Why don't you go get Lars and he can come down there with us?"

"Lars isn't here. He left early this morning to run errands."

"How about Liko, then?"

"Okay." She ran off in the direction of the guesthouse, her thin robe fluttering behind her. I dialed the police and waited for Barbie to return with Liko. When they came running, the three of us hurried toward the water. We moved quickly, but gingerly. The rocks were sharp and none of us had appropriate shoes on.

Liko was the first to reach the shoreline. He stopped short and Barbie and I almost ran into him. He stared down the steep trail to the water and pointed.

Dr. Rutledge lay in front of us, his arm flung over a rock. The tide had gone out, so the doctor's body was fully out of the water, his clothes drying in the warm sunshine.

Barbie gasped and started to sway. I took her arm and helped her to sit down on the rocky ground. She sat with her arms wrapped around her knees, rocking back and forth, tears coursing silently down her cheeks.

"I knew something bad was going to happen," she whispered, her eyes wide. Liko scrambled down to the place where Dr. Rutledge lay and felt his wrist. He glanced up at us and shook his head, then turned the body onto its back. Barbie cried harder. "Liko, don't," she called. "I don't want to see his face. Please."

Liko looked at me, as if asking for advice. "You'd better not touch him, Liko, until the police get here. They'll want to have a look at him." Barbie stared at me as if she couldn't comprehend my words.

Liko climbed slowly up the hill to where I sat next to Barbie. She was surprisingly quiet, but tears still ran down her cheeks and her nose was running. She wiped it with the sleeve of her robe. Liko put his hand on her arm.

"Are you okay?"

She shook her head from side to side slowly. We could hear sirens in the distance. What would the police do when they found a second person dead at the house? I shuddered. Could this one have been an accident? Who knew Barbie and Dr. Rutledge had been together?

Liko knew because he had seen them. Dr. Rutledge's wife suspected something was going on and mentioned it to Lars. Though Lars confronted Barbie, I didn't know for sure whether he believed that she was mingling or possibly in the bathroom while he was looking for her. He had seemed angry. I had no idea whether anyone else at the party knew about Barbie and Dr. Rutledge.

It was only a few minutes before several police officers began picking their way down the hill in front of the house. One used the radio on his shoulder as soon as he caught sight of the body lying on the rocks below.

The officers immediately sent Barbie and Liko and me back up to the house, where Marcus and Justine were just coming into the kitchen. Barbie had gone straight up to her room when we reached the house, and Liko went to the guesthouse. There were a million questions I wanted to ask him, but they would have to wait until the police had talked to all of us.

Marcus and Justine were full of questions for me. Who was it? What had happened? Did someone kill him? Had he been at the party? Were they in trouble? Did they have to talk to the police again? Where were their parents? When did it happen?

I told them as much as I dared, trying to spare them most of the details. Mostly I just had no answers for them. A detective came up to the house and asked the kids a few questions. When he had satisfied himself that they hadn't seen or heard anything, he let them go about their business. Marcus groaned. "Dad was supposed to take me surfing today. I guess that's out of the question." He went to James's house instead. I drove Justine to a friend's house up the main road.

When I returned to the house a short while later, Lars had just arrived home from his early-morning errands. He was stalking into the house with a worried look on his face when he saw me.

"Kailani, what's going on here? Are the kids all right? Barbie sent me a text to come home right away, but didn't give me any details. So now I show up and there are police cars everywhere. What's going on?" he asked again.

I relayed the story, giving him all the information I had. He turned around and ran around the side of the house.

I stood on the lanai watching the officers and Lars down by the water. The police let Lars approach, but stopped him when he got to the police tape they had strung up around the area. They stood talking for several minutes before Lars turned around and headed back to the house. He walked up and joined me and together we watched the goings-on down by the water.

"I can't believe this," he said, rubbing his temples. "First Doug, now Rutledge. Are the kids here?"

"No. I drove Justine to a friend's house. Marcus is at James's."

"Thank you. Where's Barbie?"

"Upstairs."

I returned to the kitchen, but heard shouting a moment later. It seemed to be coming from upstairs. I walked to the foot of the winding staircase leading to the luxurious master bedroom and listened. Sure enough, the shouting was coming from Lars and Barbie, and they didn't seem to care who could hear them. A police officer joined me at the foot of the stairs and started up. I turned to go back to the kitchen and by the time I reached the doorway the shouting had stopped.

Akela poked her head in the kitchen. "Why in the world are they fighting with the police here?"

I shook my head. "I have no idea. You'd think they'd keep their arguments a little quieter."

Before long the police officer, accompanied by Lars and Barbie, came downstairs. The officer sat down with Lars on the lanai while Barbie came into the kitchen.

"Kailani, could you take some coffee out to them? I think they're going to be there a while."

I took a large pot of coffee and several mugs to the table. Lars and the officer stopped talking while I was arranging the tray between them. Lars looked haggard and careworn. His tousled blond hair, which normally gave him a fun-loving surfer look, now just made him appear older and tired. The bags under his eyes were a dark gray. He certainly didn't look like the head of a popular clothing company. His authoritative air was gone, replaced with a look of defeat and sorrow.

Barbie was waiting for me in the kitchen. "Did you hear anything between Lars and the officer?" she asked.

"No. Why?"

"I just want to know how close they are to charging him with *something*. He can't just get away with this."

"You know he did it?"

"Who else could have done it? He knew I was seeing Dr. Rutledge and he was jealous. Once they charge him with Dr. Rutledge's murder, I'm sure it's just a matter of time before they charge him in Doug's death too." She looked away, sniffling.

"I'm sorry, Barbie. Can I get you anything?" I didn't know what else to say.

"No, thanks." She turned and went upstairs.

Lars and the officer talked for a long time. When the officer had finished questioning him, Lars went to his office. Akela was sent upstairs to summon Barbie. I went to the lanai to refill the coffee urn. When Barbie joined the officer, she looked confused.

"Have you charged Lars with anything?" she asked him.

"No, ma'am."

"Why not?"

"We haven't completed our investigation, ma'am." He indicated to Barbie that she should sit in the chair opposite him and he began to question her. I returned to the kitchen. Lars came in just a short while later, looking for food.

I took a tray to his office, where he sat staring toward the ocean.

"Thanks, Kailani. I don't know how I'm supposed to get any work done in this house. It's been one crisis after another lately."

"Why don't you take your laptop and go somewhere else? A change of scenery might help you."

He scratched his chin. "Maybe. I don't know where to go."

"There's a bar in Hawi that's quiet—the green one right on the main road."

"I know the one you mean. I think you're right. I'll go there."

Lars left after obtaining permission from the police. Barbie went to work after she was questioned. No doubt she would have plenty of questions to answer at the office, where the staff and Dr. Rutledge's patients would be looking for answers.

Lars returned later that afternoon. He came looking for me in the kitchen.

"Kailani, I ran into someone at that bar who said he's a friend of yours." My heart sank. Geoffrey.

"Oh?"

"Yeah. Said his name was Geoffrey. Do you know him?"

I nodded. "He came here from Washington right after I did and he's been stalking me since then," I blurted out. I hadn't meant to tell Lars about him.

"He's been stalking you?" he asked, his eyes wide.

"You could say that. He wants us to get back together and I've been trying to avoid him. But he's not getting the hint," I added ruefully.

"Have you told the police?"

"No, it's not like that. I can handle him," I answered breezily, hoping he didn't hear the uncertainty in my voice.

He looked at me doubtfully. "Let me know if you need any help with him."

"Thank you."

He went to his office and I started preparing dinner, which was to be a mainland-style Hawaiian pizza—homemade pizza dough topped with marinara sauce, ham, pineapple pieces, and fresh local mushrooms. I made a salad to go with the pizza. No one really wanted dinner, they said, but everyone ate some of it.

Barbie ate her meal late, after she came home from work. She paired her pizza and salad with a huge glass of red wine.

"I needed this tonight," she said with a sigh as I cleared the dishes from the table. "It was nonstop questions at work today. Questions from the nurses, the techs, the office staff, the other doctors, the patients, everyone. I'm exhausted." She paused. "Thanks again for your help this morning, Kailani. I appreciate it. I don't know what I would have done if you hadn't been there to go down to the water with me. I couldn't think clearly."

"You're welcome," I answered. "I'm just glad I was around to help."

"Were the police here all day?"

"No, they left after you went to work."

"I wonder what will happen next."

"Lars said they have to wait for the autopsy report before doing anything else."

"That makes sense." She pushed away from the table and went upstairs.

I cleaned the kitchen and put out the things I would need for breakfast the next morning. I was walking out to the lanai with a glass of wine for myself when I heard Liko and Marcus at the table. I stood nearby to listen.

"Were you here when they found the body?" Marcus asked him.

"Yeah. Your mom came to get me and I went down to the water with her and Kailani."

"How did he die?"

"We don't know yet."

"I asked Kailani and she didn't know, either."

"That's right. We have to wait for the autopsy. Then we'll know how he died."

"Did you know him?"

"Not really. I knew who he was, though."

"Do you think someone killed him like Dr. Doug?"

"I don't know, brah. We'll have to wait and see. I hope not."

The two of them got to work on Marcus's math assignment. I hated to listen when they didn't know I was there, but I wanted to make sure that Liko didn't say anything to Marcus that he didn't need to know.

I had my wine at the small table on the other side of the kitchen rather than disturb them at the dining table. I wanted some time to myself to think. My alone time had been horribly interrupted earlier that morning—had it really been just twelve hours ago that Dr. Rutledge's body had been found?—and I wanted to sort through some of the thoughts and emotions reeling around in my mind.

First, I still didn't know who had sent me the shark teeth. I wondered whether I was ever going to find out.

Second, there still had been no arrest in the murder of Dr. Doug. What did that mean? Were the police any closer to finding out who did it? Barbie was apparently convinced Lars had done it, but I continued to believe—possibly for my own sanity—that a stranger had been on the property and had been surprised by Dr. Doug while trying to rob the house. The police had talked to Lars several times but hadn't arrested him, so they probably didn't have the evidence they needed to charge him. Yet.

Third, there were only a handful of people who knew Barbie and Dr. Rutledge had been together during the party. Only someone with that knowledge could have killed him. But I was getting ahead of myself. It was possible that no one killed Dr. Rutledge—that he fell into the water and drowned in a tragic accident. Unlike Dr. Doug.

Finally, there was Geoffrey. I hadn't heard from him in a few days, but now that I knew he was hanging around the bar in Hawi, I figured it wouldn't be long before he appeared again.

I was right.

Chapter 13

The next morning the police were back. They had follow-up questions for Liko and Barbie and me. They talked to Barbie first. I took a cup of coffee out to her on the lanai.

"But I don't understand why you haven't made an arrest yet," she was saying. "It should be very simple. Aren't there fingerprints on Dr. Rutledge's body?"

"We're still working on that. In the meantime, we have a few more questions for you." I poured Barbie's coffee and returned to the kitchen.

My phone rang. I looked at the screen and sighed. Geoffrey again. "Hello?"

"Hi, Kailani, it's me. Geoffrey."

"I know." I refused to start any conversation with him, so I waited for him to speak.

"How's Liko?"

I had to stop that line of questioning right away. "Enough, Geoffrey. It's none of your business."

"So. I ran into someone you know yesterday."

"Uh-huh?"

"Your boss."

"Oh?"

"Didn't he tell you?"

"No, he didn't mention it." Why let Geoffrey think he was a topic of conversation?

"Oh. I told him to give you my love. He didn't say anything?"

"No." He certainly hadn't relayed *that* message, for which I was thankful.

"You busy today?"

"Yes. Very."

"What are you doing?"

"Working. I have to clean the kitchen cupboards and check all the spices for freshness." Since he owned a restaurant himself, I knew he could appreciate that sort of work, though I had no intention of doing either.

"Can that wait?"

"No, it really can't. Mrs. Jorgensen asked me to do it today." It was getting surprisingly easy to lie to Geoffrey, even though I didn't like doing it.

"Can I come over? Just for a few minutes? I have something to ask you."

"What do you want? Just ask me on the phone."

"I'd rather ask you in person."

"Well, I'm sorry, but it'll have to be some other time."

There was silence on the other end of the line.

"I heard you were attacked by a shark."

"How did you hear that?" I asked sharply.

"This is a small town. Word gets around."

A thought struck me suddenly. I don't know why it hadn't occurred to me before. "Geoffrey, did you move out of Kona? Are you staying in Hawi now?"

A little chuckle. "Yes. I felt I should be closer to you."

A chill trickled down my spine and I shuddered. I didn't know how to deal with this. I thought briefly of the police right in the house—I could ask them what to do. But I didn't want to go to the police. It seemed an overreaction to an ex-boyfriend staying nearby.

"I'm afraid I don't get up to Hawi much," I told him. "I have so much to keep me busy here that I don't really have time for anything else."

"I'll just have to come to you, then." And he hung up.

A little knot of anxiety began to build in my chest. I busied myself cleaning up the remainder of breakfast and decided that cleaning out the kitchen cupboards and going through the spices wasn't such a bad idea, after all. I needed to stay busy, to stay away from my room, where there was nothing to do but allow my thoughts to overwhelm me with fear and indecision. I got out the stepladder and started hauling down the contents of the higher cupboards first. One of the detectives poked his head into the kitchen doorway.

"Miss? Could I ask you a few more questions, please?"

I followed him out to the lanai, where we sat opposite each other. He asked me to tell him one more time what I had seen the previous morning. I went through the facts mechanically, all the time worrying about Geoffrey.

"Miss? Is there anything you haven't told me?"

I looked at him, startled. "No. Why?"

"You seem rather preoccupied." He was practically giving me the opening I needed to tell him about Geoffrey. But I didn't do it. I was so afraid that he'd think I was just being silly that I couldn't bring myself to say anything.

"I'm just thinking about all that happened yesterday, I guess," was all I managed to say.

"You'll let me know if you think of anything else?" he asked, sliding his business card across the table to me.

"Yes, I will."

The officer, Detective Alana, left and I took his card and put it into one of the drawers in the kitchen. Then I spent the next several hours rearranging the cupboards, throwing away any foods that had expired, and making lists of replacement items. I stopped shortly before lunch.

Lars came into the kitchen as I climbed down from the stepladder, wiping hair out of my eyes.

"Kailani, a friend of mine gave me this as a 'gift'," he said, making air quotes with his fingers. "I have no idea what it is." He hefted a cooler bag onto the counter.

I unzipped the bag and looked inside hesitantly. But I was pleased when I saw what was in it.

"It's *tako!*" I cried.

He looked into the plastic bag I was holding open. "It doesn't look like any taco I've ever seen."

"No, not that kind of taco. *Tako* is the Japanese word for *he'e*, or Hawaiian squid. It makes wonderful *poke.*"

"You don't have to use it. The man who gave it to me loves to fish, so I assume he caught it. It looks gross."

"I grew up eating it. It's really very good. It's all mind over matter—you have to taste it without thinking about what it is. Would you like *tako poke* for lunch? Or dinner?"

"All right, I guess," he said gamely. "How long does it take? I'm starving."

"I really should braise it before I make the *poke*, so that would take a couple hours and I could serve it for dinner. Or I could simmer it for just twenty minutes and you can have it for lunch."

"Either way, it's going to be cooked, right?"

I laughed. "Right."

"Why don't you just make it for lunch? It looks like there won't be enough for all of us at dinner, and I doubt the kids would eat that, anyway."

I simmered the squid while I prepared the onions, green onions, shoyu, ginger, sesame oil, sesame seeds, and Hawaiian salt. Lars came into the kitchen again as I was getting ready to cut the squid into small pieces.

"Can I help you with that?"

I must not have concealed my surprise very well, because he started laughing. "I like to cook, you know. It's just that Barbie doesn't let me. She wants us to have a chef, so I don't argue about it."

"I didn't know that. Of course you can help. I've prepared the other ingredients, so right now it's just a matter of dicing the squid and mixing everything together."

He looked around the kitchen. "Got tongs?" He washed his hands while I got out the tongs, then he took the squid out of the water and let it drain over the sink for a few moments, then set it on a cutting board. "You'll have to show me where to cut the squid, because I've never seen *tako poke* before."

I stood in front of him and carefully ran the knife through the fish on the board. I showed him how small to make the pieces as he looked over my shoulder. His hand brushed against the small of my back and I stiffened, feeling a tiny flutter in the pit of my stomach. He pulled his hand away and offered to take the knife so he could cut the rest of the squid.

"Sure," I said, moving aside so he could stand where I had been. I stood next to him and watched as he deftly sliced the *tako*. He glanced at me once and I smiled at him as he folded the *tako* gently into the ingredients I had already put in a bowl.

"Are you going to have some?" he asked.

"I'd love to try it, if it's all right with you."

"Sure. Grab a couple of bowls and we can eat on the lanai."

We sat across from each other at the table, much as I had done earlier with the detective. I waited to eat my squid until he tried his. Lars speared a piece of *tako* and lifted the fork to his mouth. He took a bite and chewed slowly.

"What do you think?" I asked eagerly.

"It's pretty good," he said. "It doesn't taste like I thought it would."

"The fresher seafood is, the less it tastes like fish," I noted. I picked up my chopsticks and tasted the *tako*. It was delicious.

"Do you always use chopsticks?"

"Not for all foods, but always with *poke*."

"You'll have to teach me how to use them. I'd like to learn."

"It's easy once you get the hang of it," I told him. "I've been using them since I was little. My mother is Japanese."

"Did you learn to cook when you were little?"

"Yes. I've been cooking since I was old enough to hold a spoon. I always helped my parents in their bakery."

"Can you show me how to use the chopsticks now?" He pushed his bowl across the table next to where I sat and came around and sat beside me. I went to the kitchen to get him a clean pair. I showed him how and where to hold them in his fingers. Then I took his fingers in mine and showed him exactly how to move them to get the ends of the chopsticks to come together to grasp a piece of food. Lars handled them clumsily, but laughed and didn't seem to mind. He insisted on trying again and again until he could lift a piece of *tako* from the bowl to his mouth without dropping it.

"This is great!" he laughed. "I can't believe I never learned how to use these until now!" He looked at me. "This was fun. Thanks for letting me make the *poke* and for teaching me how to use chopsticks."

"No problem. I'm glad you enjoyed it." His icy blue eyes held mine for just a moment. He opened his mouth as if to say something, but closed it again.

He returned to his office and I went back to reorganizing the kitchen. It was almost time for the kids to come home from school when I heard a noise behind me. I whirled around, startled, thinking Marcus and Justine were home early.

It was Geoffrey. "Hi, Kailani."

"How did you get in here?" I demanded.

"Walked onto the lanai from the water-side of the house. It was pretty easy. This place is wide open."

"What do you want?"

"I was just wondering what you were doing. I see you're cleaning the kitchen cupboards, just like you said you would."

"You're not supposed to be here," I told him. "You need to leave."

"Aren't you allowed to have visitors?"

"I don't like to take advantage of the Jorgensens' generosity by inviting people into their home."

"You didn't invite me, so you won't get in trouble."

"That's exactly the problem, Geoffrey—I didn't invite you. I'm afraid you're going to have to leave."

He moved closer and put his hand on my arm and squeezed. Hard. "Let go of me, Geoffrey."

"I really miss you, Kailani. Can't you just come up to Hawi for dinner one night?"

"No. I don't want to see you again. In fact, why don't you just move back to Washington? I'm sure you're needed at the restaurant."

"Nah. I'm in talks to sell it, anyway. I'm thinking of perhaps investing in one here. On the Big Island." I should have known he would do something like that.

He still gripped my arm. I shook it loose and glared at him. "Geoffrey, I want you to get out of this house. Right now. If you don't, I'll scream and everyone will know you're here."

"Don't you want everyone to meet me?"

"No. Now go away. And don't call me anymore, and don't text me, and don't visit me, and don't visit my parents. Just leave me alone. Forget you ever knew me."

"You'll regret this, Kailani."

"The only thing I regret is ever having met you in the first place. Now go."

Just then, the front door opened and I could hear Marcus and Justine talking. Thank goodness. Geoffrey let go of my arm and left quickly the same way he had come in. I found it very unsettling that he had been able to get into the house without anyone else knowing he was there. I put on a happy face for Marcus and Justine as they walked into the kitchen.

I was able to keep Geoffrey's visit at arm's length from my thoughts over the next several hours. I had to finish organizing and cleaning out the kitchen cupboards, and then I prepared and served dinner to Lars and the kids. Barbie was working late again, and I was glad because it kept me busy longer; I served her meal when she got home after everyone else had eaten.

But once the kitchen had been cleaned and the dishes were done and the breakfast preparations completed for the following day, I had nothing to think about but Geoffrey and his behavior, which seemed to be escalating to a higher level. I no longer felt guilty for lying to him about Liko. It was looking more and more like I might need Liko's help to convince Geoffrey to go away and stay away.

As I sat in my den thumbing through cookbooks, there was a knock at the door. I stiffened, suddenly afraid that Geoffrey had come back.

"Who is it?" I asked quietly.

"Liko."

A visceral feeling of relief cascaded over me and I opened the door to let him in. He took one look at my face and asked, "What's wrong?"

"Is it that obvious?" I asked with a halfhearted laugh.

"Yes. Now tell me what's going on."

"It's Geoffrey. He came here today and scared me."

"*What?*"

I nodded. "He just came into the kitchen from the lanai. He walked around toward the front of the house and stepped onto the lanai from the side lawn. I told him he had to leave, but he didn't until he heard Marcus and Justine come in from school. Thank God they got home when they did."

Liko shook his head. "K, you have to call the police. What are you gonna do when he shows up here again?"

"I'm hoping he won't."

"Hoping isn't good enough. We have to make sure he never comes back here."

"I don't know what to do. I don't want to call the police because I'm afraid they'll say I'm overreacting. I mean, he hasn't done anything except grab my arm. That's not exactly enough to put him behind bars.

"And guess what?" I continued. "He said he's trying to sell his restaurant in Washington so he can invest in one here." I covered my face with my hands. "I don't know what I'm going to do if he stays here forever," I groaned.

"Well, for one thing, I think I should pay him a visit," Liko said, gently pulling my hands from my face. "And I can't force you to call the police, but I think you should."

"It's a lot easier for you to pay him a visit now, because he's moved to Hawi, if you can believe it."

"I can believe it. Do you know where he's staying?"

"No. You wouldn't be able to find him."

"Hawi's a small town. It shouldn't be too hard to track him down."

"I don't know, Liko. I don't want you to get in trouble trying to protect me."

"Don't worry about that. I can take care of myself. I think Geoffrey could use a taste of the way we deal with his kind around here."

I smiled my thanks. "I'm not going to say go ahead and do it, but I'm not going to tell you not to, either." Liko walked through the doorway and stood at my bedroom window, looking through the slats of the blinds.

"Does Geoffrey know this is your room?"

"I don't think so."

"When you're in your room, I think you should keep the light off so that he can't snoop around—you know, so he can't look through the blinds from the outside and see you in here."

"I am not going to live in the dark because of Geoffrey."

"I'm not saying you have to live in the dark. I'm just saying for now, for a little while, until we can get him back to Washington, I think you should keep the light off in here at night. You can have the light on in the den—just keep the door to your bedroom closed."

I sighed. "All right. If it will make you feel better, then I'll do it. By the way, why did you come in here tonight?"

"I came to find out if there was any news about Dr. Rutledge."

"Not that I know of. The police were here this morning asking more questions, but they didn't say anything."

"I knew they were here. Barbie told me. But they didn't say anything about how Rutledge died?"

"No. I think they're still waiting for the autopsy report."

"Okay. That's all. G'night, K."

"Goodnight."

I lay awake for a long time that night, wondering what would happen if Liko actually paid Geoffrey a visit. On one hand, it would be nice if Liko could convince him to leave me alone, maybe even to return to Washington. On the other hand, I was worried that Liko would be hurt or get in some kind of trouble with the police and I didn't want that weighing on my conscience.

Finally, the sounds of the Pacific lulled me to sleep. I didn't sleep well, but I slept long enough to be coherent in the morning, when the brilliant orange sunrise found me on the lanai with a cup of coffee, listening to the birds singing raucously in the nearby trees. Visitors to the Big Island often remarked that the birds woke them up in the mornings; that the birds were annoying and loud, but I loved their songs and calls. I could practically set my clock to the bird sounds during the day and the insect and frog sounds at night. Lars wandered onto the lanai as I sat there. I stood up and offered him some coffee, but he waved me back into my chair.

"Looks like another beautiful day," he commented.

I nodded. "Aren't they all?"

"They are. But don't you ever get tired of the nice weather? Don't you like the rain too?"

"Sometimes, but if I want rain, I can always go over to Hilo. It rains a lot there."

"Have you ever been to the farmers' market in Hilo? I had to go to the airport up there to pick up a buddy of mine once and he wanted to stop there for fruit on our way back to Hawi. It's fantastic."

"I have been to that market. I love it. All the honey my parents use at their bakery comes from one of the suppliers at the market, and some of the fruit too."

"I have to go up there on business one day this week. You should go with me and stop at the market."

"That sounds great. I'd love to pick up some of their papayas. And some of the fresh flowers. I love the bouquets they put in the coffee cans covered with ti leaves."

"I'll let you know when I go and you can come along."

I thanked him and hurried to get breakfast ready before the kids were ready for school. They had been relatively quiet since the death of Dr. Rutledge; I often wondered what was going through their young minds. I didn't know whether Lars or Barbie had sat down with them to talk about everything that was going on, but I hoped one of them had.

Liko came in for something to eat just after the kids left for school.

"What's going on today?" I asked him.

"I'm heading up to Waimea today. Got some stuff to do," he replied.

"I have to go to one of the shops up there too. Can I hitch a ride?" I asked.

"Um, well ... I'm going to be all day. Maybe you should take your car so you don't get stuck waiting for me."

"Okay. Maybe we can have lunch together?"

"I wish I could, K, but I have plans for lunch. Sorry about that."

"No problem," I answered with a grin.

After everyone had eaten breakfast and the kitchen was clean, I drove up-country to Waimea. I picked up the pantry staples I needed at the large grocery store up there and I visited some of my favorite small shops. Waimea was home to one of the largest private ranches in the country and cowboys were a common sight; many of the local shops and businesses paid homage to the town's *paniolo* history.

I had finished my grocery shopping and wandered through several of the shops in town when I started getting hungry. I was driving past a sandwich shop on my way back to the Jorgensens, debating whether to go in and spend part of my paycheck on one of their delicious wraps, when I saw Liko sitting outside under an umbrella. He hadn't seen me. I had slowed the car to pull over and call out to him when the door to the shop opened and his face lit up. Barbie was coming out of the shop holding a small tray. She sat down next to him and placed her hand on his thigh as she leaned over and kissed him.

Had she no shame? No respect for Lars? For Dr. Rutledge? Did Liko not care who saw them together? For a brief moment I considered getting out of the car and going to confront them, but reason prevailed. Barbie would probably fire me on the spot and I could possibly lose Liko as a friend too. It was best to handle the problem another way. As much as it would hurt Liko, I wished Barbie would leave him and find someone else. Their relationship was complicating everything, and if the police found out about it, there would be no end to the speculation about Dr. Rutledge's death.

I drove back to the Jorgensens, lost in thought. Lars was in the driveway when I pulled in.

"Surf's up at Upolu," he said in greeting. "I'm heading up there now. Marcus is at school or I'd take him. And I was going to invite Liko, but I can't find him."

I bit my lip and didn't say anything. I told myself it was none of my business. The relationships among Lars, Liko, and Barbie were not my concern.

And I didn't want to hurt Lars by telling him the truth.

"If I see him, I'll let him know," I promised, then I hurried past him and into the house. I went into the kitchen, where I made myself a shrimp Caesar salad for lunch. My desire for a wrap had evaporated as soon as I had seen Liko and Barbie together in Waimea. I was feeling down; I didn't even want to eat on the lanai, where the sunshine and trade winds would mock my mood. Instead, I took a tray into my den and ate my lunch in there.

Where was Meli? She always came sniffing around when I had shrimp. I called to her, but she didn't appear. I shrugged and continued eating. I ate slowly while I flipped through the television channels, and I muted the sound when I heard a noise coming from my bedroom. I hoped Meli wasn't trapped somewhere. I remembered she had once gotten herself stuck inside the box spring of my bed back in Washington and I'd had to rescue her. She hadn't been as appreciative as I had thought she'd be and I had the scratches to prove it. I hoped she hadn't pulled the same stunt again.

I walked into my bedroom, listening for the noise again. I heard something behind me and turned just in time to see Geoffrey closing the door quietly behind me. I'm sure he heard me inhale sharply. He must have known I was terrified, but I tried to keep my voice level as I spoke to him.

"Geoffrey, why are you here?"

"I just wanted to see you, that's all."

"You can't just come here like this. You have to be invited like everyone else."

"But you're my girlfriend. I should be able to see you whenever I want."

"No, Geoffrey. I'm not your girlfriend. Not anymore." His lips were a thin white line. He took a step toward me and I backed away.

"You don't really feel that way," he said quietly. Somehow the tone of his voice was more terrifying than the fact that he was in my room.

"Yes I do. I can't be your girlfriend anymore because you are not the person I thought you were." I felt like I was talking to a five-year-old.

"I'm the same person I always was," he said in a whine, his shoulders drooping. "You have just been ignoring me because of that jerk

Liko." He spat Liko's name, as if it left a bad taste in his mouth. "I wish Liko was dead!"

"Liko has been a good friend since we were little. We grew up together," I said in a soothing voice, hoping to talk some sense into him.

"Good friend," he sneered.

"Yes. Good friend," I replied quietly.

"I'm going to kill your *good friend,*" Geoffrey hissed through clenched teeth.

I had listened to enough. I couldn't go on lying to Geoffrey about Liko, because I was afraid now that my lie might actually put Liko in danger.

"Geoffrey, listen to me. I lied about Liko. I'm not dating him. I just said that to keep you away from me. I'm sorry."

He gave a loud snort. "Ha! You expect me to believe that? You can't protect him, Kailani. Don't even try."

"I'm telling the truth, Geoffrey. He has a girlfriend, but it's not me."

He took another step toward me. His nostrils were flaring and his eyes blazed. I had backed up to the edge of the bed, so I scrambled over it to the other side.

"Kailani, I'm not going to hurt you. I just want to talk. About us."

"Geoffrey, there is no *us*. There's nothing to talk about. My life is here, and you belong back in Washington."

"My life is here too. With you." He came around to my side of the bed and grabbed my arm.

"Geoffrey, that hurts."

"You've hurt me too. In here," he said, pointing to his chest. "And if you hurt me, I have a right to hurt you."

"No you don't, Geoffrey. You have no right to hurt me." My breath was becoming shallow and ragged, when out of the corner of my eye I saw a quick movement between the bed and the nightstand. Meli. Geoffrey apparently hadn't seen her, and she obviously wasn't keen to see Geoffrey, as she had hidden from him. They say animals are better judges of people than other people are, and my thoughts flitted back for a moment to my apartment in Washington, when Meli had refused to let Geoffrey pet her. She had known, and I hadn't.

I was jerked back to the present as Geoffrey dug his fingernails into the flesh of my arm. In an instant I bent down, with Geoffrey still holding one of my arms, and snatched Meli around her midsection with my other arm. Geoffrey was so startled that he let go of me for a moment, and I seized my opportunity.

Praying that Meli would forgive me, I threw her at Geoffrey's face and ran to yank the bedroom door open. Behind me I heard the cat yowl and hiss and Geoffrey scream. I knew her claws had sunk into his skin.

Meli extricated herself from the situation rapidly, because before I could even reach the den door she streaked by me and squeezed herself under the small sofa. Knowing she was safe from Geoffrey's reach, I ran into the kitchen and jerked open the drawer that had the police officer's business card in it. There was no one else who could help me—Lars was surfing, Liko was up in Waimea with Barbie. I didn't know how much help Akela would be. Geoffrey was yelling my name and got to the den door as I turned the corner down the hallway outside the kitchen.

I ran into Lars's office and locked the door behind me seconds before Geoffrey started banging on the door. I grasped my cell phone with trembling fingers and dialed the number on the card.

"Kailani! Let me in! We need to talk!"

I explained the situation very quickly to the desk sergeant, who promised to send Detective Alana straight to the Jorgensens' home. Luckily, he was nearby in Hawi.

"Geoffrey, I've called the police," I said in a loud voice. "They're on their way."

I couldn't understand exactly what Geoffrey said after that. It sounded like a roar. I was thankful the door between us was locked. The next thing I heard was his footsteps, retreating rapidly toward the lanai. I opened the door and peeked into the hallway, then ran in the direction of the footsteps just to make sure he was leaving. I breathed an immense sigh of relief when I saw him dashing off the end of the lanai and onto the lawn. As I watched, he ran through the trees and disappeared. I could only hope he was running toward the road, but I couldn't be sure.

It was just a few minutes before Detective Alana arrived. I met him at the door and ushered him to the table on the lanai, where we sat and I related what had happened. He had lots of questions about Geoffrey: Why was he on the Big Island? Where was he from? Where was he staying now?

I could answer the questions about Geoffrey's recent past, like where he came from and why he was in Hawaii, but I didn't know where he was staying in Hawi. Lars had seen him at the bar on the main street, but I didn't know where else Geoffrey spent his time. I also couldn't give the officer any information about the restaurant-investment inquiries Geoffrey had mentioned.

Detective Alana left with a promise to be in touch once he had located Geoffrey. He didn't seem to think it would be difficult to find him. He warned me to be on my guard, though, until Geoffrey had been found.

"Why didn't you mention this earlier when I was here?" he asked.

"I was embarrassed and afraid that you'd think I was overreacting," I said, avoiding his eyes.

"These things should always be reported as soon as one party feels they're in danger," he said kindly. "I'm glad you've finally said something so we can get it sorted out and he'll stop bothering you."

He left and I went back to the kitchen where, for once, I didn't even feel like cooking to distract myself. I was anxious and edgy. I opened cupboard doors and closed them again, not knowing what to do next. Not long ago, I might have gone kayaking to burn off some of my nervous energy, but I couldn't even do that. I wasn't ready to go back in the water following the shark attack.

Finally, I decided to take a drive to help settle my mind. Along the way I stopped at a small market in the town of Kapaau to pick up fresh fish for dinner. I hadn't visited the market before, but I had heard good things about it. I walked to the fish counter at the back of the store.

I was perusing the offerings when there was a tap on my shoulder. Startled, I jumped and cried out. Apparently, the drive hadn't completely erased all of the anxiety from my mind. I turned around to see Lars staring at me.

"I'm sorry," he stammered. "I didn't mean to startle you like that."

I smiled at him. "That's okay. I've had a rough day, that's all. What are you doing here?"

"Sometimes I stop here and grab something to eat after I'm done surfing. When I'm so hungry that I can't wait to eat," he added, laughing. "What are you doing here?"

"I've heard that their fish is really good, so I thought I'd pick up something for dinner. Does that sound all right?"

"Sounds good. You've made a fish lover out of me," he said with a smile, turning to head down one of the store's cramped aisles.

I finally decided on the *opakapaka* and the man behind the counter wrapped it for me. I found Lars waiting for me by my car outside.

"What did you pick out?" he asked.

"*Opakapaka*." He looked puzzled. "Pink snapper," I explained.

"Oh." He nodded as if he knew what I was talking about. "If you don't mind my asking, what made your day so rough?"

I took a deep breath. He had a right to know, since Geoffrey had been an intruder in his home. "Remember that guy you met in the bar in Hawi when you went there to get some work done?" He nodded. "He was hiding in the house today, waiting in my bedroom when I came home from shopping in Waimea."

His jaw dropped. "You're kidding."

I shook my head ruefully. "I wish I were. But I got out and called the police."

"Did he hurt you?"

I showed him my arm, where bruises had erupted from the force of Geoffrey's grip. Small red indentations remained where his fingernails had dug into my skin. "I'm okay, but he scared me. A detective came and spoke to me and promised to start looking for him."

"Are you all right?" There was genuine concern in his voice.

I nodded. "I think so. I'm just sorry that he got in your house."

"That *is* alarming. Did he get in through the front door?"

"No, he went around the side and came onto the lanai that way."

"Let me make some calls. Maybe there's something we can do to make the sides of the house more secure. What good is an alarm system on the door if that's not how an intruder gets in?

"Are you really okay?" he asked.

"Yeah. Thanks."

He stood aside as I got into the car. Through the rearview mirror I could see him watching me drive away. I felt somehow comforted knowing Lars was watching me, keeping an eye out for me. It was so different from the way I felt when Geoffrey watched me. When Geoffrey watched me it made my flesh creep.

When I got back to the house Marcus and Justine were already doing their homework with Liko on the lanai. I got to work in the kitchen making a macadamia-nut crust for the *opakapaka*. Then I took a tray of drinks out.

"You look tired, K," Liko said after he greeted me.

"It's been a long day," I said with a smile. He raised his eyebrows at me and gave me a look that promised we'd discuss it later.

"What's for dinner, Kailani?" asked Justine.

"Macadamia-nut-crusted fish and stir-fried veggies."

"Sounds good," said Marcus, stretching and reaching for a glass of iced tea. I grinned at him.

I was in the kitchen finishing the dinner preparations when Lars came looking for me. "I talked to the security firm that wired the house," he began. He hadn't wasted any time. "They said they think they can come out here and rig up a laser security system that will protect the glass panels around the lanai from being breached."

"But there are no glass panels on the ends, and that's how Geoffrey got in."

"I know. The security firm is going to work with the architects who designed the house and get glass panels installed on the ends, then the laser system can be installed. It can all be done fairly quickly. I hope that helps put your mind at ease."

"It does," I said, letting out a long breath. "Thank you very much."

"We don't want anything to happen to you."

"I appreciate that."

He smiled at me and went back to his office. I continued working in the kitchen, feeling more relaxed than I had all afternoon.

Barbie was home in time to eat dinner with the rest of the family that evening. Liko joined them at the table. Lars told him about the waves he had missed at Upolu.

"You'll have to go with me next time," he said to Liko.

"That would be great. I'm sorry I missed it today," Liko replied. I was setting a pitcher of tea on the table and I caught Liko's eye. He looked away quickly.

Later that evening I was in my den making my peace with Meli, who appeared to have forgiven me for my behavior earlier in the day. I apologized to her for throwing her at Geoffrey's face, and I would have sworn she smiled back at me. I was sure she was trying to tell me she had enjoyed it. I knew I was officially forgiven when she jumped up onto my lap and curled herself into a ball, purring as I stroked her ears and chin softly.

A knock sounded at the door. I jumped slightly, causing Meli to glare at me. "Who is it?" I asked.

"Me. Liko."

"Come in."

"What's going on, K? You look as white as a *haole*," he said as he entered.

"Geoffrey gave me a scare today, that's all. I'm a little jumpy, I guess."

"What happened?"

I told him the story, beginning after my trip home from Waimea and including the threat Geoffrey had made against him.

He let out a low whistle when I finished talking. "Wow. That guy is nuts. I'm glad you finally told the police. I'm sorry I wasn't here to help you."

"Are you nervous that he threatened you?"

He scoffed. "Not at all. I dare him to come anywhere near me. Or anywhere near you again, for that matter. I think you need protection, K."

"Lars has already talked to the security firm about putting a laser alarm system on the lanai, and the architects who built the house are going to come out and install glass panels on the ends, so the lasers will keep intruders out."

"So you told Lars about it?"

"Yes. I ran into him in a store up in Kapaau. I didn't really want to because it's embarrassing, but he deserved to know."

"Well, I'm glad he's doing something about it right away. In the meantime, I'm not going anywhere."

"Not even to lunch with Barbie?" I arched my eyebrows at him.

"You know about that?" he asked, a touch of sheepishness in his voice.

"Yes. I was going to call out to you in Waimea today, but Barbie joined you before I had a chance. You'd better be careful, Liko."

"Don't worry about it, K."

"I've heard that before. Does it bother you that Barbie was with Dr. Rutledge the same night she was with you? Or that she began a relationship with you so soon after Dr. Doug's death? Does it ever bother you that you're fooling around with the mother of the kid you're supposed to be helping? What if Marcus finds out?"

"I'll admit that I don't want Marcus to find out. But as for Barbie and me, we have an understanding, K. I don't interfere with her life and she doesn't interfere with mine. We just have a good time when we're together."

I shook my head. It wasn't my place to judge him or Barbie, but I couldn't help criticizing the way they were approaching their relationship.

He changed the subject. "I mean it, K. I'm staying near you until the laser system is set up."

"Thanks, Liko."

He left and I got ready for bed. I assumed I would have difficulty falling asleep, but thankfully I was wrong. I must have been more tired than I thought, because I slept soundly all night. My first thought upon waking was of Geoffrey, of him in my bedroom, his face twisted and angry, but I forced myself to take several deep breaths and concentrate on preparing breakfast before the kids had to catch the bus.

An architect and men from the security firm were at the house early, getting the measurements and other information they needed for the glass panels and laser alarm at the ends of the lanai. I couldn't believe how fast they were working to get the security-system additions in place. They told me it would be only a few days before the entire house was as safe as a fortress. I could rest easy.

And true to his word, Liko stayed at the house while I was there. I didn't see much of Barbie or Lars over the next couple days. Lars had gone to O'ahu on business and Barbie was busy at work. But Liko was always around, helping me in the kitchen, lounging by the pool, reading, and helping the kids after school on the lanai. He seemed to enjoy his time at the house, and I purposely didn't pay attention to what he and Barbie did after the kids went to bed.

Chapter 14

Lars was still on O'ahu when the police came with the results of Dr. Rutledge's autopsy. Akela showed the two officers to the table on the lanai and went to get Barbie. I wanted to join them to hear the results, but once I served coffee to everyone there was really no reason for me to stay.

The police weren't at the house very long. When they left, Barbie came into the kitchen.

"The officers said Dr. Rutledge had a blood-alcohol level of three times the legal limit. They said he fell down on the lava rocks and the impact is what killed him." She sighed, then was silent for a moment. I wondered what was going through her mind. "He was such a nice man. I'll miss working with him. But thank goodness this tragedy is behind us and we can move on." She shuddered. "To die like that— can you imagine?"

"What about Mrs. Rutledge?" I asked. Very little had been said about her after she left the party that night without her husband. I wondered if the police had told her of the results before Barbie. I felt sorry for her, knowing that her husband was cheating on her the night he died.

"I don't know what they've told her," Barbie answered. "I just hope she doesn't sue us for serving her husband too much alcohol. Don't look shocked, Kailani. She and her husband didn't get along and she didn't like me, so she might view this as her chance to get back at me."

"Get back at you for what?" The minute I said it, I knew I had gone too far. Barbie glared at me.

"That's between me and her."

"I'm sorry," I mumbled.

She seemed to soften. "That's okay. We're all on edge lately." She turned and left.

Liko came into the kitchen a little while later. "I saw a police car leaving. What were they here for?"

I filled him in on the latest news and he breathed a long, loud sigh. "What a relief. I was afraid the result would be different."

"You mean that his death wasn't an accident?" I asked.

"Yeah. I figured Lars would be arrested for killing him," he said in a low voice.

"What makes you think Lars did it?"

"He knew about Barbie and Dr. Rutledge, didn't he? He was mad at Barbie that night because he couldn't find her, right? Plus, there's Dr. Doug. Barbie thinks Lars is going to be arrested for that any day now."

"I don't know how you can say that about someone you call your friend. I would defend you if someone accused you of some horrible crime."

"Of course he's my friend, K, but face facts. And I don't blame him. Who wouldn't be mad enough to kill if their wife was with some other guy?"

"Shouldn't you be asking yourself that? But to answer the question, there are other ways to express anger than killing people, you know."

He held up his hands, as if to surrender. "Okay, okay. You win. I'm sorry I said anything."

"Liko, I just don't think we should be talking about it, especially here in the house."

He shrugged. "Well, I'm just glad it's over. Seen Barbie?"

I looked askance at him. "Not since the police left. She came in here to tell me what they said and I haven't seen her since then."

"Have you heard anything about the glass panels and the laser system for the lanai?"

"Yes. Everything should be installed tomorrow afternoon."

"Good. I'll feel better when it's done."

I spent the afternoon preparing dinner and dessert for the family. I served a bouillabaisse with rouille, steamed white asparagus, grilled baguette slices, and pineapple-guava pavlova for dessert.

"You've outdone yourself tonight," Barbie said, beaming, as I cleared the dishes from the table. "It was fan*tas*tic! Even the kids loved it, and I didn't think they'd eat the soup or the veggies."

I smiled at her. "Thank you. I love making dishes with fresh fish, and the pavlova seemed a perfect accompaniment."

Later that night, I was curled up in a chair on the lanai with a glass of wine when I heard whispering. Looking over the rail onto the lawn below, I saw Liko and Barbie. Liko had his arm around her shoulders and they were deep in conversation. Something told me to back up quickly so they wouldn't see me. I couldn't hear what they were saying, but I listened as hard as I could until they were out of earshot. I only heard the words "Dr. Rutledge" and "Lars." It looked like their relationship was getting stronger, not weakening as I hoped it would. I shuddered to think how the family would be hurt if Lars or the kids found out about their many rendezvous.

I tiptoed into the darkened kitchen to finish my wine, but a noise at the front door almost caused me to drop the glass. I peered around the corner into the hallway, where a light snapped on. I was so relieved to see Lars that my knees almost gave out. He saw me before I ducked my head back into the kitchen.

"Hi, Kailani. Sorry if I startled you. I didn't want to call from the airport and wake anyone up."

"You didn't startle me," I lied.

"I haven't had dinner yet," he said quietly. "Is there anything left over?"

I heated a big bowl of bouillabaisse and some asparagus and quickly grilled more baguette on the kitchen stove. I served it to him, along with a glass of white wine, at the small table near the kitchen. I wanted to keep him away from the big table on the lanai in case Liko and Barbie were still outside.

"Tell me what's been going on since I went over to O'ahu," he said, indicating a chair opposite him.

"Not much, really. The people from the security firm called to tell me they're coming tomorrow to install the glass panels at each end of the lanai."

"They called me too. I asked them to call you and let you know. Put your mind at ease a bit."

I smiled. "Thank you. It did help me relax a little."

"Have you heard any more from Geoffrey?"

"No. Hopefully I won't."

"I'm heading up to Hilo day after tomorrow. You still want to come?"

"Sure."

When Lars was finished with dinner, he carried the dishes to the kitchen. I shooed him out and put everything away, then went to bed.

The next morning the security people and architects showed up early. They were there most of the day fitting the new glass panels and laser security upgrades on the ends of the lanai. Before they left, Lars asked them to show me exactly how they worked so I wouldn't worry about intruders anymore. They showed me in great detail how the system operated and how I could arm and disarm it myself from a new control panel they installed in the kitchen. It was very comforting for me to have all the information, though I didn't understand the engineering of the system. It was also comforting that Lars insisted that I learn how it worked so that I wouldn't have to be concerned about Geoffrey making any unwanted appearances.

I slept much better that night. I felt safe and secure and was looking forward to going up to the farmers' market in Hilo the next morning. After the kids left for school and Barbie went to work, Lars came to get me in the kitchen.

"Ready? My meeting is in just a couple hours, so we better get going."

The road to Hilo took us over to the eastern side of the island, where it was overcast and drizzly. I enjoyed watching the dazzlingly green farms as they whizzed by and the rain forests growing all around us on some stretches of the road. As we drove, the Pacific Ocean stretched away to our left, its cerulean hue looking somewhat darker under the cloudy skies.

Lars dropped me off at the farmers' market, promising to return for me after his meeting.

"You think a couple hours will be long enough to look around?" he asked.

I laughed. "I could stay here all day, but it'll do."

He drove away and I was left to my own devices at the market. I strolled slowly among the stalls of papayas, strawberries, onions, honey, lavender, guava, jams and jellies, baked goods, tomatoes of all varieties, ginger, lychees, rambutans, and scores of other kinds of fruits and vegetables. I was thrilled to be there. I took my time deciding which stalls had the best produce and goodies, then filled several bags with the choices I thought the Jorgensens would like best. I walked over to the park across the street from the market and sat watching the water as I waited for Lars. I was able to block out the noise from the traffic behind me as I followed the paths of the boats that traveled out in the bay.

Lars texted me when he was back in Hilo.

Are you still at the market?

No, across the street in the park.

It wasn't long before Lars pulled up behind me. I stood up with all my bags and he got out to help me. He was laughing.

"Did you buy one of everything?"

"I couldn't resist!"

He was looking inside the bags. "This stuff looks great. Did you eat anything at the market?"

"No. I was too busy looking around."

"Want to get a late lunch at the Thai place up the street?"

We left the bags in the car and walked past the farmers' market to the restaurant a few doors up the block. We both ordered red curry over rice and decided to get the food to go so we could eat in the park by the car.

After lunch we reluctantly headed home. Lars asked me about the culinary school where I trained and what I wanted to do after my stint as a personal chef was over. He didn't laugh when I told him my dream was to open a food truck that served healthy, high-quality breakfasts and lunches. I asked him how he became interested in clothes for surfers. He explained that he surfed in California growing up and he never liked the clothes that were marketed to surfers. He thought he could do better. Obviously, he was right.

He turned left off the highway at one point. "Where are you going?" I asked.

"I thought we'd check out Akaka Falls. I haven't been there in a while. Have you ever been?"

"Not since I was a kid," I replied, recalling a field trip there with my elementary school. "I remember it was amazing."

"I love it there. I like to visit Kahuna Falls too, even though it's not quite as spectacular as Akaka Falls."

We parked in the small parking lot and took the stairs and paved narrow path first to Kahuna Falls, winding slowly through the rain forest. Groves of bamboo grew sky-high beside rushing streams, and ferns by the thousands rustled along the path. The only sounds we could hear were the joyful cries of the birds, the water bubbling in the streams, the *whooshing* sound made by the swaying stalks of bamboo, and the soft drips of water from the trees. There were no other people around on this weekday afternoon. It was peaceful and beautiful.

When we reached Kahuna Falls, we watched for several minutes as the water tumbled in a rush, continuing its descent from the top of the cliff where the earth fell away to the dark pool below. I hadn't remembered Kahuna Falls from my elementary-school visit.

We turned to resume our hike toward Akaka Falls, reluctant to leave behind the solitude and almost secret feeling of Kahuna Falls. I stumbled on the wet path and Lars reached out to grab my arm. After that I picked my way up the path a bit more carefully, not wanting to embarrass myself again.

We heard Akaka Falls before we saw it. The tremendous power of the water as it dropped over 400 feet echoed with a thunderous roar. I quickened my step a bit as we drew closer, excited to see the source of the sound. When we came to the top of the rise in the path, I drew in my breath as the full grace and beauty of the waterfall came into view.

"I didn't remember it being this beautiful," I said in awe.

"Isn't it incredible?" Lars asked quietly. One other couple stood at the fence, watching the falls. They took turns taking each other's pictures in front of the waterfall and I approached them and offered to take one of them both. They were thrilled.

When they asked if they could return the favor, I shook my head. "Why not?" asked Lars. "I think it would be nice to have a picture of this spot. Neither one of us gets up this way very often." He handed his cell phone to the woman, who stood smiling and waiting. We stood next to the fence and Lars put his arm around my back. We smiled and the woman snapped our photo, then handed the phone to Lars for inspection.

"That's a great shot. Thanks," he told her, and she and her husband continued on the path, leaving us alone with the waterfall.

Lars leaned over and showed me the picture. "Do you like it?" he asked. "I can text it to you. Better not let Barbie see that, though. She might not appreciate it." He smiled ruefully.

"Actually, this is probably as good a time as any to tell you that I've finally asked Barbie for a divorce."

I started to speak, to tell him how sorry I was, but he held up his hand, stopping me.

"I know what you're going to say, but don't. I'm not sorry. I'm sorry for what the kids are going to have to endure in the coming months, maybe even years, but I'm not sorry for myself. Ours has been a marriage in name only for a very long time, since before we even moved to Hawaii. She never wanted to move here. I moved the family here to get her away from the men she was seeing in California. I think I even told you that I believe one of them is actually Justine's father. I thought I would make one last-ditch effort to save our family. But it didn't work. I know she's been sleeping around since we arrived on the Big Island. I just didn't have the heart or the guts to go through with it until now."

"Well, I am sorry to hear it, even if you don't want me to say it."

"Thank you. I know what you mean. It's never nice when a marriage ends, but like I said, this hasn't been much of a marriage for years. The kids deserve better. And they know Barbie and I haven't been happy since they were very little."

"What happens next?"

He sighed. "I don't know yet. The lawyers have to get involved now. That's when the real fighting will start. I don't know what we'll do about the kids or the house or anything. I love that house, but I don't know if Barbie is going to want to stay in it. If she does, I'll just let her have it and I'll go someplace else."

I didn't want to say it, but I wondered about my job. As if reading my mind, Lars said, "Don't worry about your job. You won't lose that. Unless you want to, that is."

Why would I want to?

"We should get back to the house. I have to make dinner," I said.

"You're right. Let's head out." We walked slowly up the path back to the parking lot, then Lars turned to me. "This has been such a nice day. I'm sorry to spoil it with talk about Barbie, but I thought you had a right to know."

He paused for a moment, then swallowed. "I want you to know that I've got strong feelings for you. And I'm hoping you feel the same way about me too. You are a remarkable woman and I'd like to get to know you even better, but now isn't the right time. I don't want to give Barbie any ammunition against me in the divorce proceedings." He looked down, then back up at me again. "Will you wait for me?"

I hadn't expected this from him, but I found that my stomach was doing flip-flops and I was grinning from ear to ear. I nodded. "I'll wait," I promised him.

He smiled and leaned over to kiss my lips quickly, then we got in the car and drove home. On the way he told me stories of when the kids were little, of what it was like living in California and how different the people were on the Big Island, how different the lifestyle was. I enjoyed listening to him talk so proudly about Marcus and Justine, especially knowing that Justine might be another man's child.

I ventured a question about her, hoping I wasn't overstepping my bounds. "Are you ever going to tell her?"

"I've thought about that too, and the answer is no. I don't think there's any reason to tell her. For one thing, without a paternity test there's no way to know for sure. But Justine looks exactly like one of the guys Barbie was with in California."

"So you knew who he was?"

"Yeah. They worked together."

"What are the chances he would ever show up and want to be part of Justine's life?"

Lars scoffed. "No chance for two reasons. First, he was never the fatherhood type. Second, I think he passed away from a drug overdose."

He was quiet for a few moments, then continued. "I don't think anyone would ever accuse me of not being a father to Justine exactly the way I have been to Marcus. I certainly love her as much as I love Marcus. As far as I'm concerned, I'm her dad and I always will be."

We drove a short distance in silence, then suddenly he spoke. "I know the incident with Dr. Doug hasn't been cleared up yet. I want you to know I had nothing to do with it. I keep waiting for them to arrest me just to be able to say they have someone in custody, but thank God it hasn't happened yet. I hope you'll stick by me if it happens."

Even if Lars hadn't said anything, I knew with sudden certainty that he hadn't killed Dr. Doug. "I will."

We drove the rest of the way home in silence. As we turned into the long driveway, Lars pulled the car over, out of sight of the house, and glanced at me. "I had a great day. Thank you for everything."

"I haven't done anything," I said with a laugh.

"Yes you have. You've given me hope for the future, you've listened while I talked about my kids, you've said you'll wait for me. That's more than I could have imagined. I am a very happy man right now." He reached for my hand and held it to his lips. "I'm just sorry I can't tell anyone but you how I feel."

We went our separate ways when we got into the house, me to the kitchen and Lars to his office. I was floating on air, but like Lars, I had no one with whom to share my happiness. I busied myself making dinner, using the first of the produce I had bought in Hilo. I made a delicious-looking salad with hearts of palm and lettuce that had been picked that morning, a pomegranate vinaigrette, a tropical salsa to serve with grilled pork, roasted tomatoes and onions, and a fruit salad for dessert. When I served it to the family later, they all loved it.

Liko came to my room that night. "Barbie says she thinks Lars is going to be arrested for killing Dr. Doug."

"What evidence is there?"

"You know—the jealous husband, Barbie and Doug carrying on right under his nose. It would be too much for anyone."

"I don't think he did it," I answered.

"Why not?"

"I just don't. I don't think he's capable of such a thing."

"You never know what someone is capable of until they're pushed beyond their limits."

"He's your *friend*, Liko. You don't really believe he killed Dr. Doug, do you?"

He shrugged. "I don't know what to believe. All I can say is, Barbie seems to think he did it."

"It's all her fault," I mumbled under my breath.

"What?"

"Nothing."

"You think Barbie had something to do with it?"

"I'm not accusing anyone, Liko. I just don't think it was Lars."

"Well, don't say I didn't warn you."

I didn't sleep that night, worried as I was about Lars, the kids, and their future. I couldn't believe the police had scraped together enough evidence to arrest Lars in Dr. Doug's murder. It had to have been someone else. A stranger. A burglar.

But what if Lars really did it? What if he's just lying about the future in order to get me on his side?

But why would he do that? What good would it do him to have me on his side?

My thoughts spun around and around until daybreak, when I finally dragged myself out of bed and made a large pot of coffee in the kitchen. I took a mug out on the lanai and watched the ocean come alive under the light of an orange-yellow dawn.

I was just getting ready to head back into the kitchen, when I felt a hand on my shoulder. I jumped and turned around. Lars stood there, mug in hand, smiling at me.

"Good morning," he whispered.

"Hi," I answered, a sudden feeling of happiness spreading through me.

He grinned and winked at me, then turned to go back to his office. I watched him go, feeling guilty for spending the night questioning him and his motives when I should have felt nothing but security and peace.

It wasn't long before Barbie appeared for breakfast. I served her homemade coconut-and-dried-pineapple granola on the lanai as she watched the ocean in silence.

"The ocean never changes, does it?" she asked softly. I didn't know whether she expected me to answer, so I just made an "hmm" sound.

"Everything can be going wrong in our lives, everything can be a mess, but the ocean is always there and it doesn't care what's going on."

I was surprised to hear Barbie speak that way. She didn't seem to be given to philosophical thinking. I wondered if she was referring to her divorce. She looked up at me suddenly.

"Lars and I are getting a divorce."

"I'm sorry to hear that."

"We've grown apart—far apart—over the years, so I suppose it's the only solution. What with his company and my job and the hours we both put in," she said with a sigh, "I guess it was doomed to fail. We haven't told the kids yet, so please don't say anything."

"I won't."

She pushed her bowl away and stood up slowly. She seemed thoughtful and melancholy, but I couldn't help thinking it was her behavior over the years that had finally pushed Lars away, regardless of the hours they both worked for their jobs. *Of course*, I reminded myself, *there are two sides to every story, and I'm biased.*

They told the kids that night after dinner. The tension at the table as the family ate together was palpable, and I'm sure the kids knew something was wrong. When I heard Lars suggest that they all go to the family room, I knew he and Barbie were about to make their announcement. Though the kids had known that divorce was a possibility, it was going to be a shock to them to hear their parents announce it officially.

And that's exactly what happened. I was in my room reading when there was a knock at the door. It was Liko.

"Can't you hear the shouting?" he asked, almost in a whisper.

"No. Who's shouting?"

"Marcus. And Justine, a little bit. I don't hear Barbie or Lars at all."

"Are they still in the family room?"

"Yeah. Do you know what the shouting is about?"

"I think so. They're telling the kids they're getting a divorce."

Liko's eyes widened in surprise. "They are? Really? I didn't know that. How'd you know?"

"Barbie told me this morning." I didn't feel the need to mention that Lars had told me before that.

Liko looked pensive. "I wonder what that means for us."

I knew what it meant for me, but I didn't say anything. "I guess we'll just have to wait and see."

He looked at me sharply. "You don't seem too concerned about it. Don't you worry that you're gonna lose your job?"

"If I am, there's nothing I can do about it. I'll just find something else. What about you?"

"I'll have to speak to Barbie. You know, see if she sees a future with me in it."

I didn't answer. I doubted very much that Barbie would see a future with Liko. She didn't appear to spend too much time worrying about her love interests once the affairs were over. And her affair with Liko was sure to end, just like all the others had.

After Liko left, I pondered making hot chocolate for the kids and taking it to them, but I decided against it. Marcus had been so angry the last time I tried to comfort them after their parents had talked of divorce; I didn't want to risk enraging him again.

But about an hour later both Marcus and Justine came looking for me.

"I suppose you already know," Marcus began.

I nodded. "I'm really sorry. Is there anything I can do?"

Justine's eyes were puffy and red. "No," she answered, hiccupping. "Marcus wanted something to drink and I came with him."

"How does hot chocolate sound?" I asked them.

"Okay," Marcus mumbled. Justine added, "Can I have some too?"

"Of course you can."

I busied myself making hot chocolate for them. As I heated the milk on the stove they both stood against the counter, staring at nothing in particular.

"I'll bring it out to the lanai," I offered, and they trudged out of the kitchen.

When I took the cocoa on a tray out to the table, Lars had joined them. "Got enough for me?" he asked.

"Sure." I went back into the kitchen for another mug. When I returned Justine was crying and Lars was holding her hands in his. He wasn't saying anything. Marcus just looked on, stone-faced.

I left the mug on the table and hurried away. I felt like I was intruding on something very private and personal. I went into my room and turned on the television in a feeble attempt to take my mind off the kids' grief.

There was another knock at my door just a little while later. It was Justine. "Thanks for the hot chocolate," she sniffed. "It was really good."

She looked so sad, so lost, that I gathered her to me and held her as her shoulders shook, her thin body wracked with sobs. "I don't think I'm going to live," she said in a muffled voice. I pushed her away gently so I could look her in the eyes.

"Yes, you are. I promise. Everything looks terrible right now and very sad, but it won't always be like this. You'll get through it and so will Marcus. I just know it."

"Justine?" Marcus stood in the doorway. "C'mon. You need some sleep."

"I can't sleep."

Barbie appeared just then. "I've got something that will help you sleep, Justine." She took Justine's hand and drew her away, giving me a grateful look and a sad smile. "Thanks, Kailani."

My stomach twisted with guilt and sadness. Here they were, in their saddest hour, and I was hiding my feelings for Lars from them. I felt terrible. I needed to talk to Lars about it. Once Barbie and the kids had gone off to the kids' rooms, I walked softly to Lars's office and knocked.

"Come in."

I closed the door and stood with my back against it, suddenly nervous. "Lars? Can I ask you something?"

"Sure. What is it?"

"Do you feel guilty about the things you said to me, now that you've told the kids about the divorce and seen how they're reacting?"

He stood up from behind the desk and came over to me, taking my hand in his. "No, I don't. I'm glad I said those things to you. I don't want you to think that you are the reason we're getting divorced. Like I said, this marriage has been over for a very long time. We're just making it official. We shouldn't have waited this long."

"If you're sure . . ."

He smiled at me and kissed my lips gently. "I'm sure."

I stepped back out into the hallway and closed the door softly behind me. As I turned to go back to my room, I heard a quick, soft shuffling sound. Had someone been listening at the door? I had no way of knowing who it could have been, and I decided quickly that it would be best if I didn't follow the person. It could have been anyone—Barbie, Liko, or one of the kids. I didn't relish the thought of *any* of them hearing what Lars and I had said to each other.

I spent another sleepless night, worrying about the kids. I had grown so fond of both of them that I couldn't stand the thought of them being distraught over this turn of events. Besides the divorce, there were the two bodies that had been recently discovered at their home. The kids were under a tremendous amount of stress.

It was time to take them out for ice cream again, so I decided to meet them at the bus stop after school the next day and whisk them off to Hawi for a treat.

But I didn't get the chance.

The next morning after the kids left for school the police came to the house looking for Lars. Akela let the two officers in and asked them to wait while she went to get him.

He walked out, dressed as usual in an aloha shirt, board shorts, and bare feet. "How can I help you, officers?"

They had come to arrest him for Dr. Doug's murder.

Chapter 15

I stood in the hallway listening as they charged Lars with the murder and read him his rights. I couldn't believe what I was hearing. Barbie had come down and she stood off to the side, watching and listening. I was shaking and my breath was coming in ragged gasps. Akela was standing next to me. She put her arm around my shoulders. She couldn't have known why I was so upset.

"Don't worry, Kailani. You'll be able to keep your job," she soothed, misunderstanding my reaction.

"He didn't do it," I choked. "They can't arrest him." Akela hugged me closer.

I heard Lars instructing Barbie to call his lawyer. She went to his office as the police led him away. I stood in the hallway, watching him go, my anguish plain for anyone to see. Lars smiled at me ruefully, as if trying to keep my spirits up, when it should have been the other way around. I should have been trying to buoy him, but instead he was thinking of me.

Barbie came into the kitchen just a short time later. She sighed. "How am I going to break the news to the kids? This is horrible!"

But as it turned out, she didn't have to tell the kids anything. They had heard about their father's arrest from kids at school whose parents had texted them the news. Word had gotten around quickly. And since Lars was able to post the huge bail following his arraignment, he was home by the time the kids got home from school.

As soon as they came through the front door he took them into his office and closed the door. I knew he would be able to answer some of their questions, but not the most important one: What would happen if he was put on trial for murder? I fervently prayed the charges against him would be dropped before it ever came to that, and I hoped he would be able to allay the kids' fears as well.

When the kids came out of the office, Barbie was waiting for them on the lanai. She wanted to know what Lars had told them, and they related the conversation to her. Apparently, she was satisfied with the responses he had given to their questions, because she told them not to worry and to go do their homework before she went upstairs. Asking them to do their homework under the circumstances seemed unreasonable, but they pulled out their books and sat down.

A short time later I took drinks out to them. Liko was sitting at the table, trying to help each of them with their assignments, but it was obvious that not much work was getting done. They seemed unable to concentrate and kept going over the same problems again and again. Liko was patiently explaining how to do each problem, but clearly the kids' thoughts were far away from school and homework.

Finally, Marcus pushed his books away and put his head down on the table. Justine reached over and took his hand in hers. "Don't worry, Marcus. Nothing will happen to Dad. I just know it. He would never have done such a thing," she said in her high-pitched voice.

I could have hugged Justine for the faith she had in her father. Marcus looked up at her and nodded. "I know. It stinks, that's all." He stared straight out at the ocean for several moments, then pushed away from the table. "I'm going for a walk," he announced.

"Can I come?" Justine asked.

"Next time. Right now I just want to be by myself."

Justine seemed to understand. She gave him a little wave as he walked toward the front door. He didn't wave back. Poor kid. He was devastated.

Liko asked Justine if she'd like to go for a walk with him instead, but she shook her head. "I just want to go to my room, I think." She left and Liko sighed.

"Looks like I'm not going to be earning my paycheck today."

"Maybe you'll earn it just by being a friend, not a teacher." He nodded and headed out to the guesthouse.

I went back to preparing dinner and Marcus returned from his walk about an hour later. "I need a drink," he said, pouring himself a glass of water from the pitcher in the fridge. "It's hot out there."

"Where did you go?"

"Up to the main road. That reminds me. A guy was up there and he said to give you this." He handed me an envelope with my name scrawled on the front. I recognized Geoffrey's handwriting immediately.

"Where was he?" I asked sharply, reaching for the envelope. Marcus looked startled.

"Uh, just up by the road. Do you know what's in it?" he asked, nodding toward the envelope.

"No, but I'm sure it's nothing." I put the envelope in my apron pocket to read in private later. "Did he say anything else?"

"No, he just said he had seen me coming out of our driveway and he knew I lived at the Jorgensen house. Then he asked me to give the letter to you."

"Was he just parked up there?"

"Yeah. Sitting up there in a beat-up blue car."

"If you see him again, do me a favor and come right back here and tell me. I'd like to talk to him in person."

"Why?"

"Just because," I replied noncommittally. Marcus seemed to realize I didn't want to talk about it.

"Okay." He took his water and left the kitchen.

I slipped the envelope out of my pocket and stood staring at it for a long moment. I couldn't decide if I should open it. Maybe I should just call the police and tell them about it. But what if the envelope had something completely innocent in it? What if it held an apology for the way he had been behaving? I decided to open it myself and then call the police if necessary.

My hands sweating, I drew out two photos. The first was a photo of Geoffrey and me, taken at the restaurant in Washington. We were both smiling. I remembered the night the photo was taken. We had just catered a private party for a congresswoman and her staff, and only the restaurant workers were left. We were all cleaning up the dining room, joking and laughing. It seemed a thousand years in the past. It was a past in which Geoffrey still seemed to be living.

The second picture made my blood run cold. Taken from a distance, it was a shot of Lars and me in his car in the driveway the day we had gone to Hilo. He was holding my hand to his lips. Anyone else looking at the grainy photo might not realize right away that it was Lars and me, but I knew immediately. How had Geoffrey gotten such a photo? The hairs on my neck started to prickle.

He was still watching me.

Could I show the photo to the police? I dared not. What if it got back to Barbie and she used it against Lars in their divorce? It could damage the outcome of the case between him and Barbie, to say nothing of his reputation for being a faithful husband while Barbie cheated on him.

Could I show the photo to anyone? Not Liko—he didn't know about my relationship with Lars. Not Lars—I didn't want to scare him. Not only that, but it was the last thing he needed with a charge of murder hanging over his head. I was faced with the unpleasant thought of having to keep the photo to myself. It was just between Geoffrey and me, and Geoffrey knew that. He knew exactly what he was doing.

But it was more than that. I was faced with a gnawing fear that Geoffrey was never far away. Leaving a note saying I was going for a short walk before dinner, I went up the long driveway and stood for a moment where Lars's car had been parked when the photo was taken.

I looked around, trying to figure out exactly where Geoffrey had stationed himself when he took the picture. Across the road was a large field covered with tall grass that swayed in the light wind. There was no house on the property, though I assumed the land belonged to someone. Cows that probably belonged to a nearby ranch moved slowly around the land, munching here and there on the grass. Of course, I had noticed the property every time I went in or out of the driveway, but I had never really paid much attention to it. I walked across the road and stood in the grass, my hand shielding my eyes from the sun, and scanned the field before me. My gaze was drawn to several trees that grew far from the road. They looked like *kiawe* and monkeypod trees; they had large canopies, and some of the more shade-loving cows congregated under their leaves. Suddenly I knew where Geoffrey had been perched when he snapped that photo.

I walked toward the trees, picking my way carefully through the grass and around piles of lava rock. As I got closer to the grove of trees, the cows started to get restless. They mooed at me, obviously displeased by my trespassing. They moved away in a herd, leaving the spaces under the trees empty for me. I walked under the canopy of a monkeypod tree, noticing that the cows had eaten the grass almost down to the ground. I didn't know what I was looking for, other than some evidence of Geoffrey having been there.

And I found it. Lying next to the tree trunk was a small round piece of black plastic. A camera lens cover. I didn't need a fingerprint analysis to know whose it was. I picked it up and put it in my pocket.

It was getting close to dinnertime, so I had to hurry back to the house. I would have liked a little more time to look around Geoffrey's hideout, but I didn't want to serve dinner late. I promised myself I would return.

I didn't meet anyone on the way back to the house. Dinner was on time, and no one was the wiser after my trip to the property across the road. Or so I thought.

Around 10:00 that night I was in my room leafing through cookbooks, trying to relax, when my cell phone rang. Since it was so late, I worried that something was wrong at my parents' house. I answered without even looking at the phone screen.

"We should meet so I can get my lens cap back," came the voice on the other end. Dueling emotions began battle immediately—relief that it wasn't my parents calling, and an icy fear that Geoffrey knew I had visited his tree.

"You saw me over there?" I blurted. It was somehow more frightening to know he had been watching me than if he had appeared in person under the tree with me.

"Of course. I always know when you go somewhere, even if it's just across the road."

"What do you want?"

"Just to let you know I'm thinking about you."

I hung up. I raced out to the kitchen and rummaged through the drawer where I kept Detective Alana's card. When I found it, I called him right away and left a message on his voice mail. Then I went back to my room, where I was unable to sleep and finally got up and made myself a pot of coffee. I drank it on the lanai, thankful that the security system was armed for the night and that I didn't have to worry about Geoffrey showing up.

My lack of sleep was beginning to catch up with me. My stomach was in knots and the bags under my eyes shared my tale of exhaustion with the rest of the household.

Barbie noticed it at breakfast, after the kids had left for school. I had hoped to see Lars, but he had left early for a meeting in Kona. I marveled at how he could get any work done with his future on the line.

"Kailani, are you feeling okay? You don't look so good."

"I haven't been sleeping well," I answered. "If it's okay with you, I may just rest this afternoon."

"Of course it's okay with me. I'll order out for dinner and you take the rest of the day off. You'll get sick if you don't take care of yourself. Maybe tomorrow you can come up to my office and we'll see what we can do for you there. Do you think a massage would help?"

"I don't know. I've never had a massage."

She looked shocked. "*What?* Never had a massage?" She shook her head, as if I had committed an act of depravity. "We're going to do something about that first thing tomorrow. You can come up to Waimea with me and we'll get you fixed up with my best massage therapist."

I thanked her and dragged myself through the morning, finally dropping onto my bed after lunch. I hoped to be able to sleep for a while. I was queasy and felt a migraine coming on.

Thankfully, though, the sun was beginning its descent over the Pacific when I woke up feeling much better and with only a trace of a headache. It wasn't dark in my room yet, but the shadows were lengthening outside my windows. My first thought was that I hoped I would be able to sleep again that night.

I stepped groggily into the kitchen and found Marcus and Justine bustling around getting utensils and serving dishes.

"What are you guys doing?" I asked.

"Hi, Kailani. Mom ordered takeout and we want to make it look nice," Justine answered. "How are you feeling?"

"Much better, thanks. Can I help?"

"Nope," Marcus replied. "We're doing this so you don't have to. Why don't you sit down at the table on the lanai and we'll serve tonight?"

I was touched by their thoughtfulness. I sat down and waited for them to join me.

"Where's your mom?" I asked when they sat down.

"She's still at work. She had this delivered and said she'd eat later."

"Is your dad here?"

"No, he's staying in Kona for dinner," Justine answered. Marcus gave me a quizzical look.

"What's wrong, Marcus?"

"Nothing," he answered. "Don't you want to be here with just us?"

"Oh, it's not that," I said hastily. "I just wanted to make sure that anyone who wants dinner gets it."

"Liko said he would have dinner with us too," Justine said. And as if on cue, Liko walked onto the lanai.

The four of us had a lighthearted meal, even in the face of the kids' feelings about the divorce. We talked about school, the kids' friends, and favorite weekend activities, staying carefully away from any mention of murder, accidental death, and stalkers. I think we all appreciated the relaxed atmosphere.

I was in the kitchen when Barbie came home shortly after we finished dinner. "Kailani, I've made an appointment for you tomorrow morning with my favorite masseur," she said excitedly. "How are you feeling?"

"Much better, thank you. And thanks for ordering dinner. The kids made a fancy occasion out of it and invited Liko and me to join them. It was so nice."

Barbie beamed. "I'm so glad to hear it. But believe me, we'll be happy to have you cooking for us again tomorrow. We've gotten spoiled by you."

I accepted her praise with a nod of my head, then she continued. "As a matter of fact, I've been thinking about how spoiled we are now. I haven't really talked to you about what will happen after the divorce, and I was wondering if you'd be interested in continuing on with me and the kids. As our personal chef."

I was taken aback. "Um, I—" I stammered. "I don't know for sure what my plans are. Do you need an answer now?"

"Of course not. Just think about it. We'd love to have you."

It seemed Barbie was already assuming she would have custody of the kids after the divorce was final. And she would, of course, if Lars was convicted of killing Dr. Doug. I pushed that thought away. I felt a pang of anxiety, wondering what I would say if she pressed me for an answer. She would certainly change her mind if she knew that a relationship was starting to blossom between her husband and me.

The next day was Sunday, so I didn't have to make anything for the family until dinnertime. As soon as I had checked the fridge and the cupboards to make sure I had most of the ingredients I would need, I set off for my parents' house. I hadn't seen them since the shark attack and I was happy to be spending the day with them, away from worries about Geoffrey and about the future of the Jorgensen family.

I sped south along the highway, watching carefully in my rearview mirror to make sure Geoffrey wasn't following me. I had a long stretch of road completely to myself, so I knew I was alone. It would be nice to get out from under Geoffrey's shadow.

I had told my parents I was coming for a visit, so they were waiting for me when I got there. My sister and niece and I spent the morning on the beach playing ball, swimming, and lounging on the sand. My parents closed the bakery early and joined us for a picnic lunch. I felt rejuvenated and relaxed with my family. I had to head back north by mid-afternoon, so we crammed in as much conversation and laughter as we could in our few hours together. When my father and sister took Haliaka for a walk along the beach, my mother and I sat in the shade talking.

"Is everything okay at the Jorgensen house?"

"Sure. Why do you ask?"

"I always know when something isn't quite right with you and I'm getting that feeling now."

I smiled at her. "There *has* been a lot of drama lately." I told her about the Jorgensens' divorce, about Lars being arrested—wrongly, in my opinion—for the murder of Dr. Doug, the death of Dr. Rutledge, and finally, about my feelings for Lars. I left out any mention of Geoffrey.

"Be careful," she warned. "You know as well as I do that a new relationship can be very thrilling and you want to tell the world about it, but you don't want Barbie getting suspicious."

"I know," I sighed. "I haven't told anyone but you. I certainly can't tell Liko, since I criticize him for doing practically the same thing."

"It's definitely not the same thing. Behavior like his is part of the reason they're getting divorced. Your relationship with Lars is only alive *because* of the divorce—not the other way around."

"Do you think it's wrong?"

She thought for a minute. "No, I don't think it's wrong. I just wish the timing were different." She smiled. "Go for a quick swim before you have to head north. The beach is not a place for brooding."

I took her advice and drove back to the Jorgensens tired but happy. Now that my mother knew my secret about Lars, I felt like a weight had been lifted; my secret wasn't a secret anymore, but I knew I could trust Mom.

When I turned into the Jorgensens' driveway, I instinctively looked across the road, my eyes squinting, seeking Geoffrey's monkeypod tree. Seeing nothing out of the ordinary, I breathed a sigh of relief and went inside.

Detective Alana had left a message for me, so I called him back and told him what I knew about Geoffrey's new hiding place. I didn't know how often he was there, but at least I could give the police a lead in helping to find him. The detective promised to send out officers to have a look around.

Dinner that night was a bit strained because the entire family sat around the table. There was little conversation; it must have been very awkward for all of them. They ate quickly and went their separate ways.

Marcus came looking for me after the dishes were done and the kitchen cleaned. "I saw that guy again this afternoon," he told me.

"The guy who gave you the note?"

"Yeah. He said to tell you he'll see you soon."

"Is that all he said?" I asked, hoping my voice didn't betray the fear that suddenly gripped my chest.

"Yeah. Are you okay?" So I wasn't fooling him.

"Don't worry about me," I told him, dodging the question. I was *not* okay. I was terrified and suddenly sick to my stomach.

"Is that guy bothering you?" he asked shrewdly. "You should tell my dad."

"Your dad already knows about him and I think he has other things on his mind," I said. "You need to stay away from that man. I know I asked you this once before, but please come home as soon as you see him. I don't want you near him. He's not a nice person."

"I did come home as soon as I saw him, but you weren't here. And then I couldn't tell you at dinner because everyone else was there. This is the first chance I've had. Maybe you should tell Liko about him too."

"Liko knows all about him, believe me. I just want everyone to stay away from him."

"Do you think he'll hurt you?"

"No," I scoffed, hoping he believed me.

My relaxing day off had segued quickly into a fearful and anxious evening. I called the detective and left another message for him. Since it was late on a Sunday, I hadn't expected him to be in the office. I tried sleeping, but couldn't. I went out onto the lanai, hoping the sound of the ocean would soothe my restlessness. I sat out there in the dark, trying to calm down as I focused on the waves crashing into the shore.

But before long I heard a different sort of noise, one coming from the lawn below me. I strained my ears and moved softly to the edge of the lanai, but the noise had stopped and the night had fallen silent again except for the rhythm of the breaking waves. I waited breathlessly until I heard it again—it was the sound of something snapping. A stick, perhaps.

My eyes had become accustomed to the darkness and I stood still, watching and listening. I didn't have to wait long. There was a figure moving stealthily on the lawn beneath me.

Geoffrey.

I didn't know whether to shout, to alert everyone in the house, to alert Geoffrey that I knew he was there, or to remain quiet and wait to see what he did.

I opted to wait and watch. I didn't worry that he could see me, since I was hidden in the shadows. I didn't worry that he could come any closer to me, since the lanai and all the windows and doors were armed. I didn't worry, but I was utterly terrified.

I quickly tiptoed to the kitchen and called the police, telling them there was an intruder on the property. I asked them to come quickly, but to leave their lights and sirens off so they could surprise Geoffrey and catch him. The dispatcher told me drily that the officers would consider my suggestion.

I went back out, making sure to stay in the shadows. Geoffrey was still out there. He was seated on the grass, his back to me. I wondered if he was there because he had nowhere else to go.

Several minutes went by. I was still watching Geoffrey, when out of the corner of my eye I caught movement at the end of the lanai. The police.

Geoffrey had seen them too. He bolted to his feet and crashed off through the brush surrounding the lawn, heading toward the courtyard and the pool. The police gave chase, yelling directions to each other when one caught a glimpse of their quarry.

Lights started coming on in the house. Pretty soon the whole family, Liko, and Akela had joined me on the lanai.

"What's going on?"

"Who's shouting?"

"Is everyone all right?"

"What's all the commotion?"

I asked the kids to bring a pitcher of water and several glasses from the kitchen. Once they had gone, I quickly explained to the adults gathered that I had come out, unable to sleep, and had heard, then seen, an intruder on the grounds. I called the police, I explained, without waking anyone up, because I didn't want to scare the person away. I thought the police would have a better chance of catching him if they could surprise him. I didn't mention that I knew very well who the person was.

"I can't *believe* this!" exclaimed Barbie. "I feel so *violated.*"

Lars didn't say anything; he just gave me a hard stare as if he knew I was hiding something.

Just then Marcus and Justine came back with water for everyone. I think I was the only one who had any. The rest of us stopped talking.

"What happened?" Marcus asked.

"Kailani heard—" Barbie began.

Lars interrupted her. "Kailani thought she heard a noise and called the police. That's all."

"I'm sure it was nothing," I said, sounding apologetic. I turned to Marcus and Justine. "I'm sorry. You can go back to bed. I'll talk to the police."

The kids seemed to buy my story and shuffled back to their rooms, where I'm sure they had a hard time falling asleep after all the excitement.

"What should we do?" Barbie fretted.

"Go back to bed," said Lars. "You too, Liko and Akela. I'll stay down here and talk to the police." He looked at me as if to warn me to stay silent.

"Ah, excuse me," said Akela quietly. "I just don't think I can work here any longer. It's just too much."

Lars and Barbie exchanged glances. "I understand, Akela," Lars told her. "This has been a very stressful place lately. Would you like to take some time off until things calm down?"

"I don't think so," she replied with a shake of her head. "I've been looking for another job and I think I'll just stay with my parents until I find one."

"We'll be sorry to see you go, Akela," Barbie said. Lars nodded in agreement.

Akela went back to her room and Barbie looked at Lars. "Now we'll have to find a new housekeeper."

"Can we not worry about how the house is going to get cleaned right now?"

Barbie sighed and went back upstairs and Liko returned to the guesthouse. Lars and I were left alone on the lanai.

"Was Geoffrey here?" he asked. I nodded. "What was he doing?"

"Just sitting out there on the grass. I called the police because they've had a hard time finding him. I thought if they were able to catch him by surprise, they might be able to arrest him or at least get some information out of him."

"But he didn't come onto the lanai?"

"No. I made sure the lanai was armed before I went to bed. The alarm would have gone off if he tried to get over one of the glass panels."

"Thank God you're okay," he said quietly, reaching for my hand.

We sat opposite each other at the big table until we heard a knock. I jumped in my seat, startled, but I stood up and followed Lars as he walked calmly to the front door and whispered, "Who is it?"

"Police."

I would have demanded proof, but Lars had more faith than I did. He opened the door and two officers stood there. I looked beyond them into the darkness and saw nothing.

"The suspect ran off," the first officer said with a frown. "He escaped into the growth beyond the pool and we lost him."

I looked frantically from one officer to the other. "What do we do?" I asked in a high-pitched voice.

"Do you have any idea who it was?" asked the second officer.

Everyone was looking at me. "Yes, it was Geoffrey Corcoran, my ex-boyfriend. He's been bothering me lately. Detective Alana knows all about him."

The officers nodded. One took out a notebook and wrote something down, then flipped the notebook shut. "We'll discuss this with Detective Alana when he gets in, before we go off duty. He can take it from there." He looked at his watch. "He gets in at seven," the officer added. "In the meantime, just make sure the doors are locked. Are there doors out to the lanai?"

Lars shook his head. "It's open. But the glass panels on the lanai are armed with a laser security system. If anyone tries to breach the lanai while the system is armed a loud alarm goes off."

"Good. I would keep that system armed until you've talked to the detective." The officers turned to go and Lars closed the door behind them.

"Do you think you'll be able to get to sleep?" he asked me.

"Not a chance."

"Is there anything you can take to help you? A sleeping pill or something? I'm only thinking that without some sleep, tomorrow might be hard for you. Want me to wake Barbie and see if she has anything?"

"No, I have some pills left from the shark attack. They're pretty good at making me fall asleep."

He looked at me tenderly. "I'm so sorry you have to go through this. It seems like they should have caught up with Geoffrey by now."

"Lars, there's something you should probably know," I whispered, drawing him into the darkened kitchen. "The other day Marcus came home with an envelope for me. Geoffrey had given it to him."

"Geoffrey knows Marcus?" Lars asked in surprise.

I nodded. "There was a picture in the envelope. It was a picture of you kissing my hand in the car the day you and I went to Hilo together. It had been taken from a distance. I went across the road to the property over there and found a camera lens cap on the ground underneath that huge monkeypod tree. Geoffrey must have been hiding up there."

"Do the police know this?"

"Yes. I left a message for Detective Alana last night after he had left the office. I'm sure he'll talk to me about it in the morning. I didn't tell anyone about the picture, though."

"This concerns me for a number of reasons. First, it's obvious that you aren't as safe here as we thought. Second, if he approaches one of my kids again, I'll find him and kill him myself."

"I told Marcus that he should come right into the house if he ever sees Geoffrey anywhere outside or on the road."

"Good. We should tell Justine the same thing, and they should plan to be in the house whenever they're home until this jerk is caught. And he *will* be caught. Someone can drive the kids to the bus stop every morning and pick them up after school every afternoon."

"I'll be glad to do that. This is all my fault, anyway."

"None of it is your fault, Kailani," he said softly, reaching out his finger and tracing it across my cheek. "You haven't encouraged Geoffrey in any way. We do have to protect the kids, though.

"And though this should really be the least of our concerns, there *is* a photo of you and me floating around out there. We don't want Barbie to see it."

I nodded, understanding completely. "You'd better get back to bed," I said.

"Want me to sleep outside your room?"

"No. Go to bed and sleep well." I smiled at him, hoping my eyes didn't betray that I really did want him to stay near me.

But they did give me away. "I think I'd better stay close. I've been sleeping in my office, but not tonight. I'll sleep on the lanai. It's not cold and the daybed is perfectly comfortable."

"What will Barbie say?" I whispered.

"Nothing. If she asks, I'll explain that I wanted to keep watch, so I stayed out there. Don't worry. I'll be right out here if you need me," he said gently, pointing in the direction of the lanai.

"Promise me you'll call if you need help," I said.

"I promise. Now go to bed," he said with a smile. He leaned over and brushed his lips quickly against my hair and left. I thought about trying to stay awake in my room in case Geoffrey returned and made any trouble, but I decided it would be wiser to take a sleeping pill and try to rest. I trusted Lars to protect everyone, and the morning promised to be tiring.

The pill worked. I cocooned myself under the comforter in my room and fell asleep quickly once the medicine started working. I woke up at dawn and found Lars in the kitchen. He had made a pot of coffee and poured a mug for me.

"Any more problems last night?" I asked anxiously.

"None at all," he answered. "Now that you're up, I'll go take a shower. You all right?"

I nodded. "Thanks for staying out there. I'm glad you did."

"I could tell you didn't want to be alone in this wing of the house. I wanted you to feel safe." His eyes rested on mine for just a moment and I could feel a little spark flare to life. It filled me with warmth and protection. It wouldn't take much for that little spark to turn into a raging fire.

Just then we heard footsteps on the lanai. Lars stepped away from me and refilled his coffee mug as Marcus came into the kitchen.

"I hope you were able to get back to sleep last night," I said in greeting.

"Yeah. No problem. What did the police say?"

"Not much. They didn't see anyone. They're coming back this morning to double-check," Lars fibbed.

I changed the subject. "Ready for breakfast?" I asked brightly. "Give me ten minutes and I'll have huevos rancheros on the table." Marcus grinned and went out to the lanai. Lars gave me a quick wink and disappeared down the hall.

Justine had joined Marcus by the time I took breakfast to them. I joined them at the table with another cup of coffee. They ate quickly and with gusto, not stopping long enough to ask any questions about the excitement during the night. I was a little surprised, but I thought perhaps they wanted to forget it, wanted to believe that whatever I heard had really been my imagination. For one brief moment I looked up to see that Marcus had fixed me with a thoughtful stare. I waited for him to speak, to ask me something, but he remained silent. He probably knew it had something to do with Geoffrey.

The kids finished breakfast in record time and dashed off to get their backpacks. I met them at the front door with my car keys.

"What's going on?" Marcus asked.

"Your dad wants me to drive you guys to the bus stop."

"Why?" asked Justine.

I hadn't thought about that. I decided to be as honest as possible. "The police are coming back this morning to talk to me and to double-check that the property is totally secure. I'm just driving you as a precaution."

"Do you think the house isn't safe?" Justine fretted. "Someone came to our house and killed Dr. Doug. What if that person came back last night?" Her voice was rising.

"It's perfectly safe. Remember? We've talked about this. Whoever killed Dr. Doug is long gone and will never come back. The person who was here last night was probably just curious," I hastened to assure her. "The police really just want to have a look around in the daytime and talk to me again."

She seemed to accept my explanation and we all trooped out to my car. I waited with them until the bus came, then returned to the house.

Barbie was on the lanai with her coffee, waiting for breakfast. As I set a plate of huevos rancheros in front of her, she looked at me with anticipation. "Would you still like to come in this morning for that massage?"

I had completely forgotten about my appointment with her masseur. "Oh, I'm sorry, Barbie. I have to be here to talk to the police. They're coming back this morning. Can I reschedule?"

"Of course. I'll cancel the appointment as soon as I get to the office. Let me know when you want to come in and I'll take care of it for you."

"Thanks, Barbie," I said with a smile. I didn't want to offend her by telling her that I wasn't really thrilled by the idea of a massage, and especially one given by someone who worked with her. I was happy to have an excuse to cancel and I wondered if I could just keep putting her off.

After she went to work and Lars had eaten breakfast and was working in his office, Detective Alana and another officer came to the house to talk to me. Akela had left at dawn, so I answered the door. I sat down a bit nervously.

"Miss Kanaka," Detective Alana began, "I understand Mr. Corcoran was on the property last night."

"That's right."

"Are you sure it was him? Were there any lights on?"

"No. But there was enough light from the moon for me to recognize him."

"What do you think he was doing here?"

"I have no idea."

"But he didn't make any effort to get into the house?"

"Not that I know of."

"Do you have any idea where he's staying?"

"No idea. But I did leave a message for you about the property across the road. Did you get that?"

"Yes. I wanted to talk to you about it before we go over and have a look around."

I was in a quandary. I couldn't tell them how I knew about the monkeypod tree without telling them about the photo of Lars and me in the car. I thought for a moment and then said, "Geoffrey approached Marcus Jorgensen and gave him an envelope for me. Inside it was a picture of the driveway of this house. I knew the photo had to have been taken not far away, so I went across the road and looked around myself. I found a camera lens cover under the monkeypod tree over there and put it in my pocket.

"Later on I got a call from Geoffrey. I answered it without looking at the phone screen. He said he needed his camera lens cover back. So I knew he had seen me under the tree." I shivered involuntarily at the memory of that phone call.

"The picture he gave you was just of the driveway?" Detective Alana sounded skeptical.

"I was in the driveway."

"Can I see the picture?"

"I'd rather not show you just now. It's not very flattering."

"Miss Kanaka, I've seen more unflattering pictures in my career than you can imagine. I can assure you this one won't make me blush."

He must have realized the photo was of me in a compromising position, but I knew Lars trusted me to keep the photo private. I shook my head. "I'd really rather not show it to you. Not just yet. Can you go over there without seeing the photo?"

The officers stared at me for a long moment, then looked at each other. "I suppose we can," the detective said. "I'm going to need to see that photo at some point, though," he added sternly.

"Okay. And thank you."

They excused themselves to inspect the property again, retracing the steps the officers had taken during the night, looking for Geoffrey. I watched as they picked their way through the underbrush and riotous tropical growth, stepping on plants and flowers that were so well tended by the gardeners. The officer with Detective Alana had a camera and he took pictures from time to time.

They left after they had completed their inspection of the grounds, promising to let me know what they found after they had searched the area around the monkeypod tree on the property across the road.

Barbie called after the police left. "What did they have to say?" she asked. Her voice sounded tired. I told her everything the police had said and she let out a sigh. "I do wish that Geoffrey had never come into our lives. Whatever made you want to date him in the first place?"

I was a little annoyed. "He wasn't like that in the beginning. I couldn't have known he would turn out like this."

"Mmm." She sounded doubtful. "Would you like to come into the office now?"

I couldn't think of an excuse fast enough to put her off, so I agreed. A half-hour later I was driving up to Waimea for a massage that I didn't want. I checked in my rearview mirror frequently to see if Geoffrey was behind me, and thankfully he wasn't.

When I got to her office, Barbie came out to the waiting room to greet me and then led me to the back, where the examination and therapy rooms were. Like the office in Kona, this one was large and decorated in beige and ivory. Soft Asian spa music piped quietly through hidden speakers, and the entire space was scented with a calming mixture of lavender, vanilla, mint, and tropical florals. The whole effect was supposed to be soothing and relaxing, and I'm sure it would have been if I hadn't been anxious about Geoffrey, his midnight trip to the Jorgensens, the divorce, the kids, Dr. Doug's murder, and my relationship with Lars.

Barbie introduced me to the masseur, who was breathtaking. He was tall and slim, tanned, with hair the color of caramel. I took one look at him and wondered cynically whether Barbie had slept with him too. It was likely.

The massage felt good, but not great. I was unable to relax, even with the soft scents floating around me, the music playing in the background, and the masseur's capable hands trying to knead the stress from my back and shoulders. He was doing his best, but I still felt edgy and nervous.

When he had worked some of the kinks out of my muscles for almost an hour, I could bear the stress no longer. I asked him to stop, which he did immediately. He looked at me questioningly and asked if everything was all right.

I tried to reassure him that it wasn't his work, but my mind that was keeping me from enjoying the massage.

"If you live in Barbie's house, I can see why you're stressed out," he said with a wry smile. "There's been a lot going on over there, what with the two doctors and the other thing."

"What other thing?" I asked, assuming he was going to say something about the divorce.

"Oh, you know." He looked around theatrically, then continued. "The baby," he whispered.

I was stunned. Was Barbie pregnant? I realized my mouth was hanging open and I snapped it shut.

"Oh, the baby," I answered lamely. I didn't want him to think I didn't know what he was talking about. "Yeah."

I tried paying for the massage and giving him a tip, but he smiled broadly. "It's on the house. Barbie's orders." I thanked him and then stopped to say good-bye to her before I left.

"Thanks for the massage, Barbie. Are you sure I can't pay for it?"

"Nonsense," she said, waving her hand. "I wanted you to have a treat. Are you relaxed?"

I hated to tell her the truth, but I figured the masseur would tell her that I wasn't a good client, so I said, "Almost. The masseur had a tough job getting me to relax and he did great. I feel much better than I did when I came in."

That seemed to satisfy her. "Isn't he the *best?*"

"Definitely. Thanks again," and I left her office and returned to the house.

I drove home wondering about the baby—how could I find out about it? Who was the father? *There are so many possibilities,* I thought wryly.

I served dinner to Liko and the kids that night since Barbie wasn't home from work and Lars had an important conference call that went late. I was still bewildered by the information the masseur had shared with me. And I suppose I was a little preoccupied as I came and went between the kitchen and the lanai.

"Kailani, what's wrong?" Justine asked.

"Hmm? Oh, nothing. A lot on my mind, I guess."

Marcus gave me a shrewd look. I ignored it rather than try to figure out what his problem was. I had enough to think about.

Liko came to see me after dinner. "Everything good, K?"

I shrugged. "I guess. Like I said, I just have a lot on my mind and I let it get the better of me. There's really nothing to worry about."

"Geoffrey been bothering you again?"

"Actually, no. I mean, no more than usual. Maybe the police have had a chance to talk to him. I should call them and find out," I said half to myself.

"Let me know if you need anything. Promise?"

I smiled at my old friend. "I promise."

The next morning I called Detective Alana. He answered on the first ring.

"Actually, I was going to call you in a little while," he said in answer to my question about Geoffrey.

"We had a look around the tree where you found the camera lens cover and we found some things of interest. Footprints, a candy wrapper, and a piece of paper with a phone number on it."

"What's the number?"

He recited the number and I recognized it right away. It was my sister's cell phone number. Why would Geoffrey need that?

"I was just getting around to checking out the number when you called. Do you know if Geoffrey has tried to contact your sister?"

"No," I replied, a lump of fear beginning to grow in the pit of my stomach.

"I'm going to send an officer to ask her a few questions. In the meantime, would you please call her and see if she's heard from him?"

"Yes," I choked out.

I told the detective where he could find my sister and hung up with him. I quickly called my sister's cell. There was no answer. I took several deep breaths, telling myself that there was nothing to worry about, that there were lots of reasons why Kiana wasn't answering her phone. She could be with a customer, or she could be in a meeting with the ringer off, or she could have left her phone at home, or she could have forgotten to charge it.

Or Geoffrey could have gotten to her already.

In a panic, I called the store's main number. It rang several times before someone finally answered. "Is Kiana there?" I asked in a rush.

"One moment, please."

The seconds ticked away endlessly while I waited for my sister to pick up the phone.

"This is Kiana. How can I help you?"

"Thank God you're okay," I said breathlessly.

"Kailani?"

"Yes. Has anyone called your cell this morning?"

"I don't know. I have the ringer off. Let me check. What's wrong?"

"You remember that guy I told you about, Geoffrey, the *pupule* one? He's been spying on me from across the road. When the police went to look in his hiding place, they found your cell number written on a piece of paper."

Kiana must have been stunned by the news, because she was silent for a moment. "Why does he have my number?" she asked, her voice rising. "Wait a minute. I did get a call from a number I didn't recognize. Do you think that was him?"

"What number was it?"

She told me the number and it didn't match the number I had for Geoffrey. But he could have used a different phone.

"So why does he have my number?" Kiana repeated.

"I don't know. The police are coming to the store to ask you some questions."

"I don't know anything."

"I know, but they want to talk to you anyway. Is everything all right—I mean, normal—with you?"

"I guess so," she answered slowly.

"When the police get there, make sure you tell them about the call from that number you don't recognize. Did the person leave a voice mail?"

"Hold on and I'll check." I could hear a tinny voice through the phone line as she listened to a voice mail on her cell phone. She came back on a moment later. "It's okay. It was someone from Haliaka's school. Let me call them back and then I'll call you. When are the police getting here?"

"I don't know, but probably pretty soon. I don't know if they're coming all the way from Hawi or if the Kona police are going to ask the questions."

She hung up to call Haliaka's school and I stood still, staring at my phone, willing her to call me back. When she did, I was shocked by what she had to say.

"Kailani, someone followed Haliaka to school today. She told her teacher as soon as she got there this morning and they called me right away. Do you think it could have been Geoffrey?" She sounded so worried. My hatred for Geoffrey surged.

"I wouldn't put it past him," I said grimly. "Do you have to go over to the school?"

"I told them I had to talk to the police here, then I would be over. She won't be able to take the bus anymore."

"I wish I could be there. I would drive her to and from school every day. As it is, I'm driving Marcus and Justine to and from the bus stop now. And all this fear is because of Geoffrey. My heart just breaks for the kids, and I can't stand the thought of Haliaka being scared of a man who's only on the island because of me. I'm so sorry."

"Don't blame yourself. You couldn't have known what would be put in motion when you left Washington," she assured me. "But I do have to go. I think the police are here. Call you later."

I was so nervous about Haliaka that I couldn't cook while I waited to hear from Kiana. I snatched up the phone when it rang. It was Detective Alana.

"I asked the Kona police to talk to your sister so it could be done faster," he began. "The officer who talked to her reported back to me and I understand someone followed her daughter to school this morning."

"Yes," was all I could manage.

"The school only got a vague description of the car. All the child noticed was that it's blue. Do you know if Geoffrey drives a blue car?"

I tried to remember if I had ever seen Geoffrey's car.

"I don't think I've seen—wait! Marcus told me Geoffrey was in a beat-up blue car when he gave Marcus the envelope with my picture in it. But it was probably a rental. He could be driving anything now."

"Since we know he was driving a blue car at one time, though, we will check that out. I'll stay in touch and let you know what we find out." He rang off, and I was left alone with my thoughts and fears again. I tried making something for the family for dinner, but my heart wasn't in it. For the first time since coming to the Jorgensens, my wontons were slimy, my chicken broth had too much fat in it, and I cut myself slicing scallions. I needed to get into Kona to check on Haliaka for myself. I quickly made beef-salad wraps for lunch for anyone who wanted them, put them in the refrigerator, and left a note on the counter saying I had to run into Kona due to a family emergency and I would be back in time to prepare dinner.

I gunned my car out of the driveway, squealed onto the road, and sped quickly *mauka* to the highway. Once on the highway I forced myself to slow down so I wouldn't get pulled over. Kiana wasn't answering her cell, so I didn't know where she was. I figured she was probably still at Haliaka's school.

I drove south along the Queen K highway until I came to the small town where Haliaka's school sat along the main road. There were two police cars in the parking lot and I recognized Kiana's car right away. I jumped out and rang the buzzer to be admitted.

The woman who sat behind the desk in the main office listened to my hurried story, then picked up the phone and pressed a button. She spoke quietly into the phone and when she hung up, she showed me where the principal's office was and asked me to join the group already in there.

When I went into the office, Haliaka was in there with the principal, three police officers, and Kiana. I introduced myself to the strangers in the room. The police officers appeared to know who I was. Probably Detective Alana had told them about my relationship with Geoffrey.

The principal continued talking directly to Haliaka, assuring her she did the right thing by telling her teacher about the man in the car and by telling the officers all she could remember. He sent her back to class with a reminder that she had done nothing wrong and that none of this was her fault.

I wanted to reach out and take her in my arms and keep her there until Geoffrey had been caught, but I stayed by the window where I was standing and watched her go. When she had left the room, I apologized to everyone for all the trouble Geoffrey was causing.

"We don't know for sure that it was Geoffrey Corcoran in the car that followed Haliaka to the bus stop, but it is definitely a possibility," one of the officers noted in a stern voice. He spoke quietly to one of his colleagues and that officer exited the room. The officer in charge explained that he had sent his coworker to interview the other children at Haliaka's bus stop to find out if any of them saw anything.

The principal turned to Kiana. "I'm afraid she needs to stay off the bus for a while, since we don't know who this person is and Haliaka was probably the target. Can you arrange for someone to drop her off and pick her up from school each day until this has been resolved?"

"Yes, of course." Kiana's eyes were worried, her mouth drawn. "Do you think she's in any danger?"

"I would think you can keep her safe just by having an adult with her all the time."

Kiana sighed. "I hope you're right." She turned to me. "I wish we had an alarm system at the house."

I knew it would make her feel better to have an alarm system, but my parents had discussed it in the past and had decided that an alarm signified distrust of the people in the small town where they lived. They didn't want to live that way, they said.

But maybe this incident would change their minds. And if it did, I would pay to have the alarm system installed right away.

Kiana went back to work when her meeting at the school was over. I needed to get back to work too, but first I stopped at my parents' bakery and told them everything that had happened that morning. They were shocked and upset. And fearful.

I proposed my idea of paying for an alarm system to be installed and they thought it was a good idea. True, they said, they didn't want the neighbors to feel distrusted, but obviously Haliaka's safety was a much more important concern. And they refused to let me pay for it. Before I left the bakery, my father was on the phone with a security firm that could install an alarm later in the week. I went back to the Jorgensens' house feeling slightly more at ease than I had been earlier in the day. I was furious with Geoffrey, though.

My cell phone rang while I was driving north. It was Detective Alana. He had a lead from a rental company on the car Geoffrey was driving. Apparently, Geoffrey was still driving the blue car and the police had issued an island-wide bulletin on Geoffrey and the car. He was becoming more convinced that it had been Geoffrey who had followed Haliaka to the bus stop.

If it was indeed Geoffrey who was driving the blue car, the detective noted, he was becoming bolder and an even greater cause for concern. I agreed. Though his department had not located him yet, the detective assured me it was only a matter of time before Geoffrey was caught and arrested. I was becoming more and more anxious about his whereabouts, and I asked Detective Alana if anyone had looked on the back roads around the area of Hawi. He said he had officers searching the area.

When I got home, I picked up the kids from the bus stop. Back in the kitchen, I was able to make another pot of wonton soup, this time without mistakes or injuries, because I was feeling more at ease having talked to Kiana and the police in Kona and having seen Haliaka with my own eyes. I felt even better knowing there would be an alarm system in place at my parents' home by the end of the week.

The kids and Lars loved the wonton soup later that evening and each ate two bowls of it. I served lemony broccoli rabe alongside it, as well as bread that I had brought from my parents' bakery. Barbie was home but didn't join the rest of the family for dinner.

She texted me later in the evening.

Can you bring some dinner up to my room?

I took a tray of soup and bread up to her and set it on the table next to her bed. She was just coming out of the bathroom, wearing a robe and rubbing her wet hair with a towel.

"Thanks, Kailani. I'm not feeling like myself tonight."

Her robe was tied tightly and my eyes were drawn to her waist. Did the robe hide a growing pregnancy? It didn't look like it, but many women didn't show for three or four months.

I promised to return for the tray in a while and left her to her dinner. I passed Lars on my way back to the kitchen. "Why is Barbie eating upstairs?" he wanted to know.

"She's not feeling well, I guess."

"Dinner was great tonight," he said with a smile. Then he hastened to add, "Not that it isn't great every night, but tonight it tasted even better." He sounded like a nervous teenager.

I laughed. "Thank you. I need to clean up."

He winked at me and I felt a thrill of happiness even in that tiny gesture. I briefly wondered again if Barbie was indeed pregnant. *How would Lars react to that?*

As I cleaned up from dinner I got another text from Barbie.

Do we have any ginger ale? I need something to settle my stomach.

Yes, I texted back. **Be right up**.

I took her a large glass of ginger ale and another glass of ice and set it on her bedside table, where her food sat untouched.

"Can I get you something besides the wonton soup?"

"Oh," she moaned. "Don't even mention food. I can't bear the smell of it. Can you take it with you when you go downstairs? I'm sure it's delicious, because everything you make is delicious, but I just can't stomach it tonight."

She's pregnant.

I took the food away and told her to text me if she needed anything else. Lars was going up the stairs to the master suite as I was coming down.

"You're not her maid, you know," he said.

"I know, but she's sick. I can't just let her languish up there with nothing to drink. She doesn't feel like eating." He cocked his head and studied my face for a moment.

"I'll go talk to her," he said.

He's figured it out.

He continued up the stairs and I went to the kitchen. I was cleaning the counters when I heard yelling and a crash from upstairs. I ran to the bottom of the stairs, but I didn't want to interrupt the argument that was obviously in progress.

"Is everything okay up there?" I called up the stairs.

Lars came storming down the stairs. "Come into my office," he said.

I followed him and he shut the door behind me. "She's pregnant!" he hissed.

"I was afraid of that," I admitted.

"You suspected?"

I nodded. "I remember when my sister was pregnant, she was sick in the evenings and couldn't stand the smell of certain foods. I just had a hunch about Barbie."

"How can she do this? To her own kids?"

"To you?"

"This isn't about me. I don't care if she has a dozen more kids. What I care about is that her kids are going to see her pregnant by another man while their parents are still married. It makes me sick."

"Do you know who the father is?"

He shook his head, grimacing. "She won't tell me. She probably doesn't even know that herself."

My heart felt constricted and my throat was dry. Tears sprang to my eyes. I so wanted to reach out and embrace Lars, to offer him some comfort, to tell him that things would be better soon, but I dared not. He was still married, and I worked for him. But he didn't feel the same way. To my surprise, he reached out and took my hands, then folded me into his broad chest. We stood there in silence for a moment, then he tilted my chin and kissed me. I don't know what I felt more: surprise or happiness. But it didn't last long. He held me away from him and said softly, "Not long now. You'll still wait for me, right?"

I smiled at him as I looked into his eyes. "I think you know the answer to that. But we have a lot of problems hanging over our heads. There's Barbie's pregnancy, the death of Dr. Doug, and Geoffrey. We can't be together until all those things are resolved."

"I know. But this gives me something to look forward to, to hope for. It's hard for me to keep my thoughts and my hands to myself when you're in the house all the time." He grinned. "You'd better get back to the kitchen before anyone starts to wonder what you're doing in here."

I squeezed his hands and left, again feeling an odd mixture of apprehension and happiness. Lars certainly wasn't off the hook for the murder of Dr. Doug and I wondered uneasily about the outcome of the legal proceedings. Lars hadn't mentioned it since the day he posted bail and came home, but I knew it weighed heavily on his mind and that he wouldn't be at ease until he had been exonerated.

As I walked back toward the kitchen, I heard soft footsteps in the hallway, the noise fading away as the person walked toward the back of the house. It had happened once before when I left Lars's office. Again, I opted not to follow the footsteps.

I would come to regret that decision.

Chapter 16

Things at the Jorgensens' house went on as usual for about a week. Strangely, I didn't hear from Geoffrey. I thought perhaps he had given up and hopefully gone back to Washington, but in the back of my mind I knew that couldn't really happen—if he tried boarding an airplane, the airport personnel would know there was a warrant for his arrest and he would be turned in.

Lars met regularly with his lawyer, who came to the house every three days. The lawyer, always grim-faced and serious, told him that it didn't look good for him—the jilted husband, the marriage that was going south, the wife's lover staying within yards of the main house until his death. He had motive and opportunity. Lars had hoped the charges against him would be dropped, but it seemed that the evidence against him was quite strong and the lawyer was concerned about what would happen if the case went before a jury. I know Lars was beginning to feel despondent about his chances of a quick resolution, and a dry lump grew in my heart each time the lawyer came to the door.

Good news was scarce.

Barbie came down late for breakfast several times during that week, always looking worn and haggard. I wondered how long she would be able to wait before telling the kids that she was pregnant. She'd have to tell them soon or they would see for themselves that something was different about her. If they hadn't noticed her fatigue and illness already.

Since she was feeling under the weather and I knew she needed to eat, I asked her one morning before she left for work if there was something I could make that might not upset her stomach. She thought for a moment before replying that she wanted something made with citrus fruit. I was glad to hear that she finally seemed willing to eat something, so after everyone had left for work and school that morning, I drove up to Waimea to shop for groceries. The local farms always kept the stores stocked with magnificent produce grown just a few miles away—it was the perfect place to shop for the citrus that Barbie craved.

I was so preoccupied with planning a menu in my head that I didn't notice the blue compact car following me.

I went first to the big grocery store in town to get the staples I needed, then I made a few more stops for other items. The last place I visited was a small organic farm on the outskirts of town, down a long dirt road arched with *kiawe* and plumeria trees. I stopped the car and walked to the farm stand, where the honor system was in place for anyone who wished to buy produce. I chose carefully. There were oranges, grapefruit, honey tangerines, Tahitian limes, calamondin and Kaffir limes, and tiny flame-orange kumquats. Not knowing exactly what fruits I wanted to use, I took several of each and placed them in a macramé bag I had brought with me.

As I fished in my purse for cash to pay for all the fruit, I heard a car coming up the road to the stand. I didn't pay any attention to it until the door slammed and I heard footsteps advancing toward me. I turned around to greet the person coming up behind me and was shocked to see Geoffrey. He was walking quite slowly; his eyes and the set of his mouth held the promise of menace and pain. My heart immediately started beating faster and my hands grew clammy and cold. Suddenly I didn't care about having the right amount of money to pay for the fruit. I quickly grabbed a large bill and stuffed it in the honor box and turned around.

I gasped. Geoffrey was standing inches away. Blood pounded into my ears, making a deafening sound. I saw Geoffrey's lips moving, curling, but I couldn't hear him for a moment because of the rushing noise in my head. He had seen the fear in my eyes, I knew. I tried stepping around him, but he grabbed my arm.

"This has gone on long enough, Kailani," he said quietly.

"Did you follow my niece to the bus stop?" I demanded, trying anything to distract him.

"Maybe. How else was I supposed to get your attention?"

"You could have tried calling me."

"That wouldn't have worked. You'd have called the police."

"But the police were called anyway because you followed Haliaka in your car."

"True. But I did it to let you know that I was still watching you, that I wasn't done with you yet."

Chills raced up and down my arms, my legs, up the back of my neck. What did he mean by that? I tried getting around him again, but he tightened his hold on my arm.

"What do you want, Geoffrey?"

"I don't really know yet," he mused, rubbing his chin theatrically with his free hand.

"Please let me go. I have to go back to the house."

"I can't do that, Kailani. You know that. If you get back in your car, you'll call the police and they'll be swarming over me in a matter of minutes."

"I won't call the police, I promise," I said, remembering with an inward groan that I had left my cell phone in the car.

"Do you think I'm an idiot, Kailani?" he said with a quiet laugh. "You know me better than that. Come on."

"Where are we going?"

"You'll see. I want to show you this great place that I found. Secluded, quiet, beautiful."

I tried snatching my arm away from his grasp, but he had too strong a hold. "Geoffrey, please just let me go home. You know you're going to get caught if you take me anywhere, and then what'll happen? You'll be arrested, charged, and it will be ages before you can get back to your life in Washington."

"I have no life in Washington anymore. My life is here now. With you."

"Geoffrey, we can't have a life together. There's nothing good between us anymore."

"That's your fault. We can make it work again."

There was no use arguing with him. I tried another distraction—regular conversation. It sounded crazy to my own ears, given the circumstances. "Have you found a restaurant to invest in?"

"Yes."

"Where is it?"

"You don't really care. I know that. You're just trying to stall.

Now, you're going to get into the backseat of my car and we're going for a drive."

"I don't want to."

"I don't care. Get in." As we talked, he was steering me toward his car, which was parked next to mine. When he reached for the door handle, I made one final attempt to get free. I wrenched my arm out of his grasp and ran to my side of the car.

But I had locked it. And the keys were in my purse. My hands trembled as they felt around the inside of the bag, frantically searching for the keys that I could use as weapons and to get away.

But he chased me around to the driver's side of my car and wrapped his arms around me from behind, pinning my arms to my sides. I lost hold of my purse and it fell, some of the contents spilling onto the ground.

He pulled me back to his car, where the back door was open, then shoved me into the backseat, slammed the door, and ran around to my car, where he picked up my purse. I could see him shoving my belongings back into it. I tried desperately to get out of the car, but it must have had child-safety locks—ones that couldn't open from inside the car. It was useless. I wasn't going to get away from him. I needed to think clearly, to empty my head of panic and try to stay calm.

Geoffrey jammed my cell phone into his back pocket, then thrust my purse onto the floor of the front passenger seat as he slid into the car.

"Where are you taking me?"

"You'll see." He peeled out of the parking space and hurtled down the dirt track back toward the main road. I watched my own car get smaller and smaller through the back window. One car passed us on the way back to the main road. I pounded my fists on the side window, then awkwardly on the back window as it passed us, but to no avail. All I succeeded in doing was bruising my hands and making Geoffrey angrier. I fervently hoped that someone would notice my abandoned car and call the police.

Once on the main road, Geoffrey slowed down and flowed with the regular traffic. I tried pounding on the window once, but Geoffrey reached his arm around and gave me a backhand across the face. Tears stung my eyes as my cheek throbbed, but I wasn't about to let him see me cry. I didn't try pounding on the window again, though. I watched the scenery flit by as we sped along a rather sparsely used highway that snaked through the district of North Kohala. On any other day I would have enjoyed the view and the drive. Geoffrey hit the brakes several times, as if looking for something, but eventually he pulled over to the side of the road. No other cars were in sight. I recognized the place where he stopped. To our left a wide meadow blanketed the side of a sloping hill that led *makai.* Far in the distance, the ocean sparkled in the sunshine. Closer and about halfway down the hill was a dilapidated ranch, one that looked like it hadn't been touched in years. A rusted cistern stood guard over the deserted place.

Geoffrey got out and, looking up and down the road, opened the back door and yanked me out by the arm. He stalked off down the hill, dragging me as I stumbled behind him clumsily, tripping over hillocks of tall green grass. We could hear a car approaching; Geoffrey put his arm around my shoulder tightly, so I couldn't get away from him. It probably looked to the people in the car—if they saw us at all—that we were a couple in love.

We made our way down the hill and around to the front of the largest of the abandoned buildings, which faced the ocean and away from the road. The front door had rusted and no longer hung on its hinges. It lay on the floor, dented and bent, inside the doorway. Geoffrey pushed me inside, where the only roof that remained consisted of a few rafters. The rest of the roof had probably either blown off or rusted away. The wind howled, keening through the cracks in the walls. It was the sound of fear.

Geoffrey pushed me and I stumbled over debris on the floor as I made my way across the room from him. I wasn't yet thinking of trying to escape—I just wanted to put some distance between us. I stood with my back against a dilapidated wall and stared at him, catching my breath. I wanted him to think I wasn't scared.

"You know as soon as I don't get back home someone is going to come looking for me."

"Even if they do, they'll never find you." He sneered at me. "You're well hidden up here."

"Once word gets out that I'm missing, anyone who sees your car up on the road will put two and two together and figure out that we're here. Plus, the police will know it was you. They're already looking for you."

"You say 'we' like I'm staying. I'm not staying. I'm leaving you here." He was walking toward me slowly; I edged along the wall away from him, my eyes never leaving his. Suddenly, like a cobra, he lunged toward me. I think I let out a shriek. I started to run, but he grabbed the back of my shirt. I twisted this way and that to get away from him, but his grip was just too strong. He stood over me, panting, and I felt the sting as the palm of his hand struck my face. He did it again. I kicked him in the shin, struggling to get away.

He roared with anger and pain and grabbed his shin, allowing me to scramble over more debris on the crumbling floor of the old house, getting farther away from him. But he recovered his wits quickly and came after me, crashing around pieces of metal and wood, rocks and grass. It only took a few seconds for him to catch me again, and this time I braced for his assault, which came in the form of a fist to my stomach. I doubled over, the wind knocked out of me, trying to catch my breath. I looked up into his eyes, which seemed alight with hatred and malice.

"Why are you doing this?" I croaked.

"Because you left me for some surfer loser!" he screamed.

"I didn't leave you for anyone!" I spat back, having caught my breath. "I took a new job here because I didn't want to live in Washington anymore!

"You weren't supposed to follow me," I said in a quieter voice. "You were a small part of my life for a short time, and then my life changed. I didn't leave Washington because of you—I left because of me."

He was silent, staring at me with those angry eyes.

"But now that I know the real you, the hidden you, we can never be together again," I said, thinking perhaps honesty would convince him. "You hurt me, you scare me. Those aren't the actions of someone who loves someone else."

"I only hurt and scare you to show you how much I need you. How much I miss you," he answered, his tone quiet and almost pensive.

"You're doing it the wrong way."

Suddenly his demeanor changed again, from calm to agitated and angry. "You won't listen!" he yelled. "You're not paying attention! That's why I have to do this."

"You're going to be arrested, you know."

"They have to find me first," he said with a grin.

"Where have you been staying?"

"In my car. A different place every night. Sometimes behind stores, sometimes in driveways. There are a lot of vacation homes around here, so nobody's around to throw me out. I even slept under that big tree across from the Jorgensens' a few nights. I came over, but some-one saw me and called the police. I was lucky to get away."

"What makes you think I won't tell anyone all of this?"

He stood quietly for a full minute, just staring at me. I stared back. Then, without warning, he hurled himself at me with a yell that seemed to come from the very bottom of his lungs. I leaped out of his path. He tripped and landed on his hands and knees, giving me a chance to scuttle across the broken beams and floorboards littering the ground. I reached the hole in the wall where the front door had once been and, looking behind me, crashed through onto the ground outside, stumbling just long enough for him to get to the doorway. I knew I could outrun Geoffrey if I got enough of a head start, but I kept looking behind me to see how close he was. He was catching up.

I ran straight up the hill, panting with exertion and fear, until I reached the road. I could hear Geoffrey, his feet pounding on the ground behind me. He was yelling my name. I ran along the side of the road until a car appeared in the distance. I only had to wait a minute or two until it would be at my location on the road. I stopped running and jumped up and down, waving my arms in the desperate hope that the car would see me and get to me faster.

I'll never know if the driver of the car saw me. I started running again, but stopping had cost me. Geoffrey came up behind me, breathing hard, and grabbed my arm, yanking me around to face him. He looked furious. "You'll be sorry you did that," he growled. "Come with me." He led me back to his car, threw me into the back-seat, and pulled onto the highway in a plume of gravel. I banged my head when he jerked the car onto the road. I became more alert by the time his car came to a stop again down a deserted road high above Hawi Town. I sat up higher in the seat to have a look around—we must have arrived at one of the places where he sometimes slept in his car at night. There was a folding lawn chair under a tree and sev-eral cardboard coffee cups littering the ground nearby. I wondered how he had ever found this place.

He grabbed my arm and pulled me out of the car.

"Stop pulling on me," I told him.

"You obviously intend to try getting away from me, so I have to hold onto you."

"I won't try to get away. I promise," I lied.

He made a scoffing sound. "Sit down, then," he ordered, pushing me toward the lawn chair. I sat down facing him. "I don't know what I'm going to do with you," he began. I decided to try again to appeal to reason.

"Geoffrey, you know people are going to be looking for me. Why don't you just let me go? Just drive me into Hawi and let me off on the main road. I'll tell the police I have no idea where you are. They'll believe me."

He cocked his head and looked hard at me, as if he might actually be considering my words.

"You're becoming a lot of trouble," he said, running a hand through his greasy, disheveled hair.

Sensing that he might be weakening, I pushed my advantage. "It won't be long now before someone finds my car at that farm stand and starts to wonder where I am. When they run the plates, they'll know the car belongs to me and you'll be the first person they suspect."

"Shut up, will you?" he screamed.

I shrugged. "I'm just telling you what's going to happen," I said quietly. He advanced toward me one step. I reflexively turned my face away from him, wondering at the same time how bruised and swollen I looked.

"What I need right now is time to think."

"Take all the time you need," I said unhelpfully. He sneered at me.

He paced around in the tall grass for several minutes before seeming to make up his mind. Geoffrey opened the trunk of his car and rummaged around, then turned to me, holding a length of rope. I watched him warily as he walked toward me, slapping the end of the rope against the palm of his hand.

I made the decision to run when he was about ten feet away. It was my only choice. I leaped from the lawn chair and took off in the direction of the main road. My arms pumping, I fairly flew up the dirt road, straining my ears for the sound of his footsteps behind me.

But what I heard instead were the sounds of squealing tires, of pebbles scattering, as he gunned his car. It would only be a matter of seconds before he caught me, before I became his prisoner again. I chanced a frantic look over my shoulder and saw him bearing down on me, pure fury in his eyes.

I veered off into the woods alongside the dirt track, hoping he wouldn't follow in the car. He didn't. He slammed the car to a stop and I heard him crashing after me through the trees. I didn't take the time to look behind me as I ran. I knew he wasn't far behind. I tried zigzagging around the trees, hoping it would slow him down, but it didn't. I felt something brush across my back and knew he was reaching for me. I ran faster, wondering how long I could keep going.

I hurtled out of the trees and onto the lonely road. I looked both ways in a panic, hoping a car would appear to rescue me. But there was no car in sight. I turned to my left, headed in the direction of Hawi, as Geoffrey erupted from the trees, cursing and yelling my name. I kept running, trying to focus on getting away and not think about what might happen if he caught me again.

Then he fell. Hard. I heard his body hit the pavement, but I didn't turn around. I just kept running. Another hundred feet down the road, I turned off the road, back into the trees. I finally stopped long enough to take stock of the area around me, noticing a small depression on the ground. I lay down in the tiny hollow, covering my clothes and visible skin with large leaves and fronds that had fallen from nearby trees. I lay perfectly still after that, wondering if Geoffrey would be able to hear the pounding of my heart if he came near. That is, if he didn't see me after the clumsy attempt I had made to hide myself. I held my breath and listened for his footsteps.

I heard him approaching. The sound was uneven, almost as if he was dragging his foot. Then I realized he might have hurt one of his legs or feet when he fell back on the road. Good—I hoped he was hurt.

I lay perfectly still until the steps slowed, then stopped within a few feet of my hiding place. I held my breath again. I knew he was listening. *Does he know I'm here?* He stood in place for what seemed like hours, then finally the sound of his feet began to recede. I didn't risk breathing in case he was watching and waiting. But a few moments later, I heard him calling my name softly. The sound of his voice came from the direction of the road, and I knew he had walked far enough away that I could dare to take a slow breath and release it.

I was determined to wait until it got dark to emerge from my spot. And I succeeded, though my legs began to cramp and I became panicky and claustrophobic as the hours dragged by. Dire thoughts filled my mind while I waited. What if Geoffrey came back and found me? What if I couldn't run fast enough and he caught me? What if he was waiting for me on the main road? Eventually the light filtering through the leaves covering my head began to fade. I became more and more anxious to leave my tiny space and make my way to Hawi.

Once the darkness was complete I tried moving my legs just a little bit. The noise they made under the leaves and fronds sounded deafening to my ears, but I soon realized it wasn't any louder than the fronds and leaves swaying above me in the breeze. I ventured to raise my head just above the level of the ground and scanned the area around me. It was too dark to see anything. Moving quietly on my deadened legs, I crouched awkwardly into a stooped position, hoping I would be able to bolt if I saw him. But no human sound reached my ears, no sense of him watching.

Scrambling as quickly and quietly as I could, I headed for the road. I knew I was getting closer as the trees thinned. Suddenly, I burst out of the protection of the woods and onto the road. Glancing in both directions, I hobbled across the road and stayed close to the tree line. Every few seconds I stopped moving and listened for the sound of Geoffrey's footsteps, but I didn't hear them. As my legs became used to running again, I gained confidence and speed. I hurried in the direction of Hawi, hoping the main road through town wasn't too far away.

Finally, I saw the lights of the restaurants and shops in Hawi. I ran toward them full-tilt, hope rising in my chest. I was finally going to get help.

I didn't see Geoffrey as I ran past him, hiding in the trees near Hawi's main road. I screamed when he grabbed my arm, yanking me around to look into his eyes. Even in the darkness, I could see his face was twisted with rage. It even looked like he might be missing a couple teeth.

"I knew you'd show up if I waited long enough," he growled, limping and dragging me behind him, back up the road toward the place we had been hours earlier. His voice sounded strange, like he was having trouble talking.

Then I did the only thing that my mind could register. I had to hurt him; I had to strike him where he was most vulnerable. I knew he had hurt one of his feet or legs when he fell earlier, so I started kicking him.

I kicked wildly at both legs and tried stomping on his feet. I prayed the pain would temporarily stop him from dragging me, at least long enough for me to run away from him again.

It worked. Howling with anger, he dropped my arm in shock, then flailed back toward me, trying to grasp me again.

I ran. I could hear him behind me, but he was at a disadvantage, limping from the injuries to his legs.

"I'll be watching you, Kailani! And I'll kill you!"

He continued to bellow at me, demanding that I stop, but I kept running until I reached the main road. I rushed into the first shop I came to, its welcoming lights twinkling in the large front window.

People turned and stared as I came to an abrupt stop inside the door. I hadn't thought about how terrifying I must look, but I was suddenly self-conscious.

"Can I help you?" a woman asked.

"Please, I need a phone," I gasped.

She motioned me toward the counter where two or three people waited in line to pay for their souvenirs. All the quiet chatter in the shop had come to a halt as everyone listened to my phone call.

Chapter 17

I called Liko first.

"Where have you been, K?" he demanded. "Everyone has been looking for you! The police, me, Lars, everyone! Are you all right?"

"I'll tell you everything when I see you. Can you come pick me up in Hawi?"

"I'll be there in just a few minutes. Hang tight." I told him where to find me and hung up.

I hung up the phone and turned to the woman who had let me use it. "Thank you."

"Can I call the police for you, honey?" she asked, her voice filled with concern. "Are you all right?"

"I am now, thanks. And yes, I'd like you to call the police."

It wasn't long before I heard a car speeding through Hawi and I knew Liko had come. He leaped out of the driver's side of the car and ran around to where I stood; Lars just as quickly got out of the passenger side.

Suddenly the day's pain and fear caught up with me and I stood on the sidewalk sobbing until I couldn't catch my breath, letting them take turns holding me in their arms, caressing my hair, telling me everything was okay. I had never been so happy to see anyone.

As they helped me gently into the front seat of the car, two police cars with flashing lights pulled up. I recounted for the officers the events since arriving at the farm stand in Waimea. Though they tried their best to convince me to go to a hospital to be checked out, all I wanted was to go home. They left in search of Geoffrey, though I was sure he would have found another place to hide by the time they discovered the dirt road where we had parked so many hours ago.

Finally, it was time to go home. Liko drove and Lars sat behind me, his hands on my shoulders.

Lars explained what had been happening in my absence. "There have been people out looking for you all afternoon. We got a call from the state police that your car had been found at the farm stand in Waimea, but you were nowhere to be seen. They talked to the police in Hawi and there's been a search for you since then. Everyone figured Geoffrey had something to do with your disappearance, but no one knew where he's been staying, so they didn't have any specific places to look. I'll bet they drove right past the place where you were hiding."

Liko nodded his agreement. "If I find Geoffrey, I'm going to kill him," he said between gritted teeth.

I didn't know what to say. I wanted to discourage him, but part of me found the idea appealing. We swung into the driveway and Liko parked the car. "Tomorrow we'll go up to Waimea and get your car. That is, if you're up to it," he said.

"Let's wait and see what tomorrow brings," I answered with a wan smile. I turned to face Lars. "I'm sorry I've brought all this chaos to your house. Maybe it would be better if I just went home and stayed with my parents."

"Of course you can leave if you want to, but I hope you'll stay," he said gently. "As I've told you before, none of this is your fault."

"What are we going to tell the kids when they see me?" I thought for a moment. "*I* haven't even seen me. How bad do I look?"

Lars and Liko exchanged glances. "Never mind," I said with a sigh. "You just told me everything I needed to know."

Lars started to say something, then stopped.

"What are we going to tell the kids?" I repeated.

"Marcus can handle the truth," Lars said. "And I think we can simply tell Justine that you were in an accident and you were injured. Period. Marcus won't tell her what really happened. Don't you agree, Liko?" Liko nodded.

We had reached the front door, which was yanked open by Barbie, dressed only in a nightie.

"Kailani!" she squealed. "What happened?" She peppered me with questions as she drew me into the house, then looked over my head at Lars and Liko. "I've got this. I'll get her cleaned up." She put her arm around my shoulders and walked slowly with me to my room, where she insisted on waiting while I quickly showered. When I went into my bathroom I saw my face in the mirror for the first time all day. I gasped. One eye was swollen partially shut, part of my face was purple, and dried blood crusted on my forehead and chin and pooled below my nose. I hadn't even realized my nose was bleeding. I looked away with a shudder and stepped gingerly into the shower. The water felt good on my body, but when I tried to wash my face the pain was just too much to bear. When I was done, Barbie and I went upstairs to her bathroom. I sat on a tufted stool while she dabbed at my cuts and scrapes with cotton and sterile water and ointment.

"I appreciate this, Barbie. Thanks," I told her gratefully.

"What on earth happened?"

I told her the story I had told Lars and Liko. She was horrified. "What are the children going to say when they see you?" she fretted.

"Lars already decided to tell Marcus the truth, but he thought it would be best to tell Justine that I was in an accident and not give her any more details. He thought she could handle that."

She nodded. "I suppose that's right. She's too young to hear it. It would scare her to death."

Barbie finished her ministrations to my face and stood back. "A little worse for wear, but you'll be okay. Tomorrow we can apply some makeup that will help hide the bruises. They're pretty angry-looking." I nodded ruefully.

"Now you go get some sleep," she instructed me. "I'm sure Liko will sleep near you tonight to make sure you're all right."

I hadn't thought of that, but the idea gave me some comfort. I returned downstairs, where Lars and Liko were waiting for me on the lanai. They both stood up when I appeared.

"How are you feeling?" Lars asked, concern obvious in his eyes.

"Better than I was."

"We've been talking and Liko wants to sleep in your den tonight. Do you mind?"

"Not at all. In fact, I think that would help me sleep better."

"Just let me go get my stuff," Liko said, and walked quickly down the lanai toward the guesthouse.

Lars and I were left alone on the dark and quiet lanai. He stepped forward and took me in his arms, kissing the top of my head. Silent tears rolled down my cheeks.

"I can't tell you how relieved and happy I was to see you tonight in Hawi," he said. "I have never been so worried about anything in my life." He tilted my chin up toward him. "Are you sure you're going to be all right?"

"I am now that I'm here."

He held me for a few moments, gently wiping away my tears, until we heard Liko approaching. I wished Lars and I could tell everyone how we felt about each other, but it wasn't time yet. He held me away from him. "Liko, take good care of her tonight," he said with a smile. "And Kailani, I want you to sleep all day tomorrow."

I looked at him gratefully. That sounded so tempting. I wondered if I would be able to, though. In my thoughts, I could picture Geoffrey's face looming large.

Liko led the way to my rooms and helped me into bed, pulling the sheets up to my chin. I thanked him and fell asleep almost immediately. It was very comforting to have him nearby during the night, and I'm sure that was part of the reason I slept so well.

I woke up late the next morning to the sound of a very noisy bird outside my closed bedroom window. For one brief, carefree moment I forgot the horror of the previous day, then it came back to me in a rush of dread. Lying in bed would only increase the apprehension I already felt, so I stepped out of bed cautiously, wondering whether my muscles would protest.

They did. My legs and back ached, my arms were leaden, and my shoulders were knotted and tense, as if all the stress of the last twenty-four hours had spread overnight and seeped into every corner of my body. I reached up and touched my face, wincing as my finger brushed against one of the lacerations that Barbie had treated. I looked into the bathroom mirror. The swelling had gone down a bit, but the bruises had purpled overnight.

I ventured into the den, where Liko was sitting in my armchair with the newspaper.

"K!" he greeted me. "How are you feeling?" He put the paper aside and stood up. "Can I get you coffee?"

"I've been better, thanks, but at least I'm here. I'll go out and get some coffee. I need to move around a bit. Thanks for staying with me last night. I hope you weren't too uncomfortable."

"You kidding? I can sleep anywhere," he replied with a wide

smile. We went out to the kitchen together, where the coffeemaker was on. It smelled wonderful.

"Did someone take the kids to the bus stop this morning?" I fretted.

"Lars did. Stop worrying."

"I can't help it," I replied, pouring each of us a large mug of steaming coffee. "Every time I think of how terrible yesterday was, I—"

"K, don't think about it. The kids are fine. Lars will pick them up at the bus stop this afternoon and we'll do it every single day until Geoffrey is behind bars. Or dead, which would be even better."

I shook my head, as if trying to rid myself of the memories. Liko meant well, but he didn't seem to truly understand how terrified I still felt and how edgy I would feel until Geoffrey no longer occupied a large space in my mind. I wondered if that time would ever come, even if he was caught.

"I called your parents and told them that you were in an accident. I hope that's okay," he said.

"Thanks. I don't want them to know what really happened. They'll just worry."

"They wanted to come and see you right away, but I convinced them to wait a few days."

"Thanks, Liko. I want to give the police a chance to clear this up before my parents visit."

We took our coffee out to the lanai and sat watching the Pacific change color from dark, dusky blue to a brilliant, sparkling aquamarine. A whale played lazily offshore, slapping the surface of the water with its fin and tail. It felt surreal, like there were no cares outside the walls of this house, but the nagging fear in my mind prevented me from enjoying the whale's antics, which I normally would have loved.

"I feel like I'm a prisoner here," I finally said.

"You won't feel like that once the cops catch him, K. It won't be like this forever."

Just then Lars walked onto the lanai. He saw Liko and me and his eyes lit up. "How's the patient this morning?" he asked.

"Sore, but much happier today," I answered. "I slept in and it felt so good."

"I'm glad. Do you feel like going back to sleep?"

"No—actually, I feel like getting back to work. Do you think that would be okay?"

He smiled. "I should have known that would be what you wanted to do today. If you think you're up to it—then sure. Go ahead and cook to your heart's content." Liko turned to pick up his coffee mug and Lars winked at me. I smiled at him, loving the warm feeling I got when he looked at me.

"Where's Barbie?" I asked.

Lars shrugged. "I haven't seen her."

Liko chimed in. "I saw her go upstairs earlier. She must still be up there."

"Did she have breakfast?" I asked Liko.

"I don't know. You want me to find out?"

Lars put up his hand. "Wait. If Barbie wants breakfast, let her come down and get it. You are not her servant, Liko. And as for you, Kailani, don't be going upstairs to give her food. You are supposed to be healing, not overdoing it."

"I won't overdo it, I promise."

I walked slowly to the kitchen, where the kids and Liko had already put their dishes in the dishwasher for me and where the counters sparkled. Liko followed me. "Did you do this?" I asked, waving my hand to indicate the clean counters.

He grinned. "I'm not just a great tutor, you know. Just don't ask me to make anything but coffee."

"I won't."

"You must be feeling a little better," Liko remarked. "I think I just saw a smile."

"It feels good just to be here," I answered. There was a rapping on the front door. Liko went to answer it and came back a moment later with two police officers in tow. A digital camera hung from the neck of one of the officers.

I led them out to the long dining table on the lanai, where I sat across from them.

The older-looking officer began talking. "Detective Alana filled us in on what's been going on between you and this Geoffrey Corcoran. Can you tell us what happened yesterday?"

Once again I related the events of the previous day, beginning with my trip to Waimea and ending with Liko and Lars coming to pick me up in Hawi. The officers didn't interrupt while I told my story. When I was finished, they began asking questions.

"So you think he followed you to Waimea, or did he just happen to see you up there?"

"I don't know. I didn't notice him following me, but he could have been behind me and I just wasn't paying attention."

They asked me to tell them again about being taken from the abandoned ranch on the Kohala Mountain Road to the property where Geoffrey kept me during the afternoon. I complied, shuddering at the memory.

Liko held up his hand. "Can I say something?" he asked.

The officers looked at him expectantly, saying nothing.

"Geoffrey has threatened to kill Kailani. Can you guys keep her safe?"

The older officer nodded. "We are planning on posting an officer at the end of the Jorgensens' driveway. There's not much reason to come down this road unless a person is coming to this house, so any car that comes down here will be visible to the officers and won't see the police car until it's too late to turn around and go back to the main road."

Liko looked at me, nodding. "That sounds good. What do you think, K?"

"I'm relieved to hear it."

"So tell us more about the place where you were kept," one of the officers said.

I told them everything I could remember about the place, but I still remembered little of the ride to the secluded spot, since I had banged my head so hard.

Just then Lars walked out. He needed no introduction. The officers were well aware of his legal circumstances. He offered to provide a statement and they promised to talk to him after they took Liko's statement. They turned back to me and Lars left with a reassuring smile in my direction. I smiled weakly at him.

The officers then asked me to go over the history of my relationship with Geoffrey from the time I met him in Washington. Finally, after I had given them all the information I could remember, it was time for the part of the interview I had been dreading. The younger officer needed to document my injuries by photographing them. I was self-conscious and nervous, but they let Liko stay with me. We walked over to the side of the lanai where the light was best and the officer took what seemed like a thousand photos of my face, neck, head, arms, and legs.

When the ordeal was over I heaved a long sigh of relief. We returned to the dining table and the officers asked Liko about his role in the previous day's events. They asked him what he knew about Geoffrey and about any instances during which he and Geoffrey had interacted. There had been none.

The officers then asked that Lars be called out to the lanai. Liko went to get him from his office. When Lars came out, he looked different. His forehead was creased, the corners of his mouth drawn. I looked at him inquisitively, seeking a reason for the change. He gave me a wan smile as he walked past me and sat down at the long table.

Liko and I left quietly. We returned to the kitchen, and Liko only agreed to go back to the guesthouse on the condition that I would rest before lunch and let him make sandwiches for us all. I agreed, finally feeling the exhaustive effects of the time spent with the officers. I was worried about Lars too. I hoped to have time alone to talk to him during the afternoon and find out what was bothering him.

I was able to sleep for just a little while before lunch. I went out into the kitchen to find Liko making a mess with sandwich fixings and leftover soup. I laughed. "It looks like you're planning to feed an army!"

He turned to face me, grinning. "I like this cooking thing. I think I may give it a try!"

"Well, don't do *too* good a job or I'll be out of work," I answered, smirking. "How did the interview go with Lars?"

He shrugged. "Fine, I guess. They're out there talking to Barbie right now. Probably asking about what she had to do to get you cleaned up and bandaged."

I nodded absentmindedly. I was considering whether I should go see Lars in his office while Barbie was talking to the police, but I decided against it. I didn't want Liko to wonder why I had to talk to Lars privately.

I was helping Liko arrange the sandwiches on a tray when I heard Barbie leading the officers to the front door.

"Good," said Liko, rubbing his hands together. "I'm starving."

We heard the door close and moments later Barbie came into the kitchen. Letting out a long breath, she asked, "Liko, did you make lunch?"

He held up the tray and followed her to the lanai. I rapped quietly on Lars's office door.

"Come in."

I opened the door just a bit and poked my head around it. "Do you want some lunch?"

"Is it on the lanai?"

"Yes."

"Is Barbie out there?"

"Yes."

"Then no. I'll wait until she goes back upstairs."

I was surprised. Despite having announced their divorce, Lars and Barbie had continued to eat meals together for the sake of the kids. This was the first time Lars had openly refused to eat on the lanai because Barbie was out there.

"Would you like to eat in here?"

He thought for a moment. "No, I'm not going to be a prisoner in my office because I'm mad at Barbie. I'll eat on the lanai when she's gone. You'd better not wait for me."

I wanted to reach out to him, to be the same reassuring presence for him that he had been for me. "You okay?" I asked tentatively.

He shook his head ruefully. "I'll fill you in later."

I smiled at him and finally he smiled back. "You and the kids are the sunshine in this house," he said.

I shut the door quietly behind me and joined Liko and Barbie. They were talking quietly until I came up to the table, then stopped. Barbie wiped her lips daintily with her napkin and asked, "How are you feeling today, Kailani? Better, I hope."

I pulled out a chair and sat down. "Physically, I think I'll feel much better by tomorrow. Mentally, I'm much better."

She nodded as if to prove that she was listening, but I knew her mind was elsewhere. *What was going on?*

The three of us ate lunch in relative silence. The only sounds came from the birds that sang vociferously in the nearby trees. I watched the ocean waves mindlessly, grateful for the beauty of the place and content not to contribute to any conversation. Barbie didn't eat much. She sat, looking far away, while Liko and I ate. When he was finished, the two of them got up and started to walk away. Liko turned to me. "K, do you need help?"

"No," I assured him. "I'm happy to get back to work. You go."

He nodded and caught up with Barbie, who was heading down toward the pool. *Aren't they even trying to hide their relationship anymore?* I was amazed. I knew Lars still didn't know Barbie was having an affair with Liko—otherwise Liko would have been fired and told to leave the house immediately. Liko had to be more careful if he was going to keep his job much longer.

I slowly piled the lunch dishes on the tray and carried it back to the kitchen. Lars came in a few minutes later, holding a newspaper. "I thought I heard noise in here, so I figured lunch was over. I'll grab a sandwich and eat now." He helped himself to a sandwich from the counter and poured a glass of iced tea. "We'll find a time to talk later, I promise," he said with a weak smile. I wished I could join him, but it wasn't the time. Not with Barbie and Liko nearby.

I finished cleaning up from lunch—Liko had made quite a mess—and began getting things ready to prepare dinner. I wanted to have everything close at hand so when I started dinner I wouldn't have to be running back and forth looking for ingredients. Then I went to my room to rest again.

I didn't realize how tired I was. I slept heavily for a few hours and awoke to the sounds of the kids in the kitchen, rummaging for snacks. I went to the door to help them. They seemed surprised to see me.

"Kailani! How are you feeling?" Justine asked, looking concerned. She was clearly shocked by my appearance, but was doing a good job trying to hide it.

I smiled at her. "Much better, thanks. Can I get something for you guys?"

"No, I think you should rest," she answered, sounding like a little nurse. "We can get our own snacks."

"Who picked you up today at the bus stop?"

"Dad," Marcus said. "Do you know what's up with him?" I shook my head and he changed the subject. "Want me to make dinner?" he asked eagerly.

"Sure."

"What are we having?"

"Salmon with a ginger glaze, sticky mango rice, and braised baby bok choy with mac nuts."

"Cool. What do I do first?"

"Your homework, for starters. Then when Liko says it's okay, come to the kitchen and I'll get you all set up."

He grinned. "Sounds good." Grabbing a handful of almonds and a container of yogurt, he left the room. I watched him go, smiling and shaking my head. He was definitely not the same boy who had demanded soda and cookies when I had first started at the Jorgensens' house.

"Can I help?" Justine asked.

"Of course! But you have to do your homework first. Come and find me when you're ready to help. I'll be in my room."

"Okay. Get some rest," she advised.

I eased myself into the armchair in my den, hoping to rest my eyes until the kids came to find me before dinner, but I must have fallen asleep. I woke up just a short time later to the sound of shouting coming from the lanai. Hurrying to see what the commotion was all about, I met Lars coming from his office, his eyes hard and his mouth set in a grim line.

"What's up?" I asked him.

"I can only guess," he answered.

I didn't have any idea what he was talking about, but I was soon to learn the reason he had been out of sorts all day.

Marcus was standing at the table, his homework fluttering in the soft breeze, shouting at Barbie, who was sitting across from him. Justine sat looking from her mother to her brother, eyes wide with . . . fear? Incomprehension? I looked around for Liko, but he wasn't there.

Barbie looked up at Lars, but looked away again quickly.

"How can you do this to us?" shouted Marcus.

"Marcus, darling, you simply have to calm down before we can talk about this," Barbie answered smoothly.

Marcus turned to his father. "Did you know she's pregnant? And she won't tell us who the father is!"

That's when I knew why Lars had been angry at Barbie. He knew she was planning to tell the kids about her pregnancy.

He walked over to the table and put his hand on Marcus's arm. Marcus shook it off as Lars spoke to him and Justine. "I know it's hard for you and your sister. It's hard for everyone. But we're getting a divorce and this is just what happens sometimes when marriages break up."

"But how can you stand it knowing it's some other dude's kid?"

"That's between your mother and me."

"Do you know who the father is?" Marcus demanded.

"That's also between your mother and me." Lars obviously didn't want to appear as clueless as the children were, and he was also trying to protect Barbie from having to discuss the issue in front of everyone.

Barbie nodded in agreement. "Yes, that's true. I needed to tell you two because it won't be long before I start to show and I wanted you to know before then."

"Thanks," Marcus sneered.

"When will the baby be born?" Justine wanted to know.

"In about six and a half months," her mother answered.

"That's gross," Marcus said sullenly. "And now our family is ruined. Thanks, Mom."

Barbie looked taken aback. I was even surprised to hear Marcus's reaction to her pregnancy. "Marcus, you'll see. You'll love the baby when it comes," she said, apparently trying to soothe him.

"No I won't."

"You'll see. You will, I promise."

"Just like you promised to be faithful when you married Dad?"

"Marcus, that's not fair. A lot has happened in the years since Dad and I got married."

"I don't want to talk about it," he said suddenly. He gathered up his books and stalked off, calling over his shoulder as he went, "Kailani, make dinner without me. I'm not helping. And I'm not hungry."

Justine pushed back her chair and hurried after him. Barbie remained at the table with her head in her hands. Lars looked at her with disdain. "You brought this on yourself, you know."

"I know that," she answered, looking up at him and scowling. "They had to know, though."

Lars sighed. "I guess. Too bad they have to grow up so fast." He turned and walked slowly back to his office. I expected him to go talk to Marcus, but he must have decided that Marcus needed some time alone.

I had been rooted to the spot while the angry discussion had taken place, but I was suddenly embarrassed to have witnessed it. I felt sorry for all of them—even Barbie, whose carelessness had caused all the pain.

I returned to the kitchen quietly. Barbie sat alone at the table for a while longer, then I heard her head slowly upstairs.

I didn't know whether anyone would feel like eating, but I made dinner as usual. I kept the salmon warm while I waited, sipping water with lemon on the lanai. Eventually, Liko walked up to me from the direction of the guesthouse.

"I heard all the commotion earlier and didn't want to interrupt," he said.

"That was smart."

"What happened?"

"Barbie told the kids she's pregnant."

"Didn't go over too well, then?"

I shook my head. "Want something to eat?"

"Nah. I'm not really hungry."

The question I had been dying to ask Liko—the question that hung unspoken in the air between us—remained unasked. I suppose Liko didn't know who the father was, either. It was possible that even Barbie didn't know. But I couldn't help wondering if the baby would be born with the brown skin and black hair of a native Hawaiian. Like Liko.

I knew he was thinking about it too. Somehow it seemed safer, as if we could postpone the inevitable, if we didn't talk about it. But sooner or later we would all know the answer. I didn't know what to hope for; if the baby wasn't Liko's, then Liko would know Barbie was sleeping with yet another man during their affair. But if it *was* Liko's, then the upheaval in the family could be devastating. It would be best for everyone in the long run, I supposed, if the baby were the child of some other man. Liko stood at the railing and watched the sun as it slowly descended to the west, then said "see you later" and left.

I went back into the kitchen and started putting dinner in the refrigerator. I would have to throw the salmon away because it would taste awful reheated, but Lars walked in before I got to the trash.

"Any dinner?"

I looked at him in surprise. "You're just in time. I was getting rid of the salmon. Want some?"

"Sure. Want to join me?"

"I don't think I should."

"Listen. After everything that hit the fan this afternoon, I think we can risk being seen together sitting at the same table on the lanai."

I shrugged. "If you think so."

"Come on." He took the plate I handed him and led the way to the table. I followed him with a small plate of my own. We sat opposite each other and ate in silence, both of us content to listen to the quiet sounds of the palm fronds rustling and the waves slipping in and out below us. Marcus stalked across the lanai while we were eating. "Can I get you anything, Marcus?" I asked. He stood still for a moment, looking past us out to the ocean, and answered, "I'll find something myself. Thanks."

He returned a minute later, holding a plate with a bit of salmon and some sliced mango on it. "Not hungry, son?" asked Lars.

"Not really." With that, Marcus returned to his room.

Lars sighed. "That's what I was upset about today. Barbie told me she was going to tell the kids about her baby and I wanted her to wait. I thought we should all discuss it together, but she wanted to tell them on her own. And now look what's happened. Everything is a mess." He chuckled mirthlessly. "I don't think she even knows who the father is. Can you believe it?" He shook his head ruefully. "What a wreck we made of things, Barbie and I."

I wanted to reach out and cover his hand with mine, to tell him everything was going to be all right. But I didn't dare, because I didn't know whether everything would be all right or not.

Chapter 18

The next morning I drove the kids to the bus stop. I was feeling much better and I was anxious to get outside and away from the house. As I waved good-bye to them, I considered whether to venture down to the water for a little while. Looking around, I saw no one across the road at the monkeypod tree. Two police cars sat up the road a bit, but otherwise there were no people in sight. Geoffrey must be taking a day off, I thought wryly. Touching the bruise on my face, I considered again. But the blue water was so inviting and the sound of the waves was so peaceful and mesmerizing that I went through the house and, after tidying up the kitchen from breakfast, wandered down to the water.

I spread my towel on an outcropping of lava rock to the left of the small cove in front of the house. Clasping my hands around my knees, I closed my eyes and lifted my face to the sky. The rays from the sun filled me with warmth and serenity. I heard a noise behind me and turned toward it.

Barbie was walking slowly down toward the water, shielding her eyes from the brightness with her hand. She hadn't seen me. A long white sundress hid any evidence of her pregnancy. I sat quietly, wondering whether I should say something to her. She probably wanted to be alone, so I wasn't sure if I should make my presence known. I shrank into myself, hoping she wouldn't see me.

She continued walking across the jagged lava rock to the shoreline, where the water splashed onto her sandaled feet. Her shoulders rose and fell heavily, as if something was weighing her down. I wondered how much she thought of Lars and the kids and her crumbling marriage. I wondered for the first time how she felt about being pregnant again. I remembered my sister's excitement when she was pregnant with my niece; that excitement seemed to be missing from Barbie.

I was so intent on watching Barbie that I didn't hear anyone creeping up behind me. Suddenly, rough hands grabbed my shoulders, forcing me off the ground. I gasped and somehow noticed, out of the corner of my eye, Barbie turning toward me in surprise. Then, instead of running to help me, she ran toward the house. I called to her, but she kept running, stumbling twice on the jagged rocks.

I whipped around as quickly as my bruised body would allow. Geoffrey was staring me in the face. His mouth, missing two front teeth, was twisted into an ugly scowl and his nostrils flared with anger and hatred. I took a step backward, but he held me fast.

"I told you I'd find you," he growled. His eye twitched. The man standing before me was so different from the person I had known in Washington.

I searched my mind for something to say that would calm him down, something that would help to assuage his anger. I was afraid of saying the wrong thing and enraging him further.

I looked around wildly for help, but there was no one to be seen. Not even the gardeners were out today. *Where did Barbie go?* I hoped she was getting the police who were on guard up by the main road. *Geoffrey must have hiked along the coast to avoid running into them.*

"No one is coming to help you," he sneered. "Why would they? You're a liar."

"I'm sorry you feel that way, Geoffrey." I couldn't deny it—I *had* lied to him when I told him I was dating Liko.

"I loved you," he said, his voice breaking. Suddenly he shook his head violently. "But not anymore! Now that I see who you really are, I can't believe I ever loved you!"

Without warning, he pushed me backward, toward the edge of the lava rock that fell away to the ocean that was relentlessly dashing itself on the rocks below. I fell back, scraping my elbows and back on the black shards of the ancient lava. I had to play for time. My only hope was to distract him so that I could run to safety. He took a step toward me, his hands outstretched, as I twisted slowly onto my hands and knees.

"Geoffrey! Wait!" I was surprised to hear my own voice. "You can't do this. Barbie saw you. You'll be caught and in jail by tomorrow. The police are nearby—it won't take them long to get here."

He looked behind him, and I saw my chance. I was still on my knees, so I lunged forward and pushed his legs. He buckled and fell to the ground, but was quick enough to reach out and grab my ankle as I tried to scramble past him toward the house.

I fell again, this time slicing my arm and side on the lava rock. He still held my ankle, so I tried kicking him. When a roar erupted from his throat, I knew I had hit him. I didn't know where my strength was coming from, but I was grateful for it and hoped it would last until I could get away from him.

Suddenly I heard a voice yelling my name. I looked up and saw Lars crashing through the brush, making his way toward me and Geoffrey. Barbie was hurrying behind him, threading a path more carefully through the bushes and tropical growth.

Lars reached the rocky outcropping where I was still lying, breathless and hurting; Geoffrey was struggling to his knees. As Lars took another step closer, Geoffrey reached into his pocket and pulled out a switchblade. His thumb twitched for a split second and a gleaming knife sprang from the handle. I watched with horror as Lars continued toward Geoffrey.

"Get away from her," Lars warned.

"I'll kill her first," Geoffrey replied.

"Don't, Lars," I pleaded. Barbie had reached the three of us on the rocks and screamed. I heard—rather than saw—Liko running toward us, his long black hair flying behind him.

Geoffrey brought the switchblade close to his body, then suddenly slashed out toward Lars, cutting him across the back of his hand. Blood oozing from his wound, Lars tried to grab the switchblade with his other hand. Geoffrey laughed at him, then lunged forward, missing him with the knife. I had pushed myself to a standing position, and Geoffrey headed toward me, hatred flashing in his eyes.

Lars grabbed Geoffrey by the tail of his shirt. He whipped Geoffrey around and planted both hands firmly on his chest. Before I could react, Lars had pushed him toward the edge of the lava rock. Barbie was still screaming.

Liko ran past her, yelling out to me, "You all right, K?" He dashed to the spot where Lars was struggling. Geoffrey reached out to grasp Lars's arm, but Lars yanked it out of reach.

My world was spinning in slow motion. I watched, speechless, as Lars gave one tremendous push against Geoffrey's chest and sent him tumbling backward over the edge of the lava *pali*. Geoffrey's scream died away as the wind carried it off over the Pacific.

So many things were happening at once. The police were making their way quickly down the slope to the *pali*. Liko was running toward Barbie as she slid to the ground, apparently unconscious. Lars was standing, bent over at the edge of the *pali*, his hands on his knees, breathing heavily. I stood there, stunned, by what I had just seen. Lars straightened up and turned toward me just as I started walking toward him.

"You'd better not look," he advised me. "He didn't survive. He's down on the rocks."

I slumped against his chest as he held me to him. I didn't care who saw and I don't think he did, either. When I turned around to walk back toward the house, Liko had revived Barbie and he and one of the officers were helping her to stand up. Blood trickled from a wound on her forehead where she had bumped it when she fainted.

"Is she all right?" Lars called to Liko.

"Yeah, I think so. She should probably get checked out at the hospital, though."

The other officers were standing on the edge of the *pali*, looking down at Geoffrey. One took out his radio and called for two ambulances. I had to fight the urge to go see Geoffrey's body for myself, just to make sure he was dead.

One of the officers accompanied us up to the house, where Barbie lay down on the lanai. When the ambulances arrived, three paramedics took care of her, swiftly checking her out and lifting her onto a gurney. They wheeled her out of the house and into the waiting ambulance while Lars and I spoke to the police. Lars asked Liko to accompany Barbie to the hospital.

The officer who had come up to the house questioned me and Lars while the crew from the other ambulance carefully wheeled a second gurney across the lawn in front of the lanai. I didn't want to watch Geoffrey's body being brought up from the shoreline, so I retreated to the kitchen, where I distracted myself by preparing lunch for myself and anyone else who might be hungry.

Finally, once the police had asked all their questions and the paramedics had left, I lay back against the cushions of the daybed. I closed my eyes, listening to the ocean that had so recently witnessed the violent death of a violent man. I was relieved for myself, for the kids, and even for Geoffrey, who was no longer a prisoner of his pain and anger. Tears trickled down my cheeks, but whether they were for me or for Marcus and Justine or for Geoffrey—or for all of us—I didn't know. I was startled when someone touched me.

I opened my eyes. Lars stood looking down at me, a gentle smile on his face. "How are you doing?" he asked.

I shook my head, unable to speak, the tears now falling more freely. He sat down next to me on the daybed and put his arm around me. I leaned my head into the warmth and strength of his shoulder. "It's over," he said quietly. "You don't have to worry about him anymore." I nodded, overcome with everything that had happened and longing for someone to take care of me. Lars seemed to understand just what I needed, and we sat in silence for a long time. The kids were still at school, so with just the two of us in the house we didn't have to worry about anyone else watching or wondering about the nature of our relationship.

We sat like that for a long time, until Lars got a text from Liko.

Barbie OK. We're on our way back.

He sighed. "Thank God the kids missed all of this. Poor Justine wouldn't know how to handle it."

"What about Marcus?"

Lars considered for a moment. "I don't know. Sometimes he's strong, but other times he surprises me. He feels things more deeply than I give him credit for."

He offered me his hand and helped me stand up, walking back to the kitchen with me, then returning to his office. It wasn't long before I heard the front door open and Liko's voice in the hallway. He was helping Barbie up the stairs. Lars came out of his office and took one of her arms. Together, the two men maneuvered her up to the master bedroom. When they came back downstairs, Liko told me that Barbie had asked for something to drink. I fixed a tray with iced tea and a light lunch and took it up to her.

When I had situated the tray near her bed and checked to make sure she didn't need anything else, she asked me to sit down on a long ottoman that had been placed under one of the huge windows overlooking the ocean.

She didn't waste any time before getting right to the point. "Is there something going on between you and Lars?"

I must have looked shocked, because she laughed lightly. "I knew from the way he reacted in his office this morning when I told him you were in trouble down by the water. He practically flew to help you. That's not typical employer behavior."

I opened my mouth to speak, but she stopped me. "It's okay. I'm not jealous and I'm not going to fire you. But I obviously don't want you working for me after the divorce is final."

"I know," I answered quietly.

"This makes us even," she noted, a conspiratorial tone in her voice. "Liko told me you know about him and me. So you don't tell Lars my secret and I won't make a fuss about your relationship with my husband."

I hesitated. The relationship between Barbie and Liko—it was possible that he was even the father of her baby—had moved along much further than the one between Lars and me. I couldn't start out a relationship with Lars by lying to him about Liko and Barbie.

Barbie sensed my hesitation. "You wouldn't want the kids to know you've been carrying on with their father right in their own home."

"Barbie, we haven't been carrying on. That's not fair."

"If I think you've said one word to him, I won't hesitate to tell the kids that you and Lars have been seeing each other." *And what about you, sleeping with the tutor?* I wanted to scream.

I was trapped. I didn't want the kids to know about my feelings for their father—not yet—but if Lars asked what I knew about Liko and Barbie I couldn't lie to him. I stood up and turned my back to her, leaving her room with as much dignity and confidence as my bruised body and spirit could muster.

I was fixing a tray of snacks in the kitchen when Marcus and Justine came home from school. Justine immediately noticed the bandages on my knees. "What happened?" she asked.

"Oh, nothing," I answered breezily. "I just fell and scraped my knees."

Marcus looked at me askance. "Your arm is scraped too."

"Well, I stumbled out on the lava rocks and landed on my knees, then rolled over onto my shoulder."

"I hope you feel better," Justine called over her shoulder as she skipped from the room.

"What really happened?" Marcus asked.

Lars appeared in the doorway. "Kailani was attacked by Geoffrey today and that's why she's scraped up."

Marcus turned to his father. "Where did it happen?"

"Out on the lava rocks, just like I said," I answered.

"Where's Geoffrey?"

Lars looked at me for a moment, then said quietly, "Geoffrey is dead. We don't have to worry about him anymore."

Marcus's eyes widened. "How'd he die?"

"I pushed him over the edge of the rocks and he was killed when he hit the rocks at the bottom. That's enough of the gory details. I don't want to discuss it any further and I'm sure Kailani doesn't want to relive the experience."

They both looked at me. I shook my head. "No. I definitely don't."

Marcus looked from his father to me and said, "You're lucky Dad was around to take care of the guy. He might have hurt you even worse."

I nodded, not trusting myself to say anything without going to pieces. "I'm glad you're okay," Marcus said, then he took a snack and went out to wait for Liko.

Lars stepped closer to me and brushed his hand across my cheek very lightly. "I'm so glad I was home today. I don't even want to think of what would have happened if you had been here alone when Geoffrey showed up."

I shuddered. "I don't want to think about it, either." He kissed my lips ever so gently.

"Aren't you afraid that someone's going to see?" I asked.

"Not anymore. I learned this morning that I don't care who sees." He kissed me again.

And indeed, someone did see. Justine made a tiny noise in the doorway and Lars and I turned to stare at her.

"What's going on?" she asked in her high-pitched voice.

Lars answered her. "Justine, it's probably time for you and your brother to know that Kailani and I have become very fond of each other."

"But you and Mom—" she began.

"Are getting a divorce," he finished. "Neither your mom nor I have been happy for a long time. Your mom is beginning a new life without me, and it's time for me to begin a new life too. Kailani makes me happy. And I think," he said as he looked at me, "I make her happy too."

I nodded. Justine looked from Lars to me and back to Lars. "Does Marcus know?"

"I don't think so," Lars said. "I think it's time to tell him, though."

Justine stood and nodded, not moving from the doorway.

"Move," Marcus ordered from behind her. "I have to get in there."

Justine slipped into the kitchen, watching her father. She raised her eyebrows at him, nodding toward Marcus.

"Marcus, there's something we need to discuss."

"What?" Marcus asked, shoving a handful of rice cracker mix in his mouth.

"Kailani and I are—uh—in a relationship."

Marcus cocked his head. "What do you mean by that?"

"It means that we're going to be spending a lot more time together and that I'd like you and Justine to get to know her better."

Marcus nodded slowly. "Okay. What about Mom?"

"What about your mom?" Lars asked.

"Does Mom know about you and *her*?" Marcus asked, jerking his head in my direction.

"If she doesn't, she will soon," Lars replied.

"Actually, she does know," I spoke up. All eyes focused on me. "She asked me about it earlier. She's not mad, and she understands." I looked at Marcus, hoping he too, could understand. I glanced at Lars, who was looking at me in surprise.

"I didn't know that," he said.

"I just hadn't had a chance to talk to you about it yet."

Marcus took his snack and walked out to the lanai.

I looked at Lars. "He didn't seem thrilled."

"I know, but he's got a lot on his mind. I think he'll love the idea once he gets used to it. If Barbie can get used to it, Marcus certainly can."

He kissed me again and went back to his office. Liko came looking for me just a few minutes later. "What did the doctors tell Barbie?"

"They said the baby is probably fine, since she didn't hit the ground that hard and the baby is still so tiny."

"That's a relief."

"Yeah." Liko seemed pensive.

"What's up?" I asked.

"I asked her about the baby's father on the way home."

"And?"

"She thinks it's me."

Though I had known that was certainly a possibility, it came as a shock to hear Liko say it.

"But she's not sure?"

"She seemed pretty sure."

"So what's next?"

He took a deep breath and let it out slowly. "Lars will find out sooner or later. I should probably sit down and tell him like a man." When I didn't say anything, he asked, "What do you think?"

"I agree—I guess. Is there a possibility that you and Barbie will raise the baby together?"

"I didn't ask her that."

"Do you want to be involved in raising the child?"

"Yes."

"Then tell her. Even if she doesn't want you involved, she can't keep you away from the baby if you're the father. *If* you're the father," I repeated.

"So you think I should tell the kids?"

"You and Barbie need to make that decision together, but I would think you'd want Marcus and Justine to know before the baby is born."

His shoulders slumped a bit and he looked tired. "Sort out your thoughts, and then go talk to Barbie and tell her what you want," I advised.

"I will."

I didn't see Liko again that evening except from a distance on the lanai. After he helped both kids with their homework, he vanished to the guesthouse and didn't return to the main house for dinner.

I served dinner to Barbie and the kids in the small dining area that night, because the wind was howling across the lanai. The kids and Liko had difficulty keeping their books and papers from flying away while they did homework, so I decided the small dining area would be calmer. I returned to the kitchen after I served the meal. I could hear knives and forks tinkling against the plates, but there wasn't much conversation until dinner was almost over.

"Mom, Kailani told us you know about her and Dad. How can you let her keep working here when she and Dad are fooling around?" Marcus asked.

"Because she's a very good cook and because it really doesn't bother me," she answered simply.

"Why doesn't it bother you?" Justine piped up.

"I believe your father likes Kailani because she's everything I'm not, and that makes her interesting to him. I'm a medical professional; she's basically a servant. I've got classic European features; she has the plain features of the island natives. I'm sure your father finds that exotic, at least for now."

I rolled my eyes.

She continued. "I care about the way I'm dressed, she obviously doesn't. You see? There are lots of things that separate me from Kailani."

"But he chose her," Justine said, a hint of confusion in her voice.

"That's because your father has decided he no longer wants to be married, Justine dear, and he wants to see what else is available," Barbie replied, the tiniest hint of an edge in her tone.

"How do you two feel about it?" Barbie asked after a few moments of silence.

Marcus spoke first. "I think it sucks. Everything is ruined."

"I feel funny around Kailani," Justine added.

"Well, I really don't think your father's interest in Kailani is going to last. So don't worry about that. And Marcus, you'll see that it will be better for everyone once the divorce is final. I'll be happier, and someday you'll be happier too."

The woman is so selfish.

I couldn't listen to their conversation any longer. I took a tray with plates of dessert out and set them down in silence. When I returned to the kitchen, I didn't bother eavesdropping on them—I went right to my den and sat down, flipping through television channels impatiently.

How dare she insinuate that the relationship between me and Lars was just a temporary fling? She has no knowledge of real love, real trust, real companionship. That's where we really differ. I was furious. *How dare she imply to the kids that the divorce was simply because Lars didn't want to be married anymore? That she was blameless?*

I waited to clear the table until they all went their separate ways. I couldn't look at any of them. It was no wonder Justine felt weird and Marcus was angry about the situation between me and Lars. Barbie was feeding them lies about us, letting them believe the divorce was the result of Lars's wandering eye.

Over the next few days, things were tense and quiet. I spent as little time around Barbie as I could. The kids didn't want much to do with me; Liko was only around to help with their schoolwork, and Lars was on O'ahu for business. Barbie recovered quickly, following her faint on the rocks, but she was still experiencing the sickness that went hand in hand with pregnancy.

She asked one evening if I would prepare a tray for her so she could eat dinner in her room. When I returned to see if she had finished her meal, I could hear voices from her sitting room. She was talking to Liko.

". . . to be a part of your life when the baby is born. I want to help raise her. Or him," he was saying.

Barbie murmured something, but I couldn't quite hear.

"We don't have to get married. I just want to be involved, that's all."

"How come you're going there?" Liko asked.

Where? I strained my ears to hear better.

"I'll visit you, then."

More mumbled words.

"You can't keep me away from the baby. I have a right to be involved."

I could hear a chair being scraped across the floor and I knew Liko would be heading downstairs any minute. I turned around and went down to the hallway below. When I heard his foot on the step above, I started up the stairs again. He looked glum.

"What's wrong?" I asked.

"I'll tell you later."

I continued up to Barbie's room and retrieved the tray. She thanked me from the bathroom, where I could see her puffy-eyed reflection in the mirror.

"Is everything okay, Barbie?"

"Not really," she sniffled. "I've made quite a mess of things, haven't I?"

"It'll all work out," I answered sympathetically. I felt sorry for her, despite the decisions she had made that had brought her to this place in her life.

"I'm not so sure. I'm moving to California when the baby is born," she said.

I was surprised to hear it. "Really?" I asked dumbly.

She nodded. "I never wanted to leave there in the first place, but I understand why Lars brought us here. It was partly my fault." I wanted to say it had been almost exclusively her fault, but I kept my mouth shut.

"Did Liko tell you he's the father of the baby?" she asked.

"Yes. Are you sure?"

She nodded. "Positive."

It was none of my business, but I asked anyway. "Are you going to tell the kids?"

She looked at me sideways, as if agreeing that it was none of my business, but she answered. "We'll have to. Liko and I." She put her head in her hands. "What a mess."

"When are you going to tell them?"

"When the time is right."

That was my cue to stop asking questions and leave her alone. I went back downstairs and continued making dinner for the rest of the family. Lars was due home in just a little while, and he had texted me that he'd like to have dinner with the kids.

It was wonderful to see him when he got home. He kissed me the way I wanted him to, not caring whether anyone saw us, and gave me a necklace he had bought in Honolulu.

I served dinner to him and the kids at the dining table on the lanai. He was full of stories of the surfers he had met on his business trip and some of their accomplishments. Marcus, especially, was in awe. "I'd love to spend more time on the water, Dad."

Lars looked at him pointedly. "You keep those grades up and I'll see what can be done."

Marcus grinned. I took dessert out for them and Justine noticed my necklace. "Where did you get that? It's really pretty."

I fingered the dainty silver chain. "Your dad gave it to me."

Justine beamed. "I love it. Maybe I can wear it sometime?" she asked. *Maybe she's thawing a bit*, I thought happily.

I laughed. "Of course you can." Lars watched us happily, a big smile spreading across his face.

Later that night, when the homework was done and everyone had gone their separate ways, I was in the kitchen preparing the kids' school lunches for the next day. Liko came looking for me.

"Can you talk?" he asked.

"Sure. What's up?" He walked over to where I was standing, looking out at the dark Pacific waters with the moon glinting on the waves. He took a knife and helped me slice vegetables.

"Barbie is moving to California after the baby is born."

"I know. She told me."

"What should I do?"

"About what?"

"About seeing the baby."

"I guess you'll have to move to California. Or at least visit often."

"I can't move to California. I wouldn't fit in. I belong in Hawaii. But I want the baby to grow up knowing me. I want him to know his dad. Or her dad."

"I don't know, Liko. That's a tough one."

"I know," he said miserably.

We were so engrossed in our conversation that we didn't hear someone stealing quietly into the room. By the time I noticed anyone standing behind us, it was too late.

I saw movement out of the corner of my eye and turned my head. Marcus stood with his back against the refrigerator, a small gun gleaming in his hand.

I dropped the knife I was holding. Liko, startled, turned around to see what I was looking at. I heard him inhale sharply.

"Marcus, what are you doing?" he asked.

"I came for Kailani because she's ruined everything. But it's a good thing I got here when I did, because now I know she's not the only one. You got my mom pregnant, didn't you?"

"Marcus, you have to understand something—" Liko began.

"I understand everything! Kailani stole my dad and you stole my mom and now the whole family is ruined because of you two!"

"Marcus, there's more to it than that," I said, searching for something to say that would help explain the very grown-up problems that he was facing.

He shook his head vehemently. "No, there isn't. My parents are getting divorced because of you two."

"Marcus, they were getting divorced no matter what," Liko said in a quiet voice.

"Oh yeah? I'll just bet. What I don't understand is how either of them could fall for either of you. Kailani, you're just a *cook*." He said it like the word was poison. "And you're not even smart enough to get a job as a teacher," he hissed at Liko.

"You're misunderstanding some things," I said in what I hoped was a soothing voice.

"It's pretty simple to me."

"Can we just get your mom and dad and have them explain things to you?"

"I'll kill you both if you call for anyone," Marcus warned, jerking the gun toward us.

I swallowed hard. There seemed to be no way out of this. We had to talk Marcus into dropping the gun.

"Where did you get the gun, Marcus?"

"From James's house."

"Killing us won't solve any problems. Your parents will still get divorced."

"Maybe not."

"Yes, they will. Their marriage wasn't happy for a long time, long before either Liko or I came to this house." Marcus didn't respond.

"Marcus? I think you know that. You know they moved from California to try to be happy again, but it just didn't work out. Someday you'll see that this is the right step for them. For both of them to be happy again."

He blinked. Were those tears?

"I *liked* you guys!" Marcus said through gritted teeth.

"Marcus, I'm sorry," Liko said quietly. "I didn't mean to hurt you or your sister."

"What about Dad?"

"I didn't want to hurt him, either."

"But you did it anyway."

Liko was silent. What could he say to that?

"And you," Marcus said, facing me and gesturing toward me with the gun in his hand. "You pretended everything was normal. That you were just the chef. When all the time you and my dad were . . . were . . ."

"No, Marcus. That's not true. Your dad and I wanted to wait until the divorce was final to get to know each other better. We discussed it together. We agreed it wasn't right to put you and Justine through anything else just now."

"Yeah, right," he sneered.

"Marcus, I'm telling you the truth. Please believe me. Your dad loves you and Justine and doesn't want to hurt you."

"But I heard you talking in his office those times!" So his had been the footsteps I'd heard.

"But we only talked. We didn't do anything." He studied me silently, and for just a moment I thought I saw a flicker of belief in his eyes.

Liko took a tiny step forward. "Marcus, will you give me the gun?"

To my surprise, Marcus slid down the wall and sat on the floor, his hands covering his face. He was crying. He let the gun fall beside him. Liko moved quickly to kick the gun out of the way; it skittered across the kitchen floor just as Lars appeared in the doorway, a look of bewilderment on his face.

"What's going on in here? Why is there a gun in the house? Whose is it?" he demanded.

In two steps I was at Marcus's side, kneeling next to him on the floor. I held him as he cried, speaking unintelligibly through a torrent of tears. I glanced at Lars quickly and saw the alarm in his eyes.

"Marcus? What's the matter? Are you hurt?" he asked, quickly joining his son on the floor.

Marcus shook his head, rocking forward and backward, his body trembling with sobs. Liko stood nearby, motionless.

"Marcus, tell me what's wrong. Nothing can be this bad," Lars said.

"Yes it can, Dad," he cried. He tried speaking again, but he started to choke. Lars patted his back gently while he waited for Marcus to gain some composure.

We sat there on the floor for a long time, the three of us. Liko left the room briefly to retrieve the gun from the floor in the hallway. Gradually, Marcus's breathing steadied and his tears slowed.

"Where's Justine?" he finally asked.

Lars looked at me. I shrugged. "I don't know," he said. "Probably in her room."

"I don't want her to hear," Marcus whispered.

"Hear what?" asked Lars, leaning in close.

Marcus mumbled something. "I can't hear you, Marcus," Lars said.

Marcus repeated himself. I thought I caught one or two words and my breath stuck in my throat. Lars stared at his son and then shot me a worried glance.

"Marcus, you need to take a few deep breaths. I don't think you know what you're saying."

Marcus shook his head violently. "Dad, listen. I know what I'm saying."

"But . . . but how is that possible?" Lars's voice was hollow.

"I didn't mean to kill him, Dad—I swear," Marcus gulped, the tears coursing again. Liko looked at me in alarm. I shook my head.

"How did it happen?" Lars asked.

"He was standing by the pool and I was so mad at him because I knew what he and Mom were doing and I just sneaked up behind him and hit him with a shovel that one of the gardeners left by the pool." Marcus sobbed. "I just wanted to hurt him. I didn't mean to kill him!" His voice had reached a keening pitch.

A strangled gasp came from behind us. Marcus looked up and Lars and I whirled around.

Barbie stood in the doorway, staring at Marcus in horror. "You killed him?" she asked quietly.

Marcus nodded in silence, the tears leaving wet pathways on his downy cheeks. He looked so young, so vulnerable.

"How could you?" her voice rose.

"I didn't mean to," he answered, his voice dull.

"Lars, what are we going to do?" she asked shrilly.

"Nothing at the moment," he answered. "Marcus needs sleep. We need time to think."

Barbie was breathing heavily. I thought she was going to faint, so I scrambled up and hurried over to her, but she waved me away. "I'm okay," she insisted. "Just in shock." She rested her hands on her stomach and looked around wildly. "What are we going to do?" she repeated.

"Barbie, I think you should let me handle this for now," Lars cautioned. "Please go upstairs and I'll be up to talk to you in a little while." He turned to Marcus as Barbie left.

"You need to sleep."

"I can't sleep."

"Can you at least try? Please?"

Marcus shook his head. "I can't, Dad. I don't think I'll ever sleep again."

"You will. Kailani, would you please go upstairs and ask Barbie for something to help Marcus sleep?"

I hurried upstairs, returning a few minutes later with two tablets that Barbie had said would help Marcus sleep deeply all night long. I was thankful to be in a hurry so I didn't have to discuss this development with her.

Back in the kitchen, I poured a glass of water for Marcus and handed Lars the glass and the pills. We watched as Marcus took the medicine, then Lars helped him to his feet. "I'm staying with you until you're sound asleep," he said. The two of them walked slowly down the length of the lanai toward Marcus's room.

I finally turned to Liko. "I can't believe it," he said.

I could only shake my head. I knew I wouldn't be getting any sleep that night.

Chapter 19

At dawn, I was still sitting on the lanai, staring out over the waves of the Pacific. Lars had never come out of Marcus's room. I was sure he hadn't slept, either. Justine wandered out in her pajamas, rubbing her eyes. "Where's Marcus?" She obviously had no idea what had happened the previous night.

"Still asleep, I guess."

"Can I have breakfast?"

Her words lifted me out of my bleak thoughts. "Of course." I fixed a bowl of granola with honey and yogurt, crowned with lots of fresh berries.

"I wonder why Marcus isn't up yet," she mused. "Maybe he's sick."

I shrugged noncommittally. When she was done with her breakfast she hurried to get ready for school, then I watched her trot down the long driveway toward the bus stop. What a relief that we didn't have to worry about Geoffrey anymore.

But now there was a new worry. Lars and Marcus shuffled into the kitchen a few minutes later. Marcus looked at me out of dark, hooded eyes. Lars seemed to have aged overnight. They helped themselves to bowls of cereal while I busied myself making coffee and washing more berries.

Barbie appeared in the kitchen doorway as father and son stood against the kitchen counters, eating their breakfast. She appeared to be at a loss for words, which was unusual for her.

"Lars, you have to do something," she said finally.

"What do you want me to do?"

"I don't know."

"I have to go to the bathroom." Marcus sounded so normal, so ordinary. He left the room and returned several minutes later. "I'm going to get dressed."

"Go with him," Barbie urged Lars.

"He can get dressed by himself."

"But what if he runs away?"

Lars answered her with a long shake of his head. He set his coffee cup in the sink and informed us that he too was going to get dressed.

Barbie and I weren't alone in the kitchen for long. Liko came in shortly, poured himself a cup of coffee, and turned to us. "Now what?" he asked.

"I'm going to talk to Lars," Barbie announced. "He's got to do something. He can't let Marcus go to jail." She turned and left the room without a backward glance. Liko and I stood in silence.

There was a knock at the front door. Detective Alana stood there. "May I come in?"

Unsure of why he was there, I moved aside and motioned him indoors. He cleared his throat. "I received a call from Marcus," he began.

But he didn't have to finish.

"Here I am," said a voice behind me. I spun around and there stood Marcus, facing the officer, his eyes like stone.

Lars came clattering up the stairs from the family room. "What's going on here?" he demanded.

"I called the police, Dad. I know what you're thinking. You're going to take the blame for me and Mom wants you to. But you can't. Someone has to take care of Justine."

Barbie was racing downstairs as Marcus finished speaking.

"Don't say another word until I call our lawyer," she commanded.

"Don't, Mom. I already told the detective that I killed Dr. Doug. I told him it was a mistake. I called him when I said I was going to the bathroom."

"Wait a minute. Let's all calm down," Lars said. "Detective, he's just a boy. He doesn't know what he's talking about."

"Yes, I do."

Detective Alana held up his hand. "Let's go talk about this at the station." He opened the door and took Marcus gently by the arm, helping him into the backseat of the police car that was in the driveway. Barbie and Lars followed them in Barbie's car.

Liko and I were left alone again in the house. Neither of us felt much like talking, so we went our separate ways, me to my bedroom and Liko to the guesthouse. It was hours before Lars and Barbie returned. Marcus was not with them. Barbie was crying.

"He confessed," Lars told me. "He's being transferred to a juvenile facility in Kona."

"What's going to happen?" I asked.

He sighed. "We don't know. He'll be charged with Doug's death, but there are a couple things in his favor. For one, he's a kid. For another, the fact that Doug was sleeping with Barbie will probably be considered a mitigating circumstance," he said, with a dark glance at her. "It doesn't justify killing Doug, of course, but it goes a long way toward explaining why Marcus felt like he couldn't take it anymore."

"What about Dr. Rutledge?" I asked.

"I asked Marcus about him last night. He swears he had nothing to do with it and I believe him. I think Dr. Rutledge's death was really an accident." Barbie nodded her agreement. "The lawyer met us at the station and the police were prevented from asking Marcus about Dr. Rutledge. Unfortunately, Marcus had already confessed to Doug's killing when he talked to the police on the phone."

There was nothing left to say. Lars and Barbie would have to sit down with Justine after school and tell her what had happened.

When Justine found out, she was inconsolable. Lars took her to visit Marcus the following day because she begged to see him, but she wasn't any better when they returned to the house.

So began a long, emotional period of waiting to find out what Marcus's fate would be. We visited him often, usually with gifts of homemade food. He derived a small measure of happiness from our visits, but leaving the facility and driving home without him was always heart-wrenching, especially for Justine. As the days dragged by, she became more and more despondent. Her only pleasure lay in getting out of the house: going to school, where she could be with her friends, away from the mournful atmosphere at home.

During that time, Barbie's belly continued to swell and Liko, not having to help Justine much with schoolwork, returned to Punalu'u to look for another job. He left without telling Lars about his relationship with Barbie, though I asked him several times to consider it. I suspect he was too embarrassed, too afraid of Lars's reaction, to confess to what he had done.

It wasn't as much fun cooking without Marcus in the house, even when I was making goodies to take to him, and the palpable tension over his fate pervaded every meal, every conversation. Lars and I talked at length and decided to continue waiting for our relationship to move forward while Marcus's future was in limbo.

But as sad as it was to know Marcus was behind the murder of Dr. Doug, it gave me a sense of relief knowing the search for the doctor's killer was over. There would be no more worrying about intruders, no more wondering whether the perpetrator would ever be caught. And perhaps most importantly, no more anxiety about Lars being tried for murder.

It was the birth of Barbie's baby girl that finally brought Justine back to life. Callie was born on a sunny day when the sapphire waters of the Pacific were gentle and calm. Lars took Justine to see the baby, but declined to go into the maternity ward himself. Justine came out with a big smile. She already loved her little sister. She chattered all the way home from the hospital, saying she couldn't wait for Marcus to meet the baby. It was the first time she had mentioned her brother's name without a hint of despair. "Callie's got such dark hair and dark skin!" she exclaimed as we drove through Hawi. "Not like me or Marcus."

I glanced over at Lars, who was driving. His fists clenched the steering wheel a little tighter. When we got home, Justine went to call her best friend to tell her about the new baby.

Lars went straight to his office, but later found me in the kitchen. "How long have you known?" he asked.

I knew exactly what he meant. "A while."

"Why didn't you tell me Liko was the baby's father?"

"I just couldn't do that to you. I'm so sorry."

"I don't blame you," he said with a sigh. "You were in a very tough spot."

"I just kept hoping Liko wasn't the father, even though Barbie said she was sure. And I kept hoping Liko would tell you himself. I asked him to, but in the end I think he was too afraid to face you."

He nodded slightly. "I understand. It wasn't your job to tell me. Liko should have been man enough to tell me. Or Barbie should have said something."

He gathered me in his arms and held me for a long time. Justine came into the kitchen softly and put her arms around both of us. "Everything's going to be okay," she told us.

Epilogue

A nd eventually, everything will be okay.

Marcus was sentenced to three years in a juvenile-justice center, where he currently lives and studies. He even has a new math tutor. We're allowed to visit him three times a week. He expresses deep remorse for what he did, and I believe he's relieved he doesn't have to keep his terrible secret any longer. He's also come to accept my presence in Lars's life. He's had a lot of time to think and understands now that his parents were headed for divorce long before I came into their lives.

Justine is growing into a talented athlete who loves to play tennis and swim. She eventually went kayaking again, though she was initially worried about sharks. She's become more relaxed when she's paddling and seems to enjoy both the serenity and hard work of the sport. Like Marcus, she has accepted me as part of her family and we get along beautifully. She misses Marcus, but understands that he has to face the consequences of his actions. She counts the days until he can live at home again.

Barbie and Callie moved to San Diego shortly after Callie's birth. Justine visits them twice a year, but otherwise stays with us in the house where she grew up. She tells us that Barbie dates lots of different men, but doesn't want to get married again. Barbie has not returned to Hawaii to visit Marcus, but Justine tells us Barbie writes to him regularly. Liko visits Barbie and Callie too, but never when Justine is there. I do stay in touch with Liko via email, but I never see him. It would hurt Lars too much.

The divorce was finalized about a year after Barbie moved to San Diego. We stayed in the big house with the hanging jade and the beautiful views of the Pacific. Lars was concerned that being in the house would bother me, but it doesn't. And we worried that Marcus might find it too difficult to return to the house, but he insists that he loves it there and is looking forward to returning to the home he knows. We decided not to replace Akela, so I do both the cooking and the cleaning for the three of us. I have looked into opening a food truck too. My hope is to cater to surfers by moving the truck each day, depending on where the best surf is, but that's a dream for another day.

Right now, I'm just waiting for the wedding, which won't take place until Marcus is home. But he'll join us before too long, and our family will finally be complete.

Glossary

'Aumakua: a family god (*ow-mah-koo-ah*)

Haliaka: leader (*Hah-lee-ah-kah*)

Haole: term, often pejorative, which refers to Caucasians in contrast to locals of Hawaiian ancestry (*how-lay*)

he'e: Hawaiian octopus, commonly called squid (*hay-ay*)

honu: sea turtle (*ho-new*)

Kailani: chieftain or warrior queen (*Kai-lah-nee*)

kiele: gardenia (*kee-ay-lay*)

lanai: patio, balcony (*lan-eye*)

lilikoi: passionfruit (*lee-lee-koy*)

mahalo: thank you (*mah-hah-low*)

makai: toward the sea (*mah-kai*)

malasada: Portuguese doughnut (*mah-lah-sah-dah*)

mauka: toward the mountain (*mow-kah*)

meli: honey (*May-lee*)

ono: great or delicious (*oh-no*)

pali: steep cliff (*pah-lee*)

paniolo: Hawaiian cowboy (*pah-nee-oh-loh*)

poke: raw fish salad (*poh-kay*)

Punalu'u: town on Big Island of Hawaii (*Poo-nah-loo-oo*)

pupule: crazy (*poo-poo-lay*)

pupus: hors d'oeuvres, appetizers (*poo-poos*)

tako: Japanese word for octopus (*tah-koh*)

ti: type of Hawaiian plant (*tee*)

Tutu: familiar name for grandparent (*Too-too*)

Book Club Discussion Questions

1. Two overt signs of Geoffrey's personality before he moved to the island of Hawaii were Meli's refusal to let him pet her and his behavior in following Kailani home one night after work. Did you notice any others?

2. How did you feel about Liko? Did you like him? Why or why not? How about Lars?

3. Is there anything Kailani should have done differently to deal with Geoffrey? Should she have gone to the police earlier?

4. What did you think of the setting of the book? Do you think the setting added to the story or detracted from it? Do you consider the setting to be one of the characters of the book?

5. What do you think were the themes of the story? What do you think the author is trying to say?

6. How does Kailani change and grow throughout the book? How about Barbie?

7. How would the story be different if Kailani and Liko hadn't been friends since childhood?

8. Were you satisfied with the book's ending? What do you think the future holds for Liko? Barbie? Marcus?

Turn the page for a special excerpt of Amy M. Reade's

THE GHOSTS OF PEPPERNELL MANOR

"Do you know what stories Sarah could tell you about the things that happened in these little cabins? They'd curl that pretty red hair of yours."

Outside of Charleston, South Carolina, beyond hanging curtains of Spanish moss, at the end of a shaded tunnel of overarching oaks, stands the antebellum mansion of Peppernell Manor in all its faded grandeur. At the request of her friend Evie Peppernell, recently divorced Carleigh Warner and her young daughter Lucy have come to the plantation house to refurbish the interior. But the tall white columns and black shutters hide a dark history of slavery, violence, and greed. The ghost of a former slave is said to haunt the home, and Carleigh is told she *disapproves* of her restoration efforts. And beneath the polite hospitality of the Peppernell family lie simmering resentments and poisonous secrets that culminate in murder—and place Carleigh and her child in grave danger . . .

A Lyrical Press e-book on sale now!

THE GHOSTS OF
PEPPERNELL
MANOR

The roots of evil run deep...

AMY M. READE
Author of *Secrets of Hallstead House*

CHAPTER 1

It had been a long drive to South Carolina, but Lucy and I had made the best of it, giggling through nursery rhymes, eating fast food, making silly faces at each other in the rearview mirror, and playing I Spy on every highway between Chicago and Charleston.

We arrived one sultry afternoon in late August last year. I barely remembered the back roads from Charleston to Peppernell Manor, so it was like watching the scenery unfold over the miles for the first time. Spanish moss hung low to the ground from stately trees over a century old. Perfectly still water reflected the magnolias and camellias and the hazy sky in the Lowcountry lakes and waterways that we passed. Lacy clumps of wildflowers nodded languidly as we drove by. Lucy was interested in everything that whizzed past the windows of the car, commenting excitedly on all the new sights as we drove toward Peppernell Manor.

"Look at the cows! Moo!"

"Look at the pretty flowers!" she would pipe up from the backseat in her high-pitched little-girl voice. I loved driving with her because she helped me see all the things I missed with my adult eyes.

As we got closer to Peppernell Manor, I found myself sharing her excitement. I hadn't been there since college. My thoughts stretched back to the only other time I had visited South Carolina, when Evie took me to her home for a long weekend. We had gone sightseeing in Charleston, horseback riding, boating on the Ashley River, and on a tour of an old Confederate field hospital nearby. But despite all the fun we had, it wasn't the activities I remembered best about that trip—it was her house.

Manor, actually. Peppernell Manor had been in her family for generations and even though it had seen better days and was in need of some work, it was exquisite. As a lover of art I could appreciate its romance and graceful architecture, but as a history major I was more interested in the home's past as a plantation house.

It was to this plantation house that I was returning, this time with my daughter.

Photo by John A. Reade, Jr.

Amy M. Reade is also the author of *Secrets of Hallstead House* and *The Ghosts of Peppernell Manor*. She grew up in northern New York, just south of the Canadian border, and spent her weekends and summers on the St. Lawrence River. She graduated from Cornell University and then went on to law school at Indiana University in Bloomington. She practiced law in New York City before moving to southern New Jersey, where, in addition to writing, she is a wife, a full-time mom, and a volunteer in school, church, and community groups. She lives just a stone's throw from the Atlantic Ocean with her husband and three children, as well as a dog and two cats. She loves cooking and all things Hawaii and is currently at work on her next novel. Visit her on the Web at www.amymreade.com or at www.amreade.wordpress.com.

*"You are not wanted here. Go away from Hallstead Island
or you will be very sorry you stayed."*

Macy Stoddard had hoped to ease the grief of losing her parents in
a fiery car crash by accepting a job as a private nurse to the wealthy
and widowed Alexandria Hallstead. But her first sight of Hallstead
House is of a dark and forbidding home. She quickly finds its winding
halls and shadowy rooms filled with secrets and suspicions. Alex
seems happy to have Macy's help, but others on the island, including
Alex's sinister servants and hostile relatives, are far less welcoming.
Watching eyes, veiled threats . . . slowly, surely, the menacing spirit
of Hallstead Island closes in around Macy. And she can only wonder
if her story will become just one of the many secrets of Hallstead
House . . .

56 - 3083 Puakea Bay Dr,

MLS 292652
$10.5
Kathy Christiansen
Gayle Ching

Made in the USA
San Bernardino, CA
28 April 2016